Night of Wings and Smoke

David Dalglish

BOOKS BY DAVID DALGLISH

THE HALF-ORC SERIES
The Weight of Blood
The Cost of Betrayal
The Death of Promises
The Shadows of Grace
A Sliver of Redemption
The Prison of Angels
The King of the Vile
The King of the Fallen
Legacy of the Watcher

THE SHADOWDANCE SERIES
Cloak and Spider (novella)
A Dance of Cloaks
A Dance of Blades
A Dance of Mirrors
A Dance of Shadows
A Dance of Ghosts
A Dance of Chaos

THE PALADINS
Night of Wolves
Clash of Faiths
The Old Ways
The Broken Pieces

THE BREAKING WORLD
Dawn of Swords
Wrath of Lions
Blood of Gods

THE SERAPHIM
Skyborn
Fireborn
Shadowborn

THE KEEPERS TRILOGY
Soulkeeper
Ravencaller
Voidbreaker

VAGRANT GODS TRILOGY
The Bladed Faith
The Sapphire Altar
The Slain Divine

THE ASTRAL KINGDOMS
Radiant King (2025)

LEVEL UNKNOWN
Level: Unknown (2025)

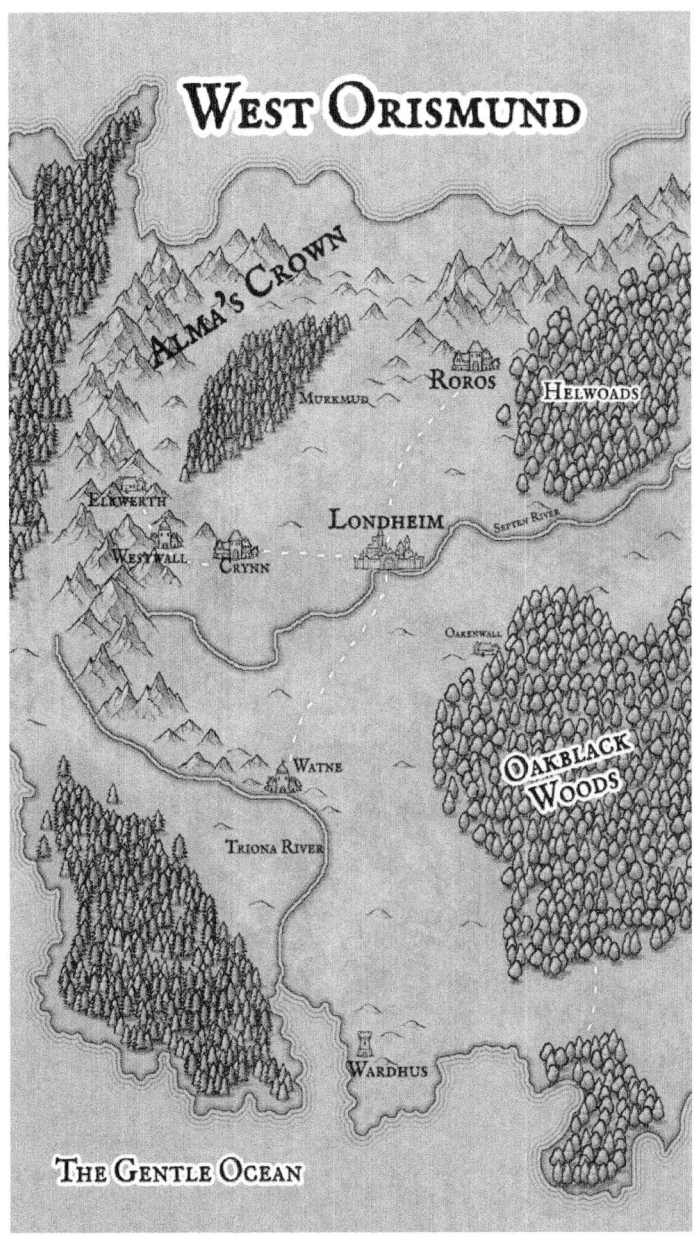

1

The mountain road is treacherous, but at last you approach its end. The ground slopes downward, the flattened path easing from the towering stone of Alma's Crown toward a more gentle, but no less cramped, pathway through a forest of towering pines, their branches freshly dusted with snow. Not far beyond them is the small village of Elkwerth, and the reason you have come all this way from the grand city of Londheim.

Elkwerth's request didn't state why they needed a Soulkeeper, but the insinuations were dire, and so you have traversed the wilds at your Vikar's request.

Keep me safe these last few miles, will you, Lyra? you pray to the Goddess of the Day as you walk the cold. *I'd hate to freeze when a fire and warm bed are finally within reach.*

It may be dark, but the stars are out and the moon is high. It is from that light you see the glint of the ambushers before they make their presence known. A hint of steel. A flicker of moonlight off a buckle. Two men. They're trying to hide behind the pines.

They're bad at it.

You halt just before the tree line, pretending all is fine and you haven't noticed them. With almost casual boredom, you draw your pistol from its holster at your hip. As your thumb cocks open the chamber, you slip your free hand into one of two pouches attached to your belt and withdraw a small red orb the size of your pinkie. It is a flamestone, and you set it into the chamber, then cock the hammer back farther, locking it in place while sliding a metal shield across the opening to prevent an early discharge.

From the other pouch you draw out a single lead shot. A ramrod is stored in a sheath underneath the barrel, and you pull it out, slide in the shot, and pump twice, finally loading the pistol.

It takes you about eight seconds to finish. During that time, the two ambushers in the trees do not leave their spots behind the pines. You catch them watching you from the corner of your eye. Are they afraid, or merely waiting?

Pistol loaded, you lower it while also tilting it slightly so its aim remains parallel to the ground. Ready, you rest your other hand on the hilt of your sword. Two men, one pistol shot. You'll need steel if the other has more bravery than smarts.

Into the forest you walk, following the path. Your senses are on edge. You hear the rustle of pine needles, then the crunch of snow that is much too heavy for any animal of the forest. Even if you hadn't seen them, you'd have detected their presence. You are at home in the wilds. They, clearly, are not.

"Halt where you are, miss," one says when you are directly between them. You calmly obey.

"How strange," you say. "I never expected a warm welcome to these woods."

The two men emerge from their hiding spots. One of them is a beefy looking fellow, strong-jawed and wielding a short sword. The other is shorter, a bit scrawny with how his skin more or less hangs from his bones. Most troubling, he has a hunting bow with an arrow nocked and ready to fly.

"Mouth shut, you hear me?" the sword wielder says. "Just open up that coin purse and give us half. That's all, half."

You glance his way. "Only half? How generous."

"Hey, we said no lip," the bow holder says, taking a step closer. You turn toward him, deciding him the more immediate threat. You trust your reflexes and training to handle the short sword. An arrow, properly aimed, however…

"Forgive me," you say, "But I'm not sure I am in a giving mood."

The bowman's eyes widen. He's seen the pendant hanging from your chest. It's a silver crescent moon tucked into the bottom third of a downward-pointed triangle. The symbol of Anwyn, Goddess of the Dusk.

"Damn it," he mutters. "Brent, she's a Soulkeeper."

To your amusement, the sword wielder, Brent you assume, retreats a step.

"No reason a Soulkeeper would be out here at the ass crack of the world," he says, but there's doubt in his voice. You decide now is the time to push them. Rely on the surprise of your profession.

"Soulkeeper Robin, at your service," you say, and lift your pistol so it aims straight at the bow holder. "Now put down your weapons and run far, far away from here. I've no desire to perform two reaping rituals tonight."

"Put…put that down," the bowman orders.

"Jack…" the other says, lifting his sword. "Jack, we should do what he says. This ain't no trader or physician."

You smirk.

"So you would rob me even if I were a physician come to heal the sick?" you ask. Your finger tightens on the trigger of your pistol.

"Just half," Brent mutters. A pitiful defense. He's not leaving, though. He's still keeping close. Whether these two are friends, brothers, or more, you don't know, but it doesn't look like either is ready to abandon the other.

"Last chance," you say, locking eyes with Jack. "Which do you think will travel faster, your arrow, or my lead shot?"

He pulls the string back the tiniest bit further. The muscles in his arms are straining. He's been holding that arrow nocked for much too long. It's affecting his posture, and his aim. There's no hiding how much the arrowhead is wobbling.

"You'll truly let us go?" Brent asks. The big man is the smarter of the two. He knows the legendary skills of Soulkeepers. He knows to be afraid.

"He's seen our faces," Jack insists. "What if Elkwerth called him here to find us and kill us?"

"I'm not here for you," you say, though you aren't certain. The village elder was cryptic in his request, but you feel confident the letter would have stated as such if the matter was only a couple of troublesome bandits robbing the mountain pass.

You take a single step toward Jack and aim directly at his forehead.

"Put. The bow. Down."

For the briefest moment, you think he will listen. And then he lets the arrow fly.

You don't move. You don't dodge. You trust in your aim and pull the trigger of your hammerlock pistol. The hammer slams down, its sharpened spike rupturing the flamestone you slotted into the chamber. It erupts, propelling the lead shot out in a blast of fire and smoke.

Your aim was true. His was not. Your bullet strikes him between the eyes, caving in the bones of his forehead. His arrow passes just over your shoulder. You feel the wind on your neck as it flies by. Jack will feel nothing as he drops, his limbs flailing, his legs buckling underneath his body.

"Jack!"

You spin in place, your whole body on the move. Your right hand shoves your pistol into its holster at your hip, while your left grabs the hilt of your sword and pulls it free of its sheath. The big man is bearing down on you, his eyes wide, his mouth twisted into a snarl that is almost feral. He's not thinking anymore, not after seeing his companion shot dead.

Your sword easily blocks his clumsy downward chop. It's all strength and brutality, and perhaps on a lesser foe, it might have worked. Your legs are properly braced, though, and your grip on your sword tight and with both hands. Steel rings out, startling in the night. He tries two more times to batter you down, as if you are a tree trunk he can split down the middle, but you hold your ground.

He's impatient and overwhelmed. He'll make a mistake soon enough.

That mistake comes when he tries to back away after his third hit fails to break your guard. You dash right into him so that he's on his heels before ever realizing you have taken the offensive. His short sword loops wildly before him. It's all panic. He has no idea where your sword will be.

One thrust, straight to his chest. He gasps as the tip slips through his ribs and into his heart. Blood dribbles down his lips, first a little, then more as you tear your weapon free. Brent collapses to his knees, the sword falling limp from his fingers as both hands clutch at the wound. He looks at you, trying to say something, anything, before the last of his strength gives out and he falls face first into the snow.

The ensuing silence is jarring, broken only by your breath and the sound of your heartbeat pounding in your ears.

"Stubborn fools," you say, cleaning your sword from a rag kept in the pocket of your long coat before sliding the blade back into its sheath. "What did you think would happen?"

Still, you cannot leave them here. You have your duty as a Soulkeeper. Their souls, no matter how tainted, deserve a better fate than remaining trapped within their mortal bodies. It will delay your travel, though. Just when you were starting to look forward to putting your feet up before a warm cabin fire.

You look to the road leading to Elkwerth, and the people waiting for your arrival.

"I hope you're worth it," you mutter, and prepare for the two robbers their pyres.

2

The reaping hour approaches. The pines encircle you, their branches softly swaying in a faint wind. The mountains of Alma's Crown form a towering wall to your west, as if reaching for the very stars. The moon is high, shining its light on the corpse laying wrapped upon the pyre. A small boy named Edwin. He'd not lived to see his ninth year.

"Thank you for coming," Elise says. She is the mayor for the nearby village of Elkwerth, and would have been responsible for leading this reaping ritual if not for your arrival. Edwin's parents stand behind her, haggard and quiet. They'd spent their tears over the past two days as the people of Elkwerth debated whether to wait for you, or hold the ritual themselves.

You're glad they waited for you. The sending of souls has grown increasingly difficult as of late.

"I only wish to offer what comfort I may," you say, and kneel before the pyre. "Now let me pray."

The words were always the same, and you know them well. It was a prayer to the Three Sisters, the goddesses that watch over all the Cradle. Gratitude for Alma in granting life, Lyra for caring over Edwin during his short years, and then a plea to Anwyn to take his soul up to the heavens for an eternity of bliss.

When the prayer ends, you scoop a handful of snow and press it over Edwin's still face. All across the Cradle, the people used the nearby elements to grant their funeral pyres.

Mud from the ocean waters for those who lived along the coast, rich black prairie soil for those among the grasslands. Here among Alma's Crown? The snow would be his pyre mask.

When the snow is packed, you remove your leather glove. This must be done by hand. Carefully you draw a triangle upon the mask and then a circle around the downward point. Each side of the triangle represents one of the Sisters and their connections to the others, while the bottom circle was both sun and moon, life beginning and ending at the same place in the heavens.

Finished, you stand and dig your hands into the pockets of your dark leather coat. There is nothing more to do than wait for the reaping hour to arrive.

"He'll go, won't he?" Edwin's mother asks. You haven't gotten her name yet. Elise had grabbed you the moment you arrived in Elkwerth late that afternoon and begged you to lead the reaping ritual.

It's been two days, and still Edwin's soul remains in his body, she'd said. *I don't want to bury him, but I fear I waited too long already.*

You insisted it was not yet too late, not when no ritual had yet been performed. And so the body was brought out to the circle of pines beyond the village and laid upon the pyre. Snow had steadily formed a layer upon him, a sick jest given his death. He'd wandered from the village, been lost for several hours unable to find his way home, and then perished of frostbite.

A cruel fate, and a sadly common one here in the far west.

"Do not fear," you say to the parents. "Anwyn's eye is forever upon us. Though you grieve now, know his suffering is at an end, and he rests within light and comfort."

You fall silent. The reaping hour has arrived, and you feel it like a touch of fingers upon your neck. The world tenses. The animals of the forest go silent and still, for even the natural world recognizes this divine hour and pays their respects. You hold your breath and stare at the symbol you drew upon Edwin's forehead.

Underneath your shirt hangs a silver pendant, a downward pointed triangle with a silver moon transcribed into that bottom edge. It is the symbol of Anwyn, goddess of the dusk, caretaker of souls, she whose hands lift the soul into the hereafter. The symbol of all Soulkeepers. You clutch it through your shirt as you stare at the body.

"By Alma, we are born," you whisper into the silence. "By Lyra, we are guided. By Anwyn, we are returned. Beloved Sisters, take her home."

A soft blue light swells from Edwin's forehead, shining as a translucent pillar reaching all the way to the stars themselves. The triangular symbol brightens, and a little orb of swirling light rises from his forehead. You relax as it begins to ascend the blue pillar. Edwin's soul had separated cleanly from the body.

Though the Mindkeepers of the Keeping Church debated a soul's true makeup, you have never wondered. Within that brilliant light was all that made up a person; their emotions, their memories, their whole life, rising into the heavens. All across the Cradle, hundreds of similar rituals were performed in kind, aiding Anwyn in reclaiming the lives granted by Alma at the moment of birth.

The orb rises upward, slowly at first, then faster and faster as the blue pillar of light lifts it heavenward. By the time it vanishes from view, the beam has faded and the reaping hour passed. Owls resume hooting, and in the distance, you hear a chorus of wolves crying to the moon.

Only then did Edwin's parents begin to cry.

"No burial, then," Elise says. She shivers in her fur coat and shakes her head. "Thank the Sisters for that. I thought…I feared I had waited too long. That I had doomed the poor boy with my doubt."

You put a hand on her shoulder and smile.

"Every reaping ritual is a burden," you say. "Do not blame yourself for your uncertainty."

With the soul departed, the body was but empty flesh. It was the cast off shell of a cicada, or the shed skin of a snake. You remove the cap to your oilskin hanging from your belt and begin splashing it across the pyre's thin, dry wood. When emptied, you put it away and withdraw two flint stones from a belt pouch.

A few quick strikes, a fall of sparks, and the oil lights. Triangular stones created the pyre's outline, with thick, braced logs to hold the body atop its bed of kindling. It'd taken you an hour to build the pyre so that it would safely burn throughout the night. All that would remain come morning would be the triangular symbol of the Three Sisters.

Elise speaks a few whispered words with the grieving parents while you watch the pyre burn.

"Is she here to help Arbert?" you overhear the father ask. "I know it's been weeks, but if anyone can find Rachel…"

The mayor shushes him quite harshly. You purposefully look away and pretend not to hear. They depart, and the mayor returns. Her gray hair hangs low over her face, and the dark circles under her eyes imply many recent sleepless nights.

"It wasn't my own failures I feared," she says as she joins you. The light of the pyre shines across you both. "It's the burial. Anwyn has abandoned us here in the Crown, Soulkeeper. That, or my own rituals are weak and useless. Most every ritual over the past five years has failed, and we've been forced to bury the dead instead."

You say nothing, just let her talk. If the soul did not depart, then the body would be buried. Sometimes, on its own, the soul would rise up from the grave during the reaping hour to ascend, but it was a rare occurrence, and even rarer over the past two decades. Most likely, the soul would remain within the decomposing body, waiting until the end of days when the Three Sisters called up each and every soul, both living and departed, to join them in the heavens.

Most Soulkeepers, whether it was right or not, felt like the failure of a soul to ascend was a judgment on their own prayers and rituals. It didn't matter that it had grown harder over the decades, to great debate amongst the Mindkeepers. If Elise had presided over that many burials, the burden she felt…it must be horrible.

"You should have summoned a Soulkeeper," you say, and then immediately feel guilty for admonishing the tired woman.

"We did, several times," Elise says. "But it's a long trip from Crynn to here, and even longer from Londheim. We make do out here in the mountains, Soulkeeper. Even if we don't like it."

"I understand," you say, and watch the pyre burn. "I'm here now. The question is, why? Your request was cryptic, and sent long before Edwin perished. What need has Elkwerth that requires my prayers, my sword, and my pistol?"

Elise glances over her shoulder, to the path the parents walked through the snow back to the village.

"Follow me to the graveyard, Soulkeeper," she says. "And I'll show you why."

*

The graveyard was almost half a mile beyond the village outskirts, built deep into the pines. They are considered ill-omened places despite all attempts of the Keeping Church to preach there was no sin or failure on the part of the deceased to cause their souls to not ascend. Still, the rumors and judgments are inevitable, and so all bodies are buried with unnamed headstones to mark their place.

You walk through two dozen such unnamed burial stones and feel a shiver work its way down your spine. The graves were dug almost haphazardly, finding space where they could amid the trees.

"So many," you say to Elise. "And all of these are recent?"

"The first dozen took fifty years," the older woman says. "Soulkeepers are a rarity out here, and we take pride in praying and caring for our dead. Those rows?" She points to at least two dozen circling a particularly tall pine tree. "All during my time. That's fifteen years. A lot of souls, Robin. A lot of emotions and memories shoved into the dirt. It feeds into the trees and turns them foul."

"Forgive me for being harsh," you say, "but that is superstitious nonsense."

"Perhaps," Elise says. She grins at you, and the hardness in her brown eyes is unnerving. "But you haven't seen what I have, Soulkeeper. You don't live at the edge of the world like us."

There's no denying a certain unease hangs around the graveyard. The air whips cold, and even the light of the stars above seems to dim as it makes its way through the pine branches. Of course, you've also spent weeks traveling here from the great city of Londheim. You're tired, haven't had a warm meal in days, and the moment you set foot in the distant mountain village of Elkwerth you we dragged to the wilderness beyond to build Edwin's pyre. Exhaustion could easily explain the way it feels like the pines are watching you.

"You know these mountains better than I," you say. "That I will admit. But I'm here, as requested, instead of asleep in a bed, like I should be. Share what you wish to share, mayor."

In response, Elise points at a tree seemingly no

different than any other.

"There," she says. "That's where we found Edwin's body, shriveled up and pale."

You frown. "The boy was lost for hours, and no one thought to check the graveyard?"

"We did," Elise insists. "Multiple times, along with the forest beyond. But when we did find Edwin, he was here, right here. And he wasn't just frozen stiff, Soulkeeper. He was buried under a full layer of snow, as if he hadn't moved since morning."

Your frown deepens.

"Then you missed him while he slept," you say. "It happens when people succumb to frostbite, they lay still and sleep, because they become tired, and weirdly warm."

"No," Elise insists, and she grabs your arm. "Look at that tree, and look at our footprints in the snow. We marched all along here, many times, and not once did anyone see him."

"Was he killed, perhaps?" you wonder aloud. "What if someone did the deed and then dumped the boy's body here once no one was looking?"

The mayor's grip on your arm tightens. It is starting to hurt.

"Killed, aye," she says. "He was killed. By the ghosts of the woods."

You know, deep down, you should be kinder. But you're tired and travel-worn, and this sort of nonsense is always worse at the farthest outreaches of civilization.

"There are no ghosts," you say, a touch louder than intended. "No monsters, no goblins, no creatures of the night or faeries of the vale. They are stories, Elise, that is all, and nothing more. The Sisters created the Cradle for us. We are their children, their *only* children." You pull your arm free of her grip. "Anything else you've heard is simply not true."

"This forest murders people," Elise insists. "And now

it's taken Rachel."

The same name the grieving parents had whispered. You cross your arms and glare at the mayor.

"Another missing child?" you ask. "If she was gone when you sent your missive, I'm sorry, Elise, but she will have perished long before I arrived."

"Except she's not missing," Elise says. "We see her at night, right here at this graveyard, but never for long. She flees from us, or rather…we flee her. The way she looks, the way she talks…"

Your bafflement is growing. What nonsense was this, that these villagers would pretend at ghosts and missing children that were not actually missing?

"I don't understand," you say, "And I do not appreciate your hiding the true reason for my arrival. Speak plainly, mayor."

Wind whips through the trees, a vicious chill descending from the mountains beyond. You pull your coat tighter about your body and pretend that you had not, instinctively, reached for your hammerlock pistol.

"The ghosts have claimed her," Elise says. "There's too many souls lingering in these woods. Too many that should have moved on to the heavens but were forced to be buried beneath the dirt. They're awake now, Robin. They're awake, and they're angry. We thought, if anyone could set the spirits at peace, it would be a Soulkeeper. If you could pray to Anwyn, if you could get the goddess to finally turn her damn eyes to the west and to our little village, we might know peace. Or at the least, Rachel would find rest. What they've done to her, what they're *doing* to her, is evil. No one should suffer so."

This fear, this certainty, it is too much to be faked. The first slivers of doubt settle into your belly.

"I'll confront her myself, and put an end to this nonsense," you say. "Souls do not become spirits or ghosts,

Elise. Anwyn takes them into her arms, and if not, they lie dormant, waiting for the goddess to claim them. There is no between. There has never been a between. When does she supposedly appear?"

"When else would souls yearning for the hereafter appear?" Elise asks. "The reaping hour."

"Then come tomorrow's reaping hour, I will be right here, waiting and ready."

3

Another cold night. Another biting wind. You stand in the graveyard, your hand resting on the hilt of your sword. You're skilled with it. You have to be. Out here in the wilds, Soulkeepers aren't always summoned for reaping rituals. Bandits, criminal trials, and legal disputes are just as often, all settled via the power granted you as a member of the Keeping Church. The Second Council of Nicus ensures Soulkeepers can serve as judge and protector in the lands where the crown did not reach.

But what good would a sword do you here?

"No ghosts, no monsters," you whisper to the night. You have traveled across more than enough miles of the Cradle to know this to be true. Every small town has its rumors and its stories, but that's all they were. Stories. And if there is one thing you know, it is that souls belong to the Sisters, and they do not falter, and they do not lose track.

Easy to think, harder to believe, when surrounded by the buried souls of dozens.

The reaping hour nears. You pull your coat tighter and kick your feet to keep them warm. In the far distance, a lone wolf howls, followed by the answers of his pack. A mile away, probably two. You're safe. You have your sword, and if necessary, your hammerlock pistol. You carry no animosity toward wolves, but you will protect yourself if you must.

A footstep, behind you. You turn, your sword already halfway out of its sheath before you realize you had started drawing it.

"Please," says a tired man wrapped in furs. "I have to be here."

You sheathe the sword. You met him earlier that day. Rachel's father. His name is Arbert.

"I am here because I must be here," you tell him. "But not because I believe your daughter haunts this graveyard. Go home, Arbert. This false hope will only lead to suffering."

"Suffering?" He steps closer. He's thin and strong, built of hard work here in the mountains. Silver mines, if you remember correctly. His hands are calloused, his eyes, nearly black from too many sleepless nights. "You think me being here is suffering? No, Soulkeeper, not knowing what happened to my little girl, where she is, whether she's cold or starving or lost needing...needing..."

Arbert looks away. Words fail him. You put a hand on his shoulder, and though he flinches, he does not pull away.

"When the day has come, and we've had our rest, I will pray with you," you tell him. "You will tell me stories about Rachel, who she was, how she smiled, and yes, we will grieve together, Arbert. All this, done in the light of day and in the warmth of a welcoming home. But not here. Not among the dead."

He looks up at you, torn between denial and surrender.

"Go home," you tell him. "Let me endure alone the reaping hour in this graveyard."

Arbert nods, and he pats your hand.

"You're right," he says. "I should never..."

His entire body freezes. His eyes are wide, and his gaze, locked over your shoulder. His lips move, but no words come forth. He has no breath to speak them.

You stand tall, telling yourself it is nothing, to not be afraid, and then turn about.

A young girl of about ten years of age stands at the foot of the tree where little Edwin was found. Her skin is paler than the moon. Her shift is much too thin to provide any protection against the cold. Her eyes are bloodshot, her hair, matted to her neck and face with snow. She stands there, her head tilted to one side, looking confused.

"Rachel," Arbert says. "Oh sweet baby, it's you."

You thrust your arm to halt his approach. The sight of the girl, the *wrongness* of her presence, sets off a thousand alarm bells within your mind.

"Arbert," you say. "Don't."

Rachel takes a single step closer. Her feet are bare, her toes, black from frostbite.

"Jason?" she asks. Her head tilt deepens. "Is that…no, not, you're…Mark? Edgar? Not…you…father, you're not father, father, name of father…"

Arbert shoves you aside. It doesn't matter the unnatural sound to her voice. It won't stop him that a strange light is seeping out of her skin, as if she were a glowing ember of moonlight floating across the graves. His daughter is here, and you feel a lump catch in your throat as he rushes past you.

His sorrow. His despair. His relief. It's all so fresh and fierce as he collapses to his knees and throws his arms around his daughter. She stands there, looking down at him with vague recollection. You have not the heart to interrupt it. He's sobbing as he clings to her.

"Daddy?" she asks, sudden clarity coming over her. Tears collect in her eyes and then start to fall. "Daddy, there's so many, so many, and they're so *loud*…"

The light about her is growing. Panic spikes through you as you guess at what it might be. It *shouldn't* be, not as you understand it, but what else could explain this miracle? But that light…you've seen that light before.

"Arbert, get away from her," you say.

He ignores you. He's too busy wiping away the tears from his daughter's face.

"We have to get her home," he says. "Goodness, girl, how have you stayed warm? Your toes, Sisters help us, your poor toes." He glances back at you. "We'll have to amputate them, won't we?"

You meet the man's gaze. He's a dead man.

"I'm sorry," you say.

The light about Rachel's skin pulses and then expands. Her head whips backwards, and though her mouth opens as if to scream, she is silent. From her body emerges not one soul, but dozens upon dozens of them, the collected mass of every single shining soul buried in this graveyard. They are a teeming mass of light, swirling with memory and emotion. Never have you see them together in such a way, trying to occupy a single body as they had with Rachel.

There isn't room, and they bleed out of Rachel as the reaping hour arrives, and Anwyn's silent call sweeps across the land. Only they don't ascend. No light pulls them. They merely swarm about Rachel's body like birds in flight.

Every Soulkeeper is warned throughout their schooling to never, ever touch a soul. It is light, it is fire, and most of all, it will burn. It will consume. And when the dozens flow silently out of Rachel, far too many push straight through the grieving father clinging to her body. Flesh peels and blackens from a fire so hot no furnace can match. Bones turn to ash as sparkling souls pierce through his chest and ribs.

Your only consolation is that Arbert dies so swiftly, so suddenly, his pain is quick, if it was even felt. His body collapses at Rachel's feet, punctured with holes and bleeding out his innards. Rachel shivers as the last of the souls exits her, and then she stares down at her father, surrounded by a halo of lost souls meant to await the time of Eschaton and Lyra's great call to the heavens. Frustration furrows her brow.

"Daddy?" she asks. Her eyes widen. Her lips quiver. "Dad?"

This time, she did scream.

You sheathe your sword and draw your pistol from its holster. Getting close to her is a death sentence. As your thumb cocks open the chamber, you slip your free hand into pouches to withdraw a flamestone, and then a lead shot. It takes you about eight seconds to fully load your pistol and have it at ready.

During those eight seconds, Rachel's scream never stops.

"I don't know what death came for you," you say as you prepare your aim. "But those souls have no claim upon you, and they are cruel to keep you alive for their purposes. By Alma, we are born. By Lyra, we are guided. By Anwyn, we are returned. Beloved Sisters, take her home."

You pull the trigger.

The hammer slams down, its sharpened spike piercing the flamestone in half. Power and flame erupt within the chamber. Your aim is true. The shot strikes her forehead with enough force to explode out the back, carrying brain matter with it.

Rachel staggers on her feet and then falls, her scream finally at an end. The souls that had hovered around her vibrate, and their swirling orbits suddenly turn wild and unsteady. You cross your arms before your face and brace yourself for the pain they might cause if they collide with you, but it seems luck is with you. The swirl out wider, wider, blasting through the pines. The trees collapse, their trunks broken. Higher. Higher. Toward the stars. Toward the places beyond.

You stand there, breathing heavily, the sound of the flamestone ringing in your ears. In the silence that follows, it is deafening. You look to the bodies, first Rachel's, then

Arbert's, and realize you have two more reaping rituals you must perform. The weight of it falls heavy upon your mind. Tonight's reaping hour has already passed. 'Tis a burden for another night.

The howl of a wolf pulls you from your thoughts. Close. Too close.

A majestic beast stands atop one of the collapsed pines to your right. His pack is behind him, nine in number. The lead wolf takes two steps toward you, moonlight sparkling off his black and silver fur. His yellow eyes meet yours, and they sparkle with intelligence.

"The mountain wakes," says the wolf. "Flee, or be prey."

Your mind threatens to break.

Wolves do not talk.

Wolves do not talk.

You run all the same.

4

It's morning. You sit on the bed of the little guest room within the mayor's cabin, lent to you for the duration of your stay in Elkwerth. You haven't decided what to do about the dead father and child. From what you leaned prior to your vigil, Arbert's wife passed years ago. There's no family left to grieve him and his daughter, only those who knew them. It feels shallow. It doesn't feel like enough.

You haven't told anyone about their deaths.

You haven't told anyone about the wolves.

Elise's cabin has a chicken coop out back, and she's cracked several freshly laid eggs into a skillet and cooked them over the fire. Upon your arrival to the kitchen, she sets the skillet down on the table with a proud smile. Waiting beside it is a glass jar, which she opens, dips in her fingers, and pulls out a mixture of shredded greens you assume are grown local. She spreads them over the eggs, then gestures for you to eat.

You're not hungry, but you take the waiting fork and give it a try. The spices are surprisingly bitter, with a kick of heat upon swallowing.

"That's the leaves of our local radishes you're tasting," Elise says as she sits opposite you at the table. She tilts her head to one side. "You look ill, Soulkeeper, and your return last night was late. Did you…well. How did your watch go?"

She's hiding it, but you see the way she's fidgeting, and how her hands clench tightly in her lap. She wants answers. She wants to know about Rachel.

"Poorly," you begin, and then tell the tale exactly as you remember it. Rachel's appearance. The emergence of souls within her body. The way they burned her father, before you put a bullet through her forehead. Elise listens silently, her skin steadily draining of color.

"Sisters help us," she says at the end. "Are they still out there? Their bodies, I mean?"

"They are," you say, and then hesitate. This part, with the wolves...perhaps you were tired. The hour was late, and your mind ragged from travel and having to kill the little girl.

No. You shake your head. It happened. Now is not the time to start doubting your own memories.

"I left them there, to go back this morning," you say. "Because of the wolves."

You tell her how they arrived, quiet and ominous, and then had their pack leader speak his warning. Her mouth tightens, the wrinkles in her face deepening.

"Absurd," she says when you finish. "And yet, we live in a land of absurdity, and I have not the stones to argue with a Soulkeeper. What do you suppose the beast meant when he said 'the mountain wakes'?"

"Perhaps they mean the creatures, like themselves, they're...awakening?" you say, your best guess at the matter. "Surely the wolves haven't been this intelligent all these years, and your village never noticed."

"They're cunning creatures, but they sure as shit don't talk," Elise says. She stands from the table, but goes nowhere. She looks uncertain. Unsteady. "What do we do with the bodies? Well, what's left of them after those wolves ate their fill?"

"I cannot say for certain, but Arbert's soul is still within his body. He deserves a reaping ritual, no matter what state his remains are in."

"Then I'll get John and Daniel to help you with the

bodies," she suggests. "They deserve their rituals, and their pyres. Get them back to town, where we can prepare them accordingly. No wolves will bother us here."

You rise from your seat. Your hand falls to the hilt of your sword by instinct.

"I pray it so," you say.

*

John is a big man, early into his thirties and well-honed by work in the mines. Daniel is his younger brother, and neither as tall nor as strong. Other than that, they are spitting images of one another, red-haired, wide-toothed, and freckled across the cheeks and arms. The pair follow you up the mountain to the graveyard, pulling a cart loaded with linens to use as wrapping. The brothers cheerfully chat with you, as if unaware, or unbothered, by their purpose. They ask you questions about Londheim, the great city on the Septen River, or if you've ever been further east, to Steeth, Oris, or even the Kept Lands ruled by the Ecclesiast in Trivika.

The answer to all of that is no. You were born in Londheim, trained in the ways of the Soulkeepers at the Grand Cathedral, and then given duties across West Orismund. It dampens the brothers' enthusiasm only a little, as does finally arriving at the graveyard.

The two bodies lay stiff in the snow. The wolves did not touch them. You can't decide if that is further proof of their otherworldly intelligence, or evidence they were a fever dream of yours.

"What a shame," John says, and he dips his head toward the bodies. "Sisters bless and keep them, the both of them. Arbert had a hard life ever since his wife died. Rachel was barely three then. We helped out where we could, we always do, but it's lonely up here in the mountains, even when surrounded by those who know and care for you. They deserved better."

"Someone should tell Lyra that, the cruel bitch," Daniel says. He immediately freezes in place, realizing he's just profaned one of the Three Sisters in the presence of a Soulkeeper. You stare at him, your gaze holding him in place stronger than any irons.

"Lyra's eye falls upon us all," you say. "Even those in the frozen wilds of the far west. I will not pretend to know her plans…nor will I deny your grief and anger. Express both how you wish, Daniel. I merely suggest you do it silently."

The younger brother blushes a fierce red and bobs his head up and down.

John punches him in the shoulder as he walks past. "Dipshit."

Wrapping Rachel's body was easy enough, if one avoided looking at her forehead. Arbert's was more difficult, given the holes throughout his body and the innards that had spilled out and then frozen overnight.

"Pile the innards, and then bury them so no scavengers can eat them," you say. "The soul is all that matters, and it resides within the mind."

Daniel glances at Rachel's corpse, opens his mouth to speak, and then wisely shuts it.

You continue with your work, wrapping the body once the brothers are busy digging with a shovel. In the clean light of day, it's easy to forget the strangeness of the prior night. You try not to dwell on the mysteries. What did it mean, for so many souls to steal a living body? You must report this to the Keeping Church the moment your stay in Elkwerth is over. The Mindkeepers will run wild with theories to explain it, if they believe you.

As for the wolves, well, perhaps you'll keep that to yourself, even from your Vikar, Forrest Raynard, the man in charge of Soulkeepers throughout West Orismund.

Halfway through wrapping Arbert's body, the ground

begins to shake. The trees sway with a deafening rustle of leaves. The violent earth shifts and sways beneath you, and you drop to your hands and knees to maintain balance. Far away, you hear a cracking of pines.

Just as suddenly as it began, the shaking halts. The three of you pick yourselves up off the ground. It's quiet now, disturbingly so.

"Do you have earthquakes here often?" you ask.

"Nothing like that," John says. He pauses as another distant rumble of noise washes over you three.

"Avalanche, a distant one," Daniel says. "Shit, do you think it hit the town?"

Shrugs all around. There's no way for any of you to know.

"Right," Daniel says. "I guess I'll have to find out for myself."

He looks about, reaches a decision, and then hurries over to his picked tree. Within seconds he's scrambled halfway up it, possessing admirable dexterity.

"Come on, now, you'll get sap all over your clothes," John calls up after him. "And it won't be you cleaning it, we both know that."

"Clothes are meant to get dirty," Daniel says as he ascends. "And it's either I climb, or I run back to see for myself. Your choice."

You linger at the bottom of the tree, your hands itching, your neck covered in cold sweat. Something feels wrong, very, very wrong. You can't place it. Invisible fingers are brushing along your spine. It's like the reaping hour has come in the daylight.

"The town's fine," Daniel calls from the top of the tree. You sigh with relief, not realizing just how worried you had been.

"Then get down so we can get these bodies ready for

their pyre," John shouts up.

"Sure, I...wait. What is...I don't understand."

You gaze up at the man. His face has gone shocked white. His expression reminds you of a rabbit spotting the shadow of a hunting hawk. He's staring west, toward the tallest, snow-tipped spires of Alma's Crown.

"What is it?" you ask.

He fights for words.

"Water?" he says at last. "Black water?"

"Start making sense!" John shouts up at him, as if that would help.

You've had enough. Whatever is going on, it seems you'll need to see it with your own eyes. You grab the lower branches and begin climbing. It's difficult, the branches are thin, the bark rough against your palms, but you hug close to it as you climb. Perhaps not as graceful an ascent as Daniel's, but you're soon a dozen feet above the ground and able to peer down the mountain, toward the town.

And then you see it.

At first, you think it a shadow, a deep one from a cloud blocking the sun. It's moving from the crossing to the northwest, the gap through the mountains you used to arrive in Elkwerth. Not a shadow, though. It's too dark, too in motion. Like water, black water, just as Daniel described. And unlike an avalanche, it is silent in its movement, and when it passes over trees, you see them bend not a wit.

"Well?" John shouts up at the both of you.

The water is not slowing. The town is in its path.

"Climb," you shout down at him.

"What?"

"I said climb!"

He looks around, baffled and as if in search of someone to argue with. Above you, Daniel gasps. You tear your gaze away from him and back to the town. It is fully submerged by the black water, and the flood is not slowing. The flow carries it higher, up the mountain, toward you.

You slide down the trunk, grimacing against the branches scratching at your face. Once halfway, you wrap your legs tight and pivot so you can offer your hand. John has begun to climb, but his weight is a heavy burden on a tree already laden with two others.

"Hurry," you shout at him. John clings to the trunk, climbing faster despite knowing nothing of the reason. He's so slow, though, too slow. He looks up at you, reaches for your hand, but he's only a few feet off the ground.

Not far enough.

The black water arrives.

5

The water, if it is water, is silent. No noise as it rushes over the land. The air does not move with its passage. Though it is midnight black, there are depths to it that emerge as you stare, captivated. Faint stars swim just beneath the surface. Strange, smoke-like things shift in purples and blues, formless and nameless. It eats the sunlight. The physical world dissolves at its touch.

All the while, silence. John's hand vanishes beneath the flow. Above you, Daniel makes not a sound.

You don't know how much time has passed. Your mind is lost to the flow, the pine needles and branches swallowed so it seems you hover above a great, abyssal ocean of space. At some point, though, it ends, and the water recedes away. When it does, a spell over your mind breaks. You gasp for air, and it feels like you've been holding your breath this whole time. Your head aches. The muscles of your neck and back are tight.

Now, finally, Daniel screams.

"John!"

He scrambles down the branches past you, despite your shouting for him to halt. What you see below, it isn't safe. It doesn't even seem real.

Where the water flowed is now black and rotting. What grass remains has lost all its color and become a uniform gray. The bark of the tree is pitch black, and it reeks of mold. The needles are the same gray as the grass, and upon Daniel touching them, they explode into a powder that fills the air. You turn away to avoid breathing it in, but there is so much of it. The powder stings your throat, and you cough as your eyes water. It feels like fire has flowed into your lungs.

Daniel collapses amid a cloud of gray, the grass also dissolving into the air. He gags, fighting for every breath. Through blurry eyes, you watch him blindly flail about, searching for his brother.

"Daniel," you say, your voice hoarse as if you had spent the last several hours shouting until your throat was raw. "Get away from it."

'It', for the shambling thing surely cannot be John any longer. His clothes are faded and weathered as if they had spent a century beneath the sun. All his hair has fallen from his head and face. His skin is the color of spoiled milk. Blood drips from his nostrils, coagulating into a thick sheen crusting over his mouth. Though his eyes are open, they are solid black, and you do not know if they can see.

You desperately want to climb down, but the strange powder cannot be ignored. Keeping your legs wrapped tightly about the tree, you draw a knife from your belt and use it to slice off a strip of your shirt. Once it is free, you tie it over your nose and mouth to form a mask. It isn't much, but you hope it will be enough. There's no protection for your eyes. You will have to make do.

"John," Daniel croaks out, still choking and blinded by the erupted powder.

"I said get away!" you shout, louder, not caring that it tears your throat. The thing that was John has turned toward Daniel. It sways unsteadily on its feet, one step, then two. Daniel is blind to him. He can't see it. He doesn't know.

No time for a pistol. You close your eyes and drop the rest of distance to the ground. More pine needles explode. You feel the little puffs of air from your passage, feel the way they make your skin burn, but then you land. You draw your sword the moment your feet are steady, and through blurred tears, glare at the walking thing that is John.

Its hands are reaching for Daniel. No sound marks its attack, for its mouth is sealed over with the crusted blood. You take one step and then thrust with your sword. The tip pierces through its back, punctures the heart, and then pushes out the other side. It halts in place, back arching, head lolling side to side. All strength leaves it, and finally it drops to its knees and then collapses to one side.

You withdraw your sword. It is slick with blood, but none like you have witnessed before. Its much darker, almost black, and much too thick. You wipe it off on John's body, sheathe it, and then finally turn your attention to Daniel.

The young man is on his knees, weeping. His eyes are clouded, and he's pointing a hand toward John's body. The whole arm is shaking.

"What happened?" he asks once he's able to form words. "Robin...what nightmare is this?"

You have no answers. You have not even guesses. The only clue you have is the cryptic words of the wolf that chased you from Rachel's and Arbert's corpses

The mountain wakes...

Fear spikes down your spine.

The corpses.

You turn to where both bodies were wrapped in preparation for bringing them back to town for a proper pyre.

Within the heavy cloth, the bodies writhe.

"Stay here," you tell Daniel, and draw your pistol.

A fresh lead shot for the head of Arbert. A second for Rachel, this one through her heart.

The writhing stops.

*

You give Daniel a moment to recover as your own

thoughts race. It is a futile act. You have nothing to work with. Given the catastrophe around you, you reluctantly admit perhaps the final age of Eschaton has come, when Anwyn will call all remaining souls, both living and the deceased, up with her to the heavens. Perhaps that is why the corpses rise.

Glancing about the forest, it is hard to believe anything else. Wherever the black water flowed, the trees are rotted. The grass and needles are poison waiting to erupt at your touch. The dead do not stay dead.

"The water killed him," Daniel says at last. He looks up at you, his eyes bloodshot from tears, the powder, or perhaps both. There is ash in his red hair. "Not you. The black water."

You nod. "I'm sorry, Daniel. The way it moved, the way it acted…I was certain you were in danger."

The man nods. His gaze is loose, his movements rigid. He's in shock. You don't blame him.

"How far does it go?" he suddenly asks. He's refusing to look at you. "I saw it rush in from the pass. That's two miles out from the town…" He startles to his feet. Horror lines his features. "The town, Robin. *The town.*"

"Stay calm, Daniel," you say, but your own calm is a lie. You saw the passage of the water from your perch. The black water washed over Elkwerth in its entirety. You think of what happened to John, recreated over the two hundred or so people living within the town.

You can't go back there.

To go back is death.

"We have to hurry," Daniel says. He lifts up his shirt so it covers his face akin to your mask. "They'll need our help!" He then stops and looks back to his brother's body. "We…we have to bury him, too, though. Or a pyre. Can we burn him, Soulkeeper? Or must we wait for the reaping hour?"

The rules and laws of the Keeping Church bubble up

through your mind, comforting in their rigid familiarity.

"A pyre come the reaping hour," you say. "It is the same for all, no matter the life a person leads."

He bobs his head up and down.

"All right. We can do that when night comes, but until then, people need us."

You don't have the heart to stop him. You only follow in his wake, your eyes squinting against the cloud of ash rising up from the grass. You tell yourself that when he sees what remains, he'll understand. He'll be ready to leave and come with you. Until then, you're careful to step on snow when possible, and to duck underneath any and all branches so as to not scatter more of the dreadful powder.

Nothing good remains within Elkwerth. The two of you pause at the edge of the woods and stare at what remains. Whatever wood the black water touched is rotting and covered with a thick black mold. Several rooftops have collapsed, the weakened structures no longer able to support the weight. The only saving grace is foot traffic has largely beaten away any and all grass so there is bare dirt to walk over.

Three bodies shamble through the street, mouths crusted over, their eyes weeping black pus.

"Elise," Daniel says, and he points. You look closer, and agree one is the mayor. You did not recognize her without her gray hair. She walks slowly, steadily, her upper body swaying with the movements. The two with her walk in stride, as if they were her escorts.

"There, you've seen enough, Daniel," you tell him. "We must leave. There is nothing left for us here."

The younger man glares at you. The look in his eye is worrisome. It's a man losing his grip.

"There has to be survivors," he insists. His voice raises with each word. "We can't be the only ones, Robin, we can't!"

Elise turns. Her eyes may not work, but her ears

appear to function. Her jaw moves. She's trying to say something but can't. The blood caked across her mouth will not let her.

"Daniel, please, come with me," you say.

Instead, he rushes into the town. He walks between broken buildings and walls reeking of rot.

"What if they're sick?" he shouts back at you. "John…you killed John before he did anything wrong. Before he said anything. You didn't know."

You retreat back into the woods. You will watch, but you will not die with him.

Daniel approaches Elise. He's calling out her name, and sure enough, it seems like she recognizes him. Her head tilts to one side. Her black eyes blink. Again, a movement of her jaw, and a churning of the dried blood, as if her tongue were pressing against it.

And then it tears. The seal of blood breaks. Her jaw pulls wide, and from within, you hear the most horrific shriek.

You load your pistol.

All three dive upon Daniel, clawing at him wildly, their hands reaching for his throat. Only Elise can bite, and she does, her now-jagged teeth sinking into Daniel's stomach as he flails. The others can only beat him with their bare fists, coating him with bruises as they steadily, mercilessly bludgeon him.

The noise is attracting more. Doors open. Windows break. What were three are soon thirty.

Despite the risk, you pull the trigger, putting a lead shot through Daniel's head to end his suffering. The sound of the flamestone is a thunder. You do not wait to see if your aim was true. You dare not let them see you, nor gain any ground.

You retrace your steps through the woods, silently whispering a prayer for Lyra to protect Daniel's soul, and for Anwyn to guide it into her arms come the fall of the sun. You are desperate to leave Elkwerth, but there is still business yet to be done.

*

You return to the bodies of Rachel, John, and Arbert. You cannot stay until nightfall, and the subsequent reaping hour, and so this will have to do. You pour a bit of oil over all three bodies, then pull out your flint stones. Once you set it alight, you move onto the next.

Let this be enough, you pray to Anwyn as the bodies burn. *I cannot do more, goddess. This must be enough.*

You have no horse. You have no supplies beyond the near empty rucksack you carry with you at all times. You do not know what animals of the wilds have survived the flood of black water. The lands beyond the mountain pass may be no better than where you are now, but you have to try.

You look the direction of Elkwerth, imagining the shambling bodies of those corrupted by the black water. They are beyond your help, and too numerous to safely grant them mercy with blade and lead shot. In whatever life, and whatever form they have now, they must endure.

"I'm sorry," you whisper, and begin your trek east.

6

You trudge across the thin layer of snow, bone-tired but unwilling to stop. To slow down was to risk the things within the village catching up to you. Not that you know they're chasing you. Nothing says they are. But you cannot shake the feeling, a nagging possibility that keeps your feet moving one step after the other.

The only blessing is that once you reach the mountain pass, the grass is thin, and the trees rare, so you no longer need to cover your mouth against the eruption of black powder that inevitably follows. Even better, you no longer must endure the sting to your eyes.

At least, for now. Beyond the pass…once free of the great mountain range of Alma's Crown…what then awaits you? How far has the black water flowed? If all the world is barren and rot, the very vegetation ready to erupt and assault…

No. You cannot think on that now. To dwell on that was to give up, and rob your feet of movement. Trudge. Cross the stone. Pass through the mountains. Find hope on the other side. That is your motivation. That is your goal, however thin, however hopeless.

You stop to rest only come nightfall. Building a fire is no easy task, given the state of the vegetation, and so you decide to do without, even if it means a chill night. Your stomach rumbles as you wrap your coat tightly about your body for warmth. It will have to do for a blanket. At least the material is rugged and warm. It was one of the reasons your Vikar, Forrest Raynard, ordered the standard Soulkeeper outfit that was predominant in the east to include a longer length and much thicker padding.

Sadly there is nothing you can do about a meal.

Your aim is solid, and you keep alert for a potential rabbit, squirrel, or even bird during your trek. A single lead shot could earn you a meal, albeit one potentially rough given your lack of fire to cook it over…but there has been none. Nature has gone into hiding.

Or been slaughtered by the black water, you think as you close your eyes. Sleep. You need to sleep. If only your mind would settle for a few moments and allow it to come to you. If only the horrors of the past few days did not seek to scrape your consciousness, denying you a peaceful rest.

If only you did not hear the soft padding of footfalls.

You do not wait for them to get closer. Your sword is ever at your side, and you bolt into a sitting position while pulling it free of its sheath. What greets you is not one of the shambling villagers, as you feared, nor a potential traveler along the road arriving from the west.

It is a lone wolf, his eyes glinting yellow in the night. His fur is in waves of black and gray, and you recognize him as the wolf you encountered in the graveyard.

He is also twice his previous size.

"Spare me your blade," he says.

Every word is a nail driven into your forehead. To hear a wolf speak breaks your every understanding of the world. But then again, how much did you truly understand the Cradle now the black water has appeared, the dead walk, and wolves talk?

You lower your sword onto your lap, but do not sheathe it.

"Forgive me my caution," you say. It is with grim

humor you realize your tone and demeanor are instinctual, the same cheerful smile and calm grace you would show strangers when newly arriving to their village. "The day has been strange, and dangerous, and I feared you come with unpleasantness in mind."

The wolf paces twice before you. The path across the mountain is not particularly wide, about ten feet from side to side. To your left is a sheer cliff. To your right, the rest of the towering spire. Before you, your newly come nightly visitor.

"If matters were changed, I would indeed taste your blood on my tongue," the wolf says. "But I am in need of your weapons of war."

You want to argue that your sword and pistol are meant to be used for peace keeping, not war, but it occurs to you that is a pointless argument to have with, well, a wolf. What did the creature even know of war?

The intelligence sparkling in his eyes makes you uncomfortable. Perhaps he knows far more of war than you do.

"I will help anyone in need," you say.

"Even a wolf?" he asks. His voice is strange, to say the least. Much deeper than expected, and lacking much range in inflection. "No, we both know that answer. You would chase us away to protect herd and coop."

"Perhaps I would not have, should you speak with me."

The wolf pants at you, and you get a disturbing feeling it is something akin to a grin.

"Then is it speech that decides a life's worth with you, human?"

"Robin," you say. "My name is Robin. Have you one of yours, that I might know the identity of the beast come to insult me while I sleep?"

The wolf snorts and shakes his head. Trying to read

his expressions is frustrating, to say the least, partly because you have never had to do so before.

"My name you cannot say," he says. "The scent of a being is a name, and beyond your nose and tongue. But a second name has come to me. It has...shaped me, these last few days. Awakened me. I remember ages past, Robin. I remember commanding great tribes of my kind numbering in the thousands. I was a king, I believe, yet what remain of my subjects?"

His head droops, and he shakes it.

"No. Memories. The past. It is too much. I cannot think." He looks back up at you. "I am the last survivor of my pack. My name is Wotri, and if either of us are to survive this night, it will be with the help of your weapons. Ready them, human. They are not far behind me."

You rise to your feet, urged on by the wolf's worry.

"Who are?" you ask.

Wotri glances back down the passage, toward Elkwerth. "My pack."

You stare that same direction, seeking what Wotri sees with his superior eyes in the moonlight. It isn't long until you spot the first sign of scurrying amid the snow. It is a wolf, just as Wotri insisted, distant and strange.

It has too many legs.

"What in the Sisters' names is that?" you ask as you ready your sword.

"The Sisters bore no part in this," Wotri says. The fur on his neck stands on end. "We witness the blessing of Viciss."

"Viciss?" you ask.

"A name. A presence. A god. It comes to me unbidden, but its meaning slips when I ponder upon it. Focus, human. My pack was more numerous than one."

Sure enough, there is a second wolf not far behind it,

and a third. You steel yourself for their approach. It's so fast, a full sprint along the mountain pass, and not on their paws. Long, obsidian black legs pierce out the center of their spines. Four of them, hooked and bent halfway down. They scurry toward you, the wolf body hanging limply beneath the legs, almost like an unneeded appendage.

It is still alive, though. You can see the glint of their eyes, hear their growls, see the whites of their teeth. Their every movement is a horror.

You sheathe your sword and quickly begin loading your pistol with lead shot.

"I was alone when the black water came," Wotri tells you. He bares his teeth against the approaching spider-wolf monstrosities. "Ascending the mountain, seeking a cave to which I could…become me. When the ground shook, and the water passed, I sought out my pack to find them changed. Broken. Become *this*."

You finish loading your pistol and draw aim to the scurrying wolves. They are silent on those long, long spider legs. You imagine a fate where Wotri did not wake you, did not give you warning, and it is terrifying.

They're so close now. More eyes stare out from their faces, some smooth and black, others shining yellow in the moonlight. At last they howl, and when their mouths open, you see what reminds you of serpent fangs dripping clear drops of venom.

"Sisters have mercy," you mutter.

"No mercy," says Wotri. "Not for them. They suffer. End it."

Their movements are quick, their scurrying uneven, but you have hit smaller, more nimble targets before. You prepare your aim, pull the trigger, and fire. The lead shot hits directly in the forehead of the nearest wolf-thing, piercing one of the additional black eyes. It lets out a high-pitched yip and collapses. The spidery appendages squirm a moment before it rolls over, the legs curling inward and growing stiff.

There is no time to load another shot. You holster your pistol, lift your sword, and prepare for the worst.

7

Only three of the spider-wolves remain, but they still outnumber you. And their speed, Sisters help you, their speed…

"Slaughter them!" Wotri snarls, and he meets their charge with a dash toward the wall of the mountain. He is twice the size of their bodies, and he uses it to his advantage, his teeth snarling and his jaws snapping for the eight-eyed faces of his former pack.

You refuse to let the wolf fight alone. With a cry of your own, you dash toward the other two. You can only guess to their intelligence, but instinct says to treat them like deadly predators. Your sword is long, almost as long as their legs. You just have to hope yours strikes first.

That hope dies the moment the nearest leaps into the air. Its legs lash forward, its mouth hangs open, and it's above you, and falling. You lift your sword rather than risk dodging. Legs braced, you accept the weight of it as it slams down on you, impaling itself upon your sword. Blood pours across your hands and the arms of your coat, disturbingly cold, and black like tar. The spider-wolf howls in pain. Your sword is deep in its chest, holding it at bay, but its mouth is so close. You see its quivering fangs as it snaps at you.

One of its legs slashes across your shoulder, and you bite down a scream. The ends are razor sharp, and you feel your own warm blood trickle down your arm. With a heave, you turn and shove the dying thing away from you so it can

NIGHT OF WINGS AND SMOKE 51

do no more damage. It slides free of your blade, rolls once, and then curls up with its legs quivering.

The impact of something heavy strikes the center of your back, and you tumble dangerously close to the edge of the cliffside pass. You let out a gasp and drop to your knees, unable to maintain your balance. A second impact hits your waist, and when you glance aside, you realize what it is.

Webbing.

The strands have latched to your coat, as well as the stone beneath you, holding you firm. You twist and pull against them, but there is no give. Trying not to panic, you look up to see the nearest spider-wolf chittering its fangs your way. Its wolf body has curled forward its lower half, and where the tail of the beast should be is instead a long spinneret.

You give one last tug, but there will be no give. Your coat. You have to remove your coat.

The spider-wolf lunges at you before you can withdraw an arm. You hold your sword in one hand, and it is a meager defense against the attack. You swing nonetheless. Maybe you'll score a lethal blow so it dies after it devours you…or wraps you up in webbing, to remain trapped and slowly rotting away as its venom does it work.

"Enough!" howls Wotri, slamming into the wretched monster mid-air. His heavy body easily shifts its trajectory, away from you and toward the cliff. It lands just beyond, with only a lone black leg outstretched to catch the rock. The hooked tip scrapes along, fails to find purchase, and then the thing vanishes from view.

"Free yourself," Wotri says as he lands and then spins around. Before you can react, he is already jumping back over you, to tackle his original foe. You slide your arms free of your coat and jump to your feet. The wind is cold, but you'll suffer its bite to help the self-proclaimed wolf king.

Wotri closes his teeth about one of those long, spidery

legs, and with a powerful crunch, he snaps it like a twig. Ichor spews across him, and his victory is short lived. The other leg slices his side, parting fur. Blood pours across him, and you can only hope the cut is not deep as you join his side, your sword thrusting.

The spider-wolf, now hobbling on three legs, does not try to dodge. Your swing slices open the wolf portion's belly and spills innards across the rock. If it cares, it does not show it, for nothing slows the quick snap of its fangs toward your leg.

You scream as they sink in. You scream louder as the first burning sensation floods your body as the venom pours into your bloodstream.

A turn of your blade, and you plunge it straight down into the thing's head, breaking the skull and piercing out the other side with the tip. The teeth relent, and you gasp. You're terrified to learn how much of the venom might be in you.

"Robin?" Wotri says, and you glance toward the wolf.

"I'm fine," you say, a thorough lie. Your bitten leg crumples, all feeling vanishing from the limb. The numbness ends at your hip, where you feel only vicious, burning pain. You take in several slow, deep breaths, trying to steady your heart and calm your mind. The faster your heart beats, the more the venom will spread, and you fear what happens if it reaches high enough to infect your lungs.

You are still on your stomach when you see the first of the black legs curl up over the edge of the cliff. The last spider-wolf. It seems the fall did not claim it after all.

"Wotri!" you shout as it vaults into the air, dark legs hooked and eager.

You may not be able to run, nor stand, but you can roll, and that's what you do as the spider-wolf lands where you were. Its legs are so close, you see the faint hairs along its seemingly smooth sides, the sharp ridges of its hooks, and the hear the scrape of them against the stone. You slice out with your sword at the end of your roll, cleaving off one of those hooks.

The thing shrieks in fury and pain, a mixture of a wolf's howl and a grating, thunderous roar more akin to a bear. It stumbles momentarily, then turns toward you. There is nothing but starlight reflecting off those six black eyes, but in the two remaining yellow, you see hunger and rage.

The fangs quiver as it snaps for you, and when you swing, it jolts back a step, avoiding the attempt. You prepare for a third, but there is no chance. Wotri lands atop the thing, his jaws closing about the neck of the monster. With one single, savage twist, he snaps the bone. The thing collapses, its legs shrivel up, and then it lays still.

Wotri releases his grip, trots aside, and then licks his tongue across the snow-covered stone. You suspect whatever blood or ichor flows through the thing's body is foul to taste. The fur of his right side is speckled crimson.

"How dire is the venom?" he asks you.

You use your arms to push away from the nearby body of the spider-wolf. The last thing you want to see is its cold, dead stare as white drops of venom leak out its fangs.

"Still just the leg," you say. "I don't think it's spreading."

"Good. Perhaps it needed more time. There is a reason for its webbing."

Again you imagine being fully wrapped in webs, those things given all the time in the world to pierce you in multiple locations with their fangs. Your stomach heaves, and you slide even further away.

"My coat," you say. With the rush of battle fading, you are aware of how cold you are with only your thick shirt and trousers.

Wotri pads over to where you left it, sniffs it once, and

then nuzzles it a bit with his nose. His teeth closed about the center of the fabric, and then he pulls. You hear a ripping sensation, and then the coat pulls free of the webbing holding it to the stone. He trots over and drops the coat at your feet.

"Thank you," you say, and slide it over your shoulders. Strands of webbing cling to the back, and you hope they will dissolve away over time. Once it is on, you slide your legs underneath you and then push up to a stand on your good leg.

As a test, you put your weight on the other, and immediately regret it. Numb it may be, but a fire spikes up your entire side, starting at your hip.

"I fear I cannot walk," you tell Wotri.

The wolf circles you once, then stops beside you. "Then let us rest here."

You glance at the bodies. "I don't think I can."

He licks his side a few times, comes away with a bit of blood on his muzzle. His head lowers, and you swear he lets out a sigh.

"So be it. Rest your weight upon me. I will be your leg."

You put your arm upon him and lean a bit his direction. Careful step by careful step, you limp down the pass, leaving the corpses of the monstrous, twisted wolves behind.

8

Wotri is quiet as he trots alongside you, bearing your weight. His injuries don't seem too bad, for which you're thankful. The wolf has not exactly been the kindest toward you, but he is far better than the monstrosities that sought to wrap you in webbing and sink in their fangs.

The size of Wotri still takes getting used to, even if it is convenient for you as a crutch. His height goes up past your waist, far taller than any wolf should be. Something about him has changed, and recently, yet it seems the black water was not the cause if he avoided its flow.

What then could it be?

"I want to thank you," you say as you slowly plod along. "For waking me."

"I do not seek your thanks," Wotri says.

"And sometimes a man does not seek water, and yet it rains on him all the same."

The wolf casts a glare your way. "I despise human sayings."

"That's rather impressive, given it's the first human saying you've ever heard."

You grin at the wolf. You're tired, hurt, cold, and hungry, but by the Sisters, you'll at least crack a smile out of this dour beast.

"You are clever, human," he says after a moment. "But that cleverness makes me dislike you even more. Is there a word for that?"

"Friendship?"

Wotri snorts. "Never mind. The trees carry more wisdom than you."

He walks the rest of the way in silence. When your tired body has had enough, you pick a spot relatively clear of snow and press up against the cliff side, hoping it will protect you from the wind. When settled, you check your other wounds. Nothing serious, but that cut on your arm worries you enough you cut a bit of your shirt and wrap it.

When finished, you count your flamestones. After that fight, you have eight left. An uncomfortably small amount, given how dangerous the world has become.

Wotri settles down near you, his head resting on his paws as he closes his eyes.

"I'm jealous of your fur," you say as you shiver underneath your coat.

"Is that why you murder us for it?"

All right, perhaps not the best choice of conversation. You let the matter drop immediately. Your breathing slows, and you close your eyes and try to forget the sound of black spider legs clacking across the mountain pass. Or better yet, stop imagining more of them climbing along the cliff side, hunting you, eager for when the pair of you let down your guard so they can sink in their fangs…

"Do you know what is happening?" you ask, deciding maybe sleep won't be coming after all. "The quake, the black water, what happened to your pack…"

You hear Wotri shuffle a bit.

"There is little I know, and much I do not. I know that I am not like I was days ago. I was…simpler. Wild. I feel new, and I feel old. Like I am an old wolf in the body of a young pup. But there are things I know. I know them like I know the scent of pine or the crunch of the snow beneath my paws."

You crack open an eye. Wotri is staring at the cliff, his

gaze distant.

"I was the king of fur and fang. The simple creatures obeyed my commands. My boundaries were loose, and all feared to cross them. My pack numbered in the thousands, and we were fierce. We were mighty."

He lowers his pointy ears.

"That was long ago. I sense it. Countless numbers of your years. Something happened to us. We were not slain. Banished. Forced into slumber. I cannot describe it, for I remember only darkness."

"Banished?" you ask.

Wotri shakes his head quickly, as if dismissing you.

"I cannot explain better. The world that was, our world, was put to darkness."

You frown and try to make sense of what the wolf is saying, and how it fits with your understanding of the world taught by the Keeping Church. The First Canon details the creation of the world, of how the Three Sisters came upon a barren rock floating within the void. Together, they birthed life upon it. They created the wolves and the deer, the bird and the fish, and then declared it good. Its inhabitants were ephemeral though, simple and incapable of worship, and so they reached across the grand emptiness known as the void and withdrew the very first light of a soul.

Within that soul were the concepts of love, forgiveness, compassion, and selflessness. The Sisters would gift this soul to their favorite amongst all their creations: the humans.

But there was one who hated this new world of light, and it was the void itself. Angered by the stars the Sisters created to hold it at bay, the void took the form of a great dragon and tried to swallow the first soul on its journey to the Cradle. They battled for a thousand years, but at last the void-dragon was defeated and fled far, far away to lick its wounds.

The Sisters delivered the first soul to the Sacred Mother, and with it, the divine right for her children to bear a new soul upon birth.

Yet to the Sisters' great sorrow, they discovered that the blood of the void-dragon had fallen upon the Cradle during their battle, and it tainted the purity of their creation. While humans now knew love and compassion, they also gained the capacity for hatred and cruelty. From that day forward, nothing was ever perfect upon the Cradle.

"The black water," you ask. "Is it the void-dragon's doing?"

"The void-dragon?"

"The darkness that lives beyond the stars. The source of all weakness and failures upon our lands. In the time of Eschaton, the Three Sisters are prophesied to descend from the stars to do battle one last time, and defeat the void-dragon so we may all be free of its corruption and live in true paradise."

Wotri turns to look at you, his mouth hanging open. Mockery, you realize, when he speaks.

"And who told you such nonsense?"

You weren't told these prophecies, of course, but instead read them in the collected writings known as Anwyn's Mysteries, penned by the famous Soulkeeper Judarius during his exile upon the Estranged Isles. They had long been debated by the Mindkeepers as to their authenticity, but the collected sentiment was that, while they may not be perfectly accurate in their predictions of the coming days, they were close enough as to have been guided by the Sisters' wisdom.

You suspect Wotri will not care about any of that.

"If not the void-dragon, then what created such a horrid thing as the black water?" you ask the wolf. "The trees rot. The grass explodes into powder, seeking to strangle and choke. The dead rise, and the living become strange, grotesque monsters."

Wotri lowers his head back down to his paws.

"All I know is that we are children distinct from you," he says. "Children...but of who? I knew, once."

"We?" you ask, still prying for information.

"They are names and flickering images, Soulkeeper, and I suspect you will not understand them. The foxkin. The avenria. The lapinkin, viridi, and dyrandar. I had a rival, the queen of the winged...Arondel. Her name was Arondel."

The names indeed mean nothing to you. The wolf could be talking nonsense, but you don't think so. After spider-wolves tried to eat you, you find it hard to argue against the possibility of things beyond your understanding.

"Who were the foxkin?" you ask, deciding to go with the simplest sounding name.

Wotri snorts. "I do not know."

"Who are the viridi?"

"I do not know. They were green. I remember plant life, the scent of grass unique only to them."

"The others then, the aven...avenria? The lapinkin? What are you talking about? Are they monsters? Creatures? Intelligent, like you, only squirrels and foxes?"

The wolf puts both paws over his face, covering his eyes.

"You ask many questions for such a late hour."

"I thought wolves are nocturnal."

He softly growls.

"I. Am. Injured. Would you have me hunt, and leave you to fend against whatever may follow us, or would you have me stay?"

Despite his grumpiness, you're surprisingly touched that he was choosing to stay with you out of concern for your safety. Maybe the cranky wolf wasn't so cold hearted as he pretended to be.

"Forgive me," you say. "My curiosity is born out of desperation. There is so much I do not understand, to an extant that leaves me feeling like I am drowning."

Wotri lifts his head once more, and he looks to the moon. He is still, very still. His eyes close. You watch and wait, giving him his moment.

"There was a name you used for us," he says at last. "A moniker that bound us. You cast it against us, as you went to war."

Another moment of silence.

"We were…we were…"

His eyes open, and he looks back to you. Their yellow glint offers no comfort.

"I remember," he says with a flash of teeth. "We were the *dragon-sired*."

9

Morning brings you no comfort. Feeling has returned to your leg, which is a relief, but it also means the pain of the bite is sharp and pulsating. Your muscles are stiff from sleeping on the hard ground, but to your surprise, your back is warm. You stir, and realize Wotri has curled up beside you. His large body is a bulwark against the swirling wind, and his fur, an extra layer of protection against the cold.

The moment you move, the wolf king stands up and trots a few feet away.

"You wake," he says. "It is about time. I thought humans rose with the sun."

The sunrise is hidden behind the mountains towering to your right, so that only orange rays of it peek over the tips. You suspect it is still much earlier than you'd prefer to be up and about if given the choice, and a warm bed to sleep in.

"It has been a long few days," you say. "Forgive my need for rest."

Wotri eyes you for a moment, then looks away.

"Your pack is light, and you have no food or water. We are in need of both."

That was putting it mildly. Your stomach is an angry knot, your tongue is painfully dry, and you feel lightheaded. Concentration is difficult, even more so than the day before. Eventually the wolf's full meaning pierces the veil.

"Did you go through my belongings?" you ask, torn between insult and amusement.

Wotri somehow looks indignant, even as a wolf.

"There was little to look through," he says. "And if we are to survive, I must know what is available to us."

You push yourself to a stand, pause momentarily for the dizziness to leave you, and then stretch your arms. The tightness in your back eases, but only a little. You take a few steps, testing your bitten leg. It holds strong, with barely a limp. At least there's that. Whatever venom the bizarre creature injected you with, it appears its purpose was to numb, not digest.

Still, you roll the trouser leg up just to check. The wound is unpleasant to look at, and reminds you of snake bites common to the men and women who work the fields east of Alma's Crown, where the grass is tall and hides all sorts of creatures. While angry, it does not look infected, for which you are thankful. No matter how kind Wotri might be, you suspect he would leave you to perish if you had to amputate the limb and hobble down the mountain pass.

"I suppose water should be our first goal," you say. "Then food, if you think there is any to be found."

"Is there another human village near?" Wotri asks.

You nod. "At the end of the pass, just beyond the mountains, there's a little trading hub named Westwall. We could reach it tomorrow, if we aren't delayed."

"Can you walk without delay?"

Your life as a Soulkeeper has worn out many pairs of boots. Under normal circumstances, you could push yourself to reach Westwall by nightfall, but on an aching leg and empty stomach?

"I can try my best," you say. You swallow, and find it difficult. "But it will not be easy."

Wotri trots over to your rucksack, sticks his nose in, and pulls out a little traveling pot by its wire handle. He sets it down on the rock.

"We cannot eat the snow," he says. "We must melt it. To do that, we need a fire."

You reach down and grab the little pot you bring with you everywhere, plus the rucksack, and hoist both onto your back.

"If we could build a fire, I would have already," you say. "But I have nothing to burn."

Wotri tilts his head slightly.

"Do you now?"

*

With a bit of oil, and a minute of striking your flintstones together, your rucksack steadily burns. You position the cooking pot beside it, using its heat to steadily melt the snow you dump inside it. The rest of your belongings are strewn about the cliff side, that which will not fit inside the pockets of your heavy coat.

Luckily for you, you have two separate waterskins, and as the morning drags on, you fill them both to near bursting. After that, you melt even more snow so that you and Wotri can drink your fill from the pot itself. The water is unpleasantly lukewarm, but that is a mild complaint against the warmth spreading in your belly and the absolute relief you feel in slaking your thirst.

"Those waterskins will have to carry us to Westwall," Wotri says when you finish, and your rucksack is down to smoldering embers. "As for food, we must hope little creatures are on our path, and that they escaped the black water's flow. Otherwise, we put our hopes upon your human village."

As much as you hate leaving comforts behind, you tell yourself you can make do without most of it. You keep your needle and thread, to fix both clothing and stitch flesh, depending on the need. The same goes for your skinning knife, sharpening stone for your sword, repair tools for your pistol, and the cook pot. The rest, things like rope, hunting traps, and several empty containers meant to store dried and salted food, you leave behind.

Westwall is a trading town, and it thrives on supplying goods to those making the trip to and from Elkwerth and its silver mines. It would surely have everything you need to replace what was left behind.

Assuming the village has survived, you think, but do not voice the dour thought. You still do not know the extent to which the black water has buried the world. Hope may await you at Westwall, or a horde of disfigured, ashen-skinned things the people became like in Elkwerth.

You won't know until you arrive, and so you try not to dwell on it. For now, it is time to put one foot in front of the other. Together, you and Wotri travel the path carved out along the mountainside. No hint of more spider-wolves, so there is that, at least. High above, you catch the sight of several vultures, as well as a hunting hawk. Seeing life, normal, untouched life, warms your chest more than the sun rising over the crests of Alma's Crown.

"What does it mean to be dragon-sired?" you ask Wotri after a bit. As comfortable as you are to travel in silence, your curiosity is stronger.

"It means what it means," he says. He trots a little faster ahead of you, for the path has been sloping downward for a good part of the last hour.

"As in, the void-dragon?" you ask. That something as majestic as Wotri could be made by the great corrupter upsets you, but the rest of what you have seen, the ruined wolves, the twisted humans, and the choking grass, all very much fit perfectly.

"I do not understand your obsession with this void-dragon," Wotri says. He glances back at you and licks his lips. "There *are* dragons, but not of the void. Why do you believe this so?"

You decide you definitely do not wish to argue the merits of Soulkeeper Judarius's work on Anwyn's Mysteries.

"It's what the Keeping Church teaches," you say, purposefully vague. "What is it that you believe, wolf king?"

Wotri snorts, but you can tell by the way he stands a little taller during his trot that he likes you calling him 'king'.

"It is not belief. It is knowledge. Five dragons. Five creators of this world. We are their children."

"You certainly do not look like the children of dragons."

"They did not birth us as pups. They...made us. Made everything. And then the Sisters came, and they made you, and they..." He shakes his head. "I do not know. It is hazy still. When I think on the Sisters, I feel rage, but I also feel betrayal."

"And the dragons?"

Wotri breathes in long and deep, and then lets it out in the wolf equivalent of a sigh.

"I remember not even their names. It vexes me. Give me time. I do not yet feel...complete."

You can't imagine what that means. Does he plan to grow bigger? It doesn't seem possible, but you swear his size is even greater than when you went to sleep. When walking side by side, the top of his back is just above your hip. If you thought he wouldn't eat you for suggesting it, you'd have requested a ride like he were a small, furry horse.

The hours pass. You stop occasionally to sit and rest your legs as well as drink from your waterskin. It's a bit tricky for Wotri to have his share, and you end up pouring it slowly above his head as he licks at the opening.

"Demeaning," he says afterwards, and leaves you alone for a bit.

The slope grows steeper downward, and it feels like

you spend more time tumbling forward than actually walking. Your first blessing arrives just after midday, at the sight of a pine forest sprouting before you. You've reach the end of the mountain pass, and while the spires are still tall about you, there is vegetation now, and a path slicing through the woods toward Westwall.

A forest, you pray, means potential game.

The black water, though, has beaten you here. It swept halfway up the trees, turning the needles to little gray barbs and trunks into rotting black poles weeping a disturbing, inky sap.

"The rage of it," Wotri says as he carefully walks the center of the worn path. It is the only place where you are safe from brushing against the needles and the awful explosion of ashen powder that occurs when they are disturbed. That it happens only by your touch, and not the rustle of branches against branches, or the blowing of the wind, adds a strangely sentient nature to its hostility.

"The water did not reach the top," you say. "That means we can burn those portions, and that maybe some birds or squirrels survived."

"Have you a means to chop the trees down?" Wotri asks.

"Forgive me, I did not pack an ax during my panicked flight from Elkwerth."

"A shame." He pauses, lifts his nose toward the trees, and begins to sniff. "But your optimism has merit."

Another few sniffs, and he trots off the path. You have to crouch to follow, and you're quick to replace the mask you fashioned to protect against the occasional brush of needles and the ashen mist that results. You do not know where Wotri is leading you until he stops before a tree no different than any other.

"Ready your pistol," he says.

You scan the tree, and after a moment, you spot the squirrel amid the still green portions of the pine. It is clinging to a branch, wary and silent.

"I have few flamestones left," you say as you start the process of loading a lead shot into your pistol.

"Is one stone worth one meal?" Wotri asks.

"It is," you say, and prepare your aim.

The shot strikes its head, cleaving off the poor creature's skull. It falls limp to the ground. Wotri picks it up by the tail, then lowers his ears.

"This way," he says, voice slightly muffled. He leads you to another tree, and after searching, you find another squirrel atop the branches. A shot, and it falls. Wotri leaves it for you to grab.

"Back to the path," you say, tired of crouch-walking slowly to avoid the constant threat of the ashen needles. Once in the clearing, you set the squirrel body down and draw your skinning knife. You've plenty of experience hunting and cleaning squirrels, though there still remains the issue of what to burn for you to cook it. The grass has mostly died underneath a layer of pine needles and snow, and you've no intention of digging it up with your hands to discover what the black water did to it.

Wotri, however, does not have that problem. He lays down in the center of the path and starts chewing away, swallowing half of the squirrel, bones and all, before you've even finished peeling the chest and back.

"I'm not sure how I'll cook mine," you tell the wolf.

"Is your hunger not great enough to dine raw?"

You wince. "I'd prefer not to, if I may. Now is not the time to catch illness or disease. I need a fire. The question is, what do I burn?"

"Have you need of your coat?" he asks in return. At your glare, he lowers his head and ears. "It was a jest, human.

I thought your kind favors those."

He finishes the last of the squirrel, even the tail to your mild surprise, and then trots off. When he returns several minutes later, he has an enormous branch between his teeth. The black water has clearly washed over it, and bits of black tar ooze across his teeth when he spits it out in front of you.

"Foul," he says. "Sour. Sick."

"What am I to do with it?" you ask.

"Burn it," he says as he rubs his tongue against the fur of his chest.

You've not actually tried to burn anything touched by the black water, and you're running low on precious oil. You shrug and decide to give it a try, although without any oil. With how wet it appears from the sap, you hold doubts it will burn well, and you're not willing to waste the resources on a fool's hope. Instead you ready your flintstones and shower it with a few sparks.

The branches catches instantly, with such fury it was as if the entire branch were soaked in oil. The flames sweep across its entire length, burning a strange, violet color. What smoke that rises off it is pale and white, but there is no questioning the heat. You frown and wish you'd actually broken the branch and layered the pieces atop one another, but you'd been hesitate to place your glove upon the rotted substance.

"It burns well," you say lamely to Wotri. The wolf nods as he watches.

"Keep it from the other trees," he says, and you have to agree. With how easily it caught fire, the entire forest could be quickly overwhelmed. You wince at the memory of you firing your flamestone pistol so carelessly earlier. What might have happened if one of the sparks had landed on the pine needles?

Cooking the squirrel is a bit tricky, but you use your

sword to spear the body on the tip and then hold it above the flame. Minutes later, you're devouring the meat, the grease sticky on your face and fingers. It tastes divine, and is a welcome heaviness in your stomach. As you suck what little bits you can from the bones, you feel the first inklings of true, honest hope.

The world was not yet over. Maybe, just maybe, your life can continue.

Wotri lays beside you, his eyes closed and his head near the fire to enjoy the warmth. You doubt he is asleep, even if he appears to be. Now that you're in the woods, you do a quick mental check of distances, comparing it to your trip to Elkwerth. Reaching Westwall by sunset appears unlikely. You'll need to spend another night beneath the stars. Thankfully, with how well the trees inflicted by the black water burn, you will not suffer without a fire.

Knowing you will not reach the village today, you decide to relax and let the meat settle in your otherwise empty stomach. It is a good time to refill your waterskins, and so you set up your little cooking pot, pile in some snow, and wait for it to melt down so you might safely store it.

"What did you mean earlier?" you ask Wotri as you add a bit more snow to the pot. He cracks open a yellow eye and glances your way.

"With what?" he asks. "You question many things incessantly, and know even less."

You hold back a smirk.

"When you say the trees," you clarify. "The rage. You referenced rage when looking at the black water. Whose rage?"

Wotri closes his eye, and after a pause, lets out a snort.

"Something of the change around me *feels* similar. Not by appearance. Not by destruction. The aura about it. The magic. It is…familiar. Almost comforting. But it is different, for unlike how I remember it, this is angry, so angry."

You glance about the ruined forest, and remember the cursed things the black water has made.

"If something is angry at us, and let loose this black water, then they are a vile being, indeed," you say.

He pushes up to his paws. "Or your crimes are unfathomable."

"Crimes?" you ask. "What crimes did these trees commit? What blame falls upon the members of your pack that they must suffer pain and misery, to be twisted into…" You pause, and realize you have gone too far. "Into what they became," you finish.

Wotri does not argue with you, not at first. He looks to the swaying gray branches above you, a smoky cloud to blot out the sun.

"The rage of the imprisoned," he says, his deep voice soft and distant. His tail wags once. "Our father. His name. I know his name. I feel it on my tongue. I smell it in the air. I saw it in the black water. It moves. It changes. Change. He *is* change. And his name…his name…"

Wotri's eyes open, and they are no longer yellow. They are swirling silver stars suspended in orbs of black. His fur ripples, not just gray and black anymore. The fur shifts, becoming red and gold, but only in waves before the color fades. He opens his mouth, and a mist of light leaks from his teeth. Where it lands beneath him, the grass turns red, like blood.

"Viciss," he says, and at the word, all the trees tremble. "The Dragon of Change."

And then he howls.

You see it.

The howl.

It flows out of him in a rainbow of color, sparkling like the spray of a waterfall. It floats upward into branches of increasing number. Reverberations shake through it with the howl, so fierce and high pitched, you fear your ears will bleed. It grows larger, blooming into an enormous tree of light and sound that somehow has taken physical form and absorbed every color of the spectrum visible to your eyes.

And when it touches the ashen needles of the pines, they wither away, not into a choking dust, but thick red drops. Crimson rain falls upon you, and there is no denying the choking scent of blood. They slide off Wotri's fur, unable to stain or wet him.

"Wotri," you whisper, at a loss for words.

The tree blooms with leaves, each as red as the setting sun. What they are born of, you do not understand. What keeps them aloft, you do not know. They are broad, like an oak, unlike the thin pines surrounding you, and then they fall. Some scatter to the distance, but nine leaves settle down upon Wotri's head and ears, latching together from ear to ear.

His howl ends. The tree dissipates. The leaf crown remains, hardening, becoming something akin to gold.

"I was and forever am the King of Fur and Fanged," Wotri proclaims to the sudden quiet. "These mountains were my borders, the lands beyond, my hunting ground. I oversaw a rule of might, and a truth found only in the prowl. I held no crown of silver or gold as man bore, but the trees themselves gave me their blessing. I wore it with pride, Robin, for the years did not touch me with their passing, and through generation upon generation, hunt and birth, nest and den, my kingdom flourished beneath my loving gaze."

He lowers his head. The stars remain in his eyes, but they twinkle now with a sudden flourish of tears.

"Where now is my kingdom? Why now are the nights silent, and my pack, gone to me? To what end was my punishment? What purpose, my absence?"

He remembers you are there, watching him, and he looks away.

"Leave me to my despair, human. Follow the path, and I shall not be far."

10

You give Wotri his space, and alone you walk the beaten path through the forest leading to Westwall. There is so much for your mind to process, you feel a bit lost in a dream. You acclimated to a talking wolf companion quicker than you know you should have, but even with that, witnessing such…wonder as the re-crowning of the wolf king, has reawakened you to how much the world has changed.

Continues to change, you tell yourself as you walk. Whatever has happened, whatever caused the black water and Wotri's return, it is not some isolated incident. It hearkens to something old, something forgotten, and you suspect all the Cradle is about to learn it anew.

Assuming there is more left alive, you remind yourself as you dip your head underneath some low-hanging ashen branches that would choke you if you let them. Still, your dour mood has steadily improved in Wotri's presence. The world has changed, yes, but not all for the worse. That shimmering rainbow tree, the bloody leaves, the physical presence of an audible howl…the majesty of it stole your breath away.

There has to be more like that. There has to be beauty unearthed amid the darkness.

As if to mock your optimism, a foul smell hits your nostrils like a sledgehammer. Your stomach immediately seizes, and you fight off a sudden need to vomit. It's coming not far off the path, and after a few steps, you see the cause.

A large buck lays on its side in the snow. Its tongue

hangs out of its mouth, its eyes milky and open. Flies buzz around its body. Its belly is remarkably swollen, and looks fearfully close to bursting. What might have been beautiful red and brown fur is now drained of all color, so the beast is a gray and sickly sight.

The deer is clearly dead. It is also still breathing.

"What monstrosity is this?" you ask aloud. You debate whether to use your sword or pistol, but before you can decide, the thing stirs. A little moan drones out its throat as it shifts and turns, alerted by the sound of your voice. Its trying to stand, but the weight of its bloated belly is preventing it.

Given its limited movement, and what few flamestones you have left, you draw your sword and carefully approach. It does not appear to have been so horribly changed as the wolves had been, but you are not eager for new discoveries, either. A quick blow to the head should end the poor creature's misery.

The buck lunges to its feet before you can close the distance. To its feet…and only its hind feet. It staggers a few steps, its weight horribly off-balance and its swollen, protruding belly hanging low. It lifts its front legs higher, higher, until the shoulder joints pop and shift. You hear the crack of bone. The hooves split, once, then twice, to form four black fingers ending in hard nubs. Blood leaks between them, black and thick.

It opens its mouth. You expect the distinct call of a deer. Instead, you hear words.

"Free," it speaks as it takes a lumbering step toward you. "Free."

You slam your sword deep into its chest and then cut. The swollen belly ruptures, and a massive tangle of intestines spill onto the ground between you. They writhe and twist as if they are alive. Smoke rises from them. The buck shows not a care to the wound, and steps closer.

"Free. Free. Free."

You decide you've heard enough of its mindless speech and swing for its throat. Your sword easily parts the flesh, strikes the spine, and then wedges halfway through. Such a hit would have impaired any living creature, but this shambling monstrosity shows no care. It takes another step, its hoof smashing the spilled intestines. When they pop, black worms come crawling out by the dozens.

"Freeeeeeeeee."

You plant your feet and yank with all your strength, dislodging the sword from the bone. The monster swings those bleeding, cracked, broken things that resemble hands for your chest. You counter with your own attack, a thrust for the face. The fist hits your ribs, and you gasp at the pain. Only your training keeps you moving, keeps the sword thrusting forward to pierce through its gaping mouth and hanging tongue. The tip punches into where the brain should be, and finally, blessedly, the thing goes silent and still.

"Sisters have mercy," you mutter as you stagger away from the rotting mess that was the deer. Your chest aches, and it hurts to breathe. Hopefully no ribs were broken, but given the level of pain, you suspect that is a fool's hope. You look to the forest path and imagine how many more deer must be out there amid the trees.

New plan, you think to yourself. *We hurry through this forest, fast and silent.*

Wotri's absence worries you, now knowing what might lurk out there. You tell yourself he's strong enough to take care of himself, and more than fast enough to outrun the weird deer things. Given their powerful stench, they certainly wouldn't be sneaking up on the wolf, either.

After a quick check of your chest (and seeing the already-growing bruise), you stick to the center of the path and march the quickest pace your tired, battered, and hungry body can manage. Hours pass, thankfully uneventful, though you start to wonder if Wotri will ever return. The change that came over him, and the magic spilling out of him, felt significant. Who he is now, it may not be one willing to spend time protecting a random human struggling to make his way across a mountain pass and through a forest path to some small, unimportant village.

Such concerns end when, an hour before nightfall, he comes trotting toward you from within the ashen trees.

"Welcome back," you say, and force a smile to hide your shock. He is larger than ever, his spine as high as your elbow. The leaf crown remains between his ears, looking like nine blood-red oak leaves dipped in clear wax to harden and then brushed with a thin layer of gold. His eyes have returned to their more normal yellow color, though the pupils shimmer with silver light as if the moon hides within them.

"I have scoured much of the forest," Wotri says. "It is empty of life. The black water spared nothing. Viciss spared no mercy upon his waking."

Again that name, Viciss. The wolf king referred to him as the Dragon of Change, but what exactly that means, you can only guess. Hopefully you'll have a chance to get those answers from the wolf, but for now, you're glad to no longer be alone.

"What of Westwall?" you ask as he joins your side.

"I did not reach the village," he says, and glances your way. "Hold hope, or fear, as is your choice. I cannot say what fate befell the village until we arrive."

"Did you find the end of the black water's destruction?"

Wotri shakes his head. "I did not, but do not despair. Viciss created much of this world. He would not condemn it to ruin, not at the moment of his waking. We walk only in a sliver of his wrath."

"You certainly don't make Viciss sound like the most pleasant of people."

The enormous wolf glances your direction. "You have always feared our gods. Little changes."

Again you fight to hide your reaction. This is the first time the wolf has referred to this dragon as not just a dragon, but a god. Then again, perhaps that is your own fault for not making the realization. Wotri referred to Viciss as his creator, after all. And for a being to make something as majestic and strange as Wotri, well…

"We'll need somewhere safe to sleep," you say.

"Will the path not suffice?"

"I presume you did not encounter any deer?" you ask in response.

"A few, dead and bloated. Their stench was unpleasant to the extreme, and I gave them a wide berth."

You explain what happened when the one you encountered heard your speech and came alive. Wotri listens quietly, and does not speak until you finish.

"Such cruelty, to birth such creations," he mutters. "Imprisonment does not excuse it."

At least in that, you agree.

"I'd like to sleep without fear of waking to one of those things stumbling for me," you say. "Any ideas?"

Wotri is silent for a long moment.

"Build me a fire," he says at last. "I will give you safety."

*

You do your own searching this time instead of forcing Wotri to carry one of the rotten branches between his teeth. Your gloves will suffice for protection. It doesn't take long to find an entire tree tumbled over onto its side. By your guess, it had already been leaning, and when the black water swept across it, the weakened trunk could not endure.

You hack at the longest of the branches with your sword, careful to keep your head turned and your mask on tight. The pine needles explode and float through the air, and despite the mask, they coat your throat raw. The pain is awful, but you endure.

Thankfully the wood burns as easily as ever, and this time, you've broken the branch into about six pieces layered atop one another to form a proper fire in the center of the road. When that is done, you sit before it, enjoying the warmth while you sip from your waterskin. It's not food, but it is something. You pray that, come tomorrow, you'll find a proper meal in Westwall. A proper meal, survivors, and an end to the reach of the black water.

Wotri paces a circle around you, and has for the past half hour. He says nothing, and you leave him be, not wanting to interrupt whatever strange ritual guides him. His eyes are locked on the stars. He circles, and circles, his enormous paws carving a path through the snow and dirt.

Night falls, and it is unsettlingly silent. No song of the crickets, no croak of frogs, no hoot of the night owls. Even if the creatures survived, they did not remain here, but departed for elsewhere. The only noise is the faint rustle of the wind through the trees, and the padding of Wotri's paws.

"I was made to be more than a king," he says as he circles, the sound of his deep voice startling you from a tired daze.

"We are all more than the roles we play," you say. "Just as I am more than a Soulkeeper."

"But you were born," Wotri gently admonishes. "I was not. I was made, crafted and beloved by the Dragon of Change. His gifts run through me, Robin. They were granted with a purpose. To shape the Cradle. To make new that which was old and breaking."

You have no reason to doubt the majestic creature.

After what you saw earlier, it is clear unknown magic resides within the beast.

"What does that mean?" you ask.

In answer, Wotri pauses by the nearest tree, opens his mouth wide, and breathes upon it. When finished, he goes to the next, and the next. One after the other, he gives the trunks his breath. When finished, he dips his head and retraces the path he has worn. One final revolution, and then he stands at your side beside the fire.

"I am master of the wilds," he says, and though he speaks to an audience of one, you feel as if you were in a grand court, and he, announcing a royal proclamation. "King of wood and den. Forest shaper. Field breaker. Bring forth the vines. Make green the desolation. Grow, I command. Grow, and become life."

The wolf king tilts his head to the sky. His eyes resemble stars once more. His crown shimmers with light, and then he lets loose his howl.

Again a rainbow of light pours forth from his throat, but this time it flows like water, and it branches immediately into dozens of shimmering rivers. They flood the area around you, some dropping to the worn path Wotri walked, the rest floating to the trees he marked with his breath. The color settles into them, pale and light, in stark contrast to the black.

And then, the rot recedes. The black falls from the bark. Color returns, as healthy as ever. It spreads up the trees, along their branches, and to their needles. What was ashen turns green. What was deadly and choking becomes vibrant and *alive*. From the path sprouts vines, thick and hearty. They lash themselves to the trunks, sprouting with otherworldly speed, and crisscross in opposite of those nearby so they form an interlaced pattern. Higher and higher they grow, until you sit in the center of a walled-off portion of the forest, protected by vines and nestled within a green canopy.

"You healed it," you whisper, overwhelmed with awe.

"The black water is change," he says. His voice is heavy, and his eyes, fading back to yellow. There is no hiding his exhaustion. "As am I. I have revoked the dragon's gift, and given it my own. I pray he will not condemn me for such blasphemy when we next meet."

You approach the vine wall and try to see through the other side, but cannot.

"The forest?" you ask. "Can you heal it all?"

He shakes his head.

"It takes much of my strength to do what you have seen. To repair the entirety of the woods? It would take many, many years. Perhaps, in time, I will dedicate a portion of my life to doing so. I know not yet the extent of Viciss's rage, nor the needs of my eventual kingdom."

You return to the fire, and to your surprise, all the snow about it has melted, revealing a soft blanket of grass. You sit upon it, find it supple and gentle. A bed, made in preparation. You look to the wolf king and find your throat constricting. Within these walls, you are safe. You are warm. You have a bed, and companionship.

Tears come to your eyes. The exhaustion of the days, the hopelessness and despair of a world made into nightmare, is a bleeding wound you are all too aware of. This moment, this place; it is more than you are capable of handling. You have been strong. It is time to break, if only so you may heal.

"Thank you," you say. "You are a most gracious king."

Wotri sits beside you, and he crosses his paws and lowers his head upon them. The fire flickers within his star-lit irises.

"With each passing day, I remember more," he says. "And with each passing day, I fear I will learn to hate you, or that you have always hated me."

You keep silent. This is not a time for your words.

"I hope that never comes to pass," he says after a time. "Humanity's hatred flows in great rivers of its people, but kindness is unique and precious among that flow. I would call you friend, Soulkeeper, should the world never deign us enemies, nor call upon you to hate my kind."

"Why would I ever hate you?" you ask.

Wotri closes his eyes.

"I do not know, but there was a time, in an age past, when we warred. I know this. I feel it in my bones."

His eyes open. They are stars. The fire, which had dwindled, burst back to roaring life.

"And I fear, little Soulkeeper, that those days of war will soon be upon us again."

11

You wake, and Wotri is gone. The vine walls surround you fully. Groaning, you sit up and wipe the sleep from your eyes. Based on the sunlight filtering in from above, it is morning, if not several hours passed sunrise. You suspect you have slept better than you have in a while.

"Wotri?" you ask. Nothing. You push to your feet, adjust your coat so it rests correctly upon you after being shifted during sleep, and then ask again. "Wotri?"

The vines suddenly part, and trotting along the path from the direction of Westwall is the true King of Fur and Fanged. The crown that rest between his ears has expanded, now fifteen leaves, five resting atop a lower layer of ten. Little silver vines weave through them, and they continue beyond the crown itself to rest like a lace along the sides of Wotri's face, down his back, and to his legs, where they loop around his ankles into rings. There is no yellow to his eyes any longer, only sparkling stars within a sea of black. There is blood on his teeth, and more on his claws.

He is as tall as you now, if not taller.

"Was your night restful?" he asks. The remaining vines collapse at his arrival, revealing the circle of healthy trees forming a green oasis amid the blackened and rotting forest.

"Better than I could ever hope for," you say. "You didn't by chance catch me something to eat for breakfast, did you?"

The wolf stares at you for a moment. "I have come

from Westwall."

Your stomach twists and tightens.

"And?" you ask, meaning so much and more. Survivors. Supplies. Food. Civilization.

"And you will not like what you find."

He does not elaborate further, only turns and begins the walk to the village. Before you follow, you bow your head and pray your morning prayer to the Sisters.

"Blessed be the morn, and the Sister who gave it," you say, and then add to the end. "You'll keep me in mind, won't you Alma? I'm not ready for Anwyn to take me into her arms, but if she does, make it quick and painless, if you'd please."

You have nothing to eat, so you drink what is left of your water so your stomach has something and then follow the wolf king. You want to ask questions, but if Wotri did not volunteer an explanation, it was for a reason. Westwall is not far. You will have your answers soon enough.

Even with his warning, you are not prepared when you step out from the forest and into the field leading to Westwall.

The village is ruined, its buildings toppled and wood warped just as it had been in Elkwerth. The ankle high grass that made up the field is a uniform ashen color, and it bursts into choking smoke from the slightest touch of your boot. All across the roads, you see corpses, familiar in their ruination. Their limbs are torn and broken, and even from afar, you can tell their throats were ripped open.

"The black water," you say. "It spared nothing."

"I found none when I searched for survivors," Wotri says. His tone is gentle. "As for the things the people had become, I ended their misery. It was a task you need not be present to witness, I felt."

Your head feels light. The world is spinning.

"No," you say. "I suppose I didn't need to be, did I?"

You don your mask, close your eyes, and walk straight

through the field into Westwall. A bit of the sting still reaches your eyes, and they are watering by the time you exit the grass onto the beaten dirt paths that crisscross through the pine log cabins that made up the trading village.

Once there, you glance back to see Wotri following in your wake. The grass does not erupt at his touch. Is it because of his royal status, or do the changed creations not hate him as they hate you?

"If this is a trading village, there should be a place with supplies," Wotri says. "Much would be prepared for travel, jarred and dried. Find it, and you should have all you need and more to reach your next destination."

"Yes, my next destination," you say, trying to ignore the bodies Wotri has killed. Trying not to see their pale, sickly skin or the oozing black blood that has crusted over their mouths and nostrils. You imagine a map of West Orismund in your mind. The nearest and largest city by far was Crynn. From there, it would be a lengthy trek to the capital, the majestic city of Londheim.

Getting to Crynn would take over a week, and involve crossing a lot of ashen grass tainted by the black water. The potential journey inspires only exhaustion and trepidation in you. 'Next', Wotri says, as if it will be so easy to continue. As if there is a reason to keep moving.

Foul thoughts, and you shove them aside. Giving up so easily has never, ever been your thing and you have no plans to start now.

"All right," you tell Wotri. "If we're looking for storage, we want the biggest buildings located somewhere along the most well-traveled roads."

"I will search the northern portion of the village," Wotri says. "Search the south."

He leaves you, and after the departure, you close your eyes and slowly breathe out.

"Keep moving," you whisper. "Keep stepping forward. Stay with me, Sisters. I need you now, more than ever, for the path I see is dark and unwelcome."

Normally you'd suspect a storage barn or building would be easily noticeable above the homes, but with how many have collapsed, their walls and rooftops giving way, the matter is not quite so simple. You follow what appears to be the main road at first, then deviate when none catch your eye as befitting your expectation.

You could always loot some homes, of course, but anything useful would have to have been stored in a high shelf somewhere to escape the black water's flow. You'll do it, if you must, of course. But given how much you need, it seems wisest to start where there should be plenty, prepared for a long journey either to or from Crynn. Plus, there's always the hope a sealed jar protected against the black water's influence.

The sound of your footsteps is the only noise as you walk. The stillness is disturbing in a way you did not anticipate. Around you are homes, and you instinctively anticipate the sounds of life. Children playing, adults chatting, the passing of carts and occasional sight of a stray dog or cat. Instead, silence. Silence, and the murdered corpses as Wotri made the village safe for your arrival.

Even having warned you, you cannot help but feel the weight of it sink your shoulders. Though you never voiced it, never dared even acknowledge the thought in your head, you had hoped that reaching Westwall would be the end of the black water. The end of the change, the corruption, and the despair. The end of your solitude.

It was not to be. You're strong enough to endure, but that doesn't mean it doesn't hurt as you wander Westwall's empty streets. The signs of life only make it hurt worse. Toppled brooms. Discarded tools. A bin of laundry, spilled over on its side. The rope the clothes were to hang from is encased in what looks like tar.

You do find a well, though, situated near the center of town. When you glance within, you see what, as far as you can tell, is clean water. The rope and bucket meant to draw water from within it has collapsed from rot, however. Frowning, you make a mental note of it, then continue onward.

Your search halts when you hear a sound, then another. Distinct. Two moans, echoing together from within the nearby home whose door has crumpled in on itself.

"Hello?" you ask. Again, a pair of cries, clearly in some sort of pain. Despite the danger, you kick the door, easily crumpling it, and then step inside.

You hold back a gag upon entering. Everything, from the floor to halfway up the walls, reeks of a particular sort of rot. It's akin to wetness and mold, only stronger, and more bitter on the back of your throat.

"Is anyone here?" you ask. It's dangerous to talk. You know that. You've learned that multiple times now, but you cannot help yourself. Your need for other humans overrides your good sense. The pained cries are your only answer. Steeling yourself for the worst, you follow them toward the back of the house. The floor boards groan underneath you, and you fear they cannot support your weight for long. Already they bow slightly, and quiver with a disturbing vibrancy unbecoming of cut pine. The further from the door, and fresh air, the worst the smell becomes, until you pull out your mask and tie it around your face in a futile hope it blocks some of it from entering your nostrils.

There is another door at the end of the short hall, its hinges barely clinging to the wall. After a debate, you draw your pistol, load a lead shot and flamestone into it, and then hold it at ready. With how dilapidated everything is, there is no opening the door normally. Instead you give it a solid kick with your heel, then step back as it breaks in half and crumples, revealing the bedroom within.

The black water spared nowhere, and no one. Upon the bed is a couple, married, perhaps, or merely lovers. They were sleeping when the black water flowed, their arms entangled, the sides of their hips pressed to one another in repose.

That flesh is now merged together into one. It is stretched, and so pale it is nearly translucent. Their legs have warped into three long appendages. What blankets had covered them have rotted away. Their hair has fallen out, and their arms, sunken into the body of the other.

They see you and writhe, and moan, but cannot leave the bed. Blood dribbles down their lips to their necks, leaving a long black trail.

No words come to you, not at first. You're too stricken with horror. They twist and turn, trying to reach for you, trying so hard that the flesh starts to tear along their waist and chest. It reveals, not muscle beneath, but bone.

You lift your pistol.

"By Alma, we are born," you whisper, and pull the trigger. The lead shot bursts through the forehead of what had once been a woman. Her half of the combined body goes still, but the other writhes all the harder. One of his arms manages to tear free, and it is a barren reach of bone and fleshy tendrils that might have once been muscle.

You load the second flamestones, your mind blank, your actions routine.

"By Lyra, we are guided. By Anwyn, we are returned."

You point the pistol at the man's withered pale skull. Your throat is dry. This. This was the civilization you hoped to find. This mockery of life was your comfort against your loneliness. The bitterness of it is far beyond any scent of rot emanating from the walls around you.

"Beloved Sisters, take them home."

You pull the trigger.

When you exit the home, all is silent once more. Silent, perhaps forever.

12

It is Wotri who finds you the supplies that will sustain you for the coming days. What had once been a storage shed for some traders is now a collapsed husk of rotting wood, with only the roof having avoided the touch of the black water. The building is much smaller than you anticipated, and by the looks of it, its door had been locked using a key, something no doubt expensive to have set up, requiring a locksmith to travel all the way from Crynn, if not Londheim.

Not that the lock means much anymore, with the walls and door broken. Wotri has shoved aside half of the building, revealing collapsed shelves that are now slanted at a sharp angle against one of the enduring support beams. Upon those shelves are rows upon rows of jarred beets, squash, and rhubarb.

You pick up one and, with a bit of effort, twist it open. Within are pickled squash. Your fingers are shaking as you slip your fingers into the brine. The black water clearly rushed over the jars, but it seems it had no affect on the glass. You pull out a piece and take a bite.

It crunches between your teeth, the flavor instantly waking your stomach. You taste garlic cloves, peppercorn, and a hint of onion, all mixed into the brine as flavoring. Before you can finish chewing, you've already shoved the entire thing in your mouth and reached for a second. The taste is divine. You could almost cry. There are over a dozen similar jars, of just yellow squash alone.

"Carrying so much will be difficult," Wotri says, watching you from the road. "But if you follow me, I found what I believe was a smithy shop that endured better than most."

You follow him, the jar tucked into the crook of your arm. A bit of brine spills across your coat, and you could not care less. While still munching on the squash, you arrive at the shop, and sure enough, there is an obvious open air forge. Just like the glass of the jars, the metal appears to have endured far better than the wood. From one of the racks, you loot yourself another knife, plus a fresh sharpening stone.

The true treasure, though, is a rucksack stashed on a high shelf, safe from the passage of the black water.

"Thank you," you whisper to the previous owner. "I hope you don't mind me taking this."

You remember the slain bodies all throughout Westwall, and that one of them likely is the previous smith. No, they will not mind, but neither do you feel like joking about it so glibly, even with your dire circumstances.

Your next task is obtaining water from the well. You scour the smith's shelves, at least the high ones, and find a small pail. A glance inside shows it was likely used to haul coal, but a bit of wiping with part of your shirt cleans it up enough you aren't afraid to drink from it. A bit more searching locates a suitable length of rope. You return to the well, send the pail down, and then lift it back up. To your naked eye, nothing appears out of the ordinary, so you lift the pail to your lips.

The water is pure. Untainted. You drink deep, then send the pail back down for more.

Food. Water. A way to carry your supplies. You slide to a sit with your back against the well as Wotri joins you. You offer him a drink from the pail, which he gladly accepts.

"What now are your plans?" he asks when finished. The pail is small compared to the size of his mouth, and much of the water is left to drip from his dark nose. He licks it with his tongue.

"I suppose Crynn would be our next destination," you say.

"Is it?"

There's something about his tone you don't quite understand. You let it drop. There's enough on your mind.

"I have to stay the night, though," you say. "Just one night, that's all."

Wotri stares at you with his star-filled eyes. "And why is that?"

You want to say it's to rest. You want to say it's so you can recover from what you saw in the cabin. The truth, though, will suffice.

"Because I have my duty as a Soulkeeper."

*

It is a gruesome task, but thankfully Wotri is willing to help. Road by road, and home by home, you find the bodies the wolf king has slain. Without cart or stretcher, you rely on your gloved hands to drag the bodies mutilated by tooth and ruined by black water to an enormous pile in the center of Westwall.

Not all need dragged. Some are small enough to be carried.

Though you don't count an exact number, you suspect nearly three hundred bodies are in that enormous pile by the time night falls. Wotri helped with over half, lifting bodies between his teeth far more gingerly than he assaulted them that morning. You wish you had more time, and far more helping hands, but this will have to do.

A glance at the sky. You have two hours. Best get to work.

You go from body to body, all of whom lay on their backs. You will not use snow, nor blood, nor cut the symbol with a knife. Instead, you use a thick tar-like substance from the smith shop you've half-filled the pail with. A quick dip, and it coats your fingers. One by one, you draw the downward pointing triangle of the Three Sisters, along with the circle at the bottom.

Each and every one of these bodies possesses a soul, and you will not leave them unattended in ruined bodies. They deserve to be lifted in Anwyn's hands, and you will do your best to grant them that gift.

Body after body, triangle after triangle. The tar grows thicker on your thumb, the symbol more rushed and ugly as you press along. It has to be done before the reaping hour. The thought of staying another day here is too much for you to bear. You have kept sane through constant movement. To lose that among a village of the dead? Surely you could not endure.

No. Cowardly thoughts. You have your work, your responsibility, and you will do it no matter how long it takes. Let the world end. Your faith will remain strong.

Wotri lays nearby and quietly watches. There is not much else he can do.

At last you are done. You stand and stretch your back, groaning as it creaks and your muscles spasm. So much bending over. So much squinting in the fading light of the setting sun.

"Do you seek to honor your dead?" Wotri asks as you trudge to join him.

"Honor them, and usher their souls to the stars," you say.

"How so?"

You frown at the wolf.

"Through the reaping ritual. Do you not remember it?" When he shakes his head, you decide to explain. "When the reaping hour comes, I will preside over the dead, and offer my prayers to the Sisters. Through the ritual, and the drawn marks upon their foreheads, I will empower Anwyn to take the souls of the departed into her hands, to carry up to the stars, and then across the void to join them in their paradise."

"And if you do not perform this ritual?"

"Then often the soul remains, to await the final call at the end of the world."

Wotri turns his attention to the enormous gathering of dead bodies, lined up in columns and rows in the center of town.

"That the Sisters would have need of you to perform their allotted task?" he says. "What fate befell the Cradle, I wonder, to harm them so? Or perhaps it was our own imprisonment that burdened them."

You don't like the presumption that the reaping ritual should not be necessary, given that the history of it predates even the earliest writings available to the Keeping Church. Neither can you deny the obvious fact that its *need* has grown tenfold just over the past years, though. You cannot discount the possibility there was a point where the reaping ritual went from being a ritual act of grief and honor, to something required by the Sisters to aid them in the harvesting of a soul.

"Have you ever performed a ritual for so many?" Wotri asks, pulling you from your thoughts. You look upon this field of the dead and shake your head.

"Never before," you say. "And I pray, never again."

You feel the whisper-touch of otherworldliness brush across your neck. The air grows still. The stars seem to shine that much brighter. It is time. The reaping hour has come. You clutch the pendant of Anwyn underneath your shirt and take a deep breath.

"By Alma, we are…"

Light blasts your eyes, interrupting you. The symbol of the Sisters flares like blue flame, burning across the tar you used. It shines from each and every forehead, and with so many, it is nearly blinding. You hear a strange noise in your mind, like the ringing of a bell, yet its sound comes from everywhere and nowhere. Wind blows across you, sudden and cold from the west.

First a few, then dozens, and then hundreds of thin blue pillars shine across the foreheads. The sparkling, burning white star that is their souls lift from their bodies, cleanly separating. The sight leaves you breathless. So many. There's so many. Memories. Emotions. Entire lives, shimmering in a spiritual, physical manifestation the Scholars and Mindkeepers still debate to this day.

And then they rise to the heavens, slow at first, then faster, faster, falling stars in reverse order to join the dark canopy above the world.

Your fear fades away, and you walk toward them, your arms wide and your head tilted skyward. You watch the great burst of lights, and you bathe in the wonder washing over you. Never before have you felt Anwyn's presence so keenly. There is sorrow in the death, and yet glory in the miracle awaiting the end of one life and the beginning of another.

The black water may have turned the world foul, but your goddesses remain with you, ever watchful, ever waiting the end of your days. In this, there is comfort, as you watch the parade of souls leap to the stars.

The reaping hour ends. In their absence, the town is dark and quiet. You shiver, overwhelmed by a sudden, gripping dread and loneliness upon your heart.

"What now?" Wotri asks, and you cannot express how glad you are to hear his voice.

"Now, we burn them."

13

You spend much of the next day going home by home, inspecting for anything useful to be added to your rucksack. You find a few more sealed jars, these of rhubarb, to give yourself a bit of variety. Sadly you find no flamestones, but you do add another knife to your collection, along with some rope, eating utensils, and most exciting, a bedroll for you to actually lay on when night comes.

"No more sleeping on my coat with a rock for a pillow," you tell Wotri upon finding it. He only snorts and continues his own search for things that might benefit you.

Come the afternoon, the two of you stand on the road east of the village. Your pack is heavy on your back, and you adjust its weight in preparation for travel to the much larger town of Crynn.

"Are you ready?" you ask.

"Forgive me, Robin, but I have held my tongue too long," he says in answer.

You arc an eyebrow his direction. "How so?"

The wolf king stares west. "I will not be going with you any farther."

His words are a dagger between your ribs. A dozen responses flit through your mind.

"Is that so?" you say, pretending not to be as upset as you are.

"Take this as no insult, Soulkeeper," he says. "But the mountains we have crossed mark the limits of what was once my domain. I will go no farther. I have a responsibility to reclaim what was mine, and scour the extent of its breadth to reform my kingdom."

So far as you know, Alma's Crown marks the farthest extent that West Orismund has settled. Everything beyond was supposed to be wild and untamed, and perhaps that was exactly what Wotri hoped to find upon his arrival. Assuming, of course, the black water had not washed it all away and turned his subjects into monsters.

"Travel will certainly be less safe without you," you say, if only to fill the sudden, awkward silence.

"Hence why I kept with you so far as Westwall," he says. "But you have food, supplies, and a destination. And for what it is worth, know that in my heart I believe Viciss's destruction will not have traveled much farther. You will find safety soon. You need only keep the strength to find it."

You swallow down a stone that has suddenly lodged in your throat. Your first meeting with Wotri was certainly not the most pleasant, but much about the world has changed since then, as has his form. And whatever dismissive attitude he might have first shown has since softened.

"I will miss you," you say. Anything else would be dishonest.

Wotri turns toward you, and his eyes close as he leans his forehead toward you. His fur presses to your chest, and you lean your own head against his, taking in the softness.

"Perhaps this will be our final meeting," the wolf king says. "Perhaps our paths shall cross again. I pray they do. Though our time together was short, I found you amusing, Soulkeeper, and better company than I expected."

"And I found you so much more proud and arrogant than I thought possible in a wolf."

You make sure to grin wide when he pulls back, ensuring he knows you only jest.

"And yet you were exactly as stubborn and annoying as I expected of a human," he says. Before you can react, he licks you, his enormous tongue coating your face and hair with his saliva. You groan and wipe your eyes with your coat sleeve.

"Farewell, Soulkeeper Robin," he says. "May the moon ever shine upon you, and light your path."

And with that, he trots northward, to where, you cannot say. Perhaps he will find his subjects in the forests of Murkmud, if they were spared the wrath of the black water. You only know that your path to Crynn awaits you, and that you will travel it alone.

Alone.

"Chin up, Robin," you tell yourself as you take that first step. "You traveled this whole way to Elkwerth, and you can make it back to Londheim the same."

At least the road has two clearly marked ruts from wagon wheels, sparing yourself the wrath of the corrupted grass. You walk within them, one foot after the other, and tell yourself you will be fine. You need no other companion. You need no protection of the wolf king.

You aren't sure if they're lies, but they feel like lies as the miles steadily pass, and you leave the mountains of Alma's Crown behind and enter the gently rolling plains on your journey southeast.

*

The days pass uneventful. Your nights are cold but quiet. At no point do you encounter other travelers, nor find sign of them. You tell yourself that is a good sign, that people might have survived and immediately headed east for safety. You tell yourself Crynn would be the obvious bastion for everyone in the far northwest corner of West Orismund, the place all would go who could not safely reach the capital in Londheim. If anywhere survived, it would be there.

So it is with painful trepidation that you stand before

the field between you and the walls of the city.

"What happened here?" you wonder aloud.

The space between you, a good quarter mile of distance, is entirely ash. Fire has consumed it fully, of such strength and fury only blackened dirt remains for hundreds of yards in either direction of the city entrance. Strangely enough, it seems to have focused solely on the grass, and left the buildings untouched.

Somehow it caught fire, you think, and remember the ease in which a rotted branch had caught flame when you used it for firewood. If a branch burned so easily, then how might a swaying field of grass?

The proof is before you. Not a hint of the grass remains, but that is not what inspires your horror. No, what does is the bodies you find amidst the grass.

They number in the hundreds. They are nothing but skeletons, their flesh burnt to ash, their blood, charred away. They lay in various poses, aimlessly scattered throughout the grass. Some were crouched, others collapsed onto their backs, and still others clearly died on their hands and knees.

You walk through the desolation, your head on a swivel. None move. None live.

Why were you here? you wonder. What would possess so many to wander just outside the gates of the city? Why wouldn't they take safety within its walls?

You pause just outside the city. Your fear has grown with each passing step. Perhaps these people lingered outside because they were twisted and changed by the black water, as the people of Elkwerth and Westwall were? Or maybe they had fled, because whatever was now inside the city was worse?

You stare through the front gates off the city's outer wall. Within is a similar sight as Westwall, just on a larger scale. Homes are collapsed onto their sides due to rotted supports and walls no longer able to support the weight of their roofs.

Their sides are blackened and warped, and even from here, you smell the now familiar moldy scent.

Nothing good awaits you within, you tell yourself. For a long time, you stand there, looking, but you see nothing. No people. No signs of life. You hear no rattle of wheels, no shouts, no hint that this once bustling hub of travel connected all of the frontier lands of West Orismund contains a single survivor.

You want to stay. You want to search. But your food is limited, and you feel you will find nothing but corpses inside…if not worse.

"To Londheim," you mutter to yourself, and skirt wide around the city. From there, you'll have to travel dozens of miles east, but at least the road, once you reach it, is large and well-maintained. You walk with your head low and your heart lower. When you reach the road, it takes you a long moment before you glance aside and realize something is amiss.

The decayed grass has burst and dissipated for several feet on either side of the road. Footprints, dozens upon dozens, mark the dirt. You see wheel ruts, too, from wagons or carts. The sight sets your insides to trembling. You'd almost given up hope, but there is no denying the evidence before your eyes.

Survivors.

You follow after them, now with a clear goal in mind. You'll catch up with them. You'll end your solitude. Among other people, you'll be able to discuss the insanity of the changed world. You'll grieve together the lost and the dead, and shudder in mutual horror at the newly come dangers.

A spring enters your step. The hour is late, but you find yourself jogging more than walking. Perhaps they're only a few miles ahead of you. Perhaps you might even catch up to them.

So focused are you on your haste you don't notice the change at first. In many ways, it is everything you would expect before you, only the realization doesn't hit immediately. You crest a hill, and splayed out before you is a sprawling valley. Near the center is a small pond, its waters sparkling with the light of the stars glinting into view as the sun sets. A few trees sway in the gentle evening wind, forming a circular copse around a third of the pond. Their leaves are lit a faint blue by the shine of the moon.

Green. Blue.

Not gray.

"The black water," you whisper, and turn about. "It ended."

Not a hundred yards behind you, the grass is still blackened and rotted, but with a sudden, unexplainable limit, its passage simply ends. Nothing beyond suffers its touch. The grass is a faded greenish yellow from the approaching winter. The trees are healthy and strong. When you inhale the wind, it carries no scent of rot.

Your legs go weak. You collapse to your knees, and a thousand prayers to the Sisters rattle unspoken through your mind. Exhaustion and relief war within you, so you want to laugh as much as cry.

"It ended," you whisper again. Saying so seems to make it more real, more believable. "It ended. The black water ended."

The world lives on. The lands of the east, Londheim and beyond, the Oakblack Woods, Steeth, Oris, the Kept Lands…they were spared, surely they were spared.

You stagger to your feet, and you remember once more the caravan of survivors up ahead. If you hurry, you can catch up to them, for surely you are much faster than any mixed group of survivors. You walk, then jog, then run.

The world is suddenly alive, the stars unusually bright, and the thought of sleep, a million miles away.

14

Despite the tribulations of the past few days, your exhaustion, and dwindling supplies, you jog far more than you walk. A singular need drives you, and that is to catch up to whoever these survivors are. You're tired of being alone, and Wotri's absence hangs heavy over you the first night you unroll your bedroll and camp in the center of the road toward Londheim.

You set no fire for fear of alerting whatever might be out there in this new world. Just your bedroll, and your coat. Sleep comes, slow to arrive despite your exhaustion, for with every rustle of wind you imagine wolves prowling with spider-legs curling out from their spines.

It is on the second day you see them in the distance. Hundreds of people, together forming a caravan of survivors. Your elation knows no bounds. The horrors of Crynn feel like a lifetime away. Your jog becomes a sprint, and you cross the remaining valley in less than an hour to finally reach the tail end of the caravan.

A family of five riding in a wagon pulled by a donkey are the first to greet you.

"Did we leave you behind?" an older woman among the family asks, grinning wide. You grin right back. You haven't felt this happy in months.

"Just a little," you say. "Had to run a bit to catch up is all."

A man walks beside the donkey, and he nods at you.

"Good to see another Soulkeeper join us," he says.

"Another?" you ask.

He points ahead, to where the majority of the caravan is clustered closer together, several hundred in number at the least.

"You'll find him up ahead, leading the charge. Name's Devin, Devin Eveson. He's the reason we fled Dunwerth when we did."

You thank the man and continue onward. You pass by tired families, weary couples, and numerous groups of children laughing and complaining in equal measure as they trudge along. Many greet you, always happy to see a member of the Keeping Church in their dire hour. Many ask you to stop and pray with them. They are haggard, and tired, and you are all too happy to comfort them in any way you can.

It isn't until nightfall that you find Soulkeeper Devin at the very front of the caravan. He has settled down for the night, without tent or canvas to protect against the chill wind. A little fire burns beside him, and he is not alone.

"Greetings," you say as you approach their fire. "Devin?"

The middle-aged man looks up at you, and it takes a moment before realization sets in.

"Robin?" he asks. A grin spreads across his fine features. "Lyra have mercy, you survived this mess?"

"I did," you say as he lurches to embrace you. You wouldn't consider Devin a friend, but only because you see him too irregularly for that. You two are the Soulkeepers most often assigned to the far western reaches of West Orismund, and it is a rare occurrence for the both of you to be home in Londheim at the same time. He's a good man, though, trustworthy even for a Soulkeeper.

"You've seen better days," you tell him. His face, normally clean-shaven, carries a thick shade of stubble. His brown hair is cut short, and it sticks to his forehead with sweat and carries the indent of his tricorn hat. His silver pendant to Anwyn hangs freely from his neck, reflecting the light of the fire.

"All the Cradle has," Devin says, pulling away from the hug. "I pray your travels were calmer than mine?"

"Where were you when the black water arrived?" interrupted the man seated with Devin. He is young, with a bit of acne still on his cheeks. His blond hair is long, and roughly combed to keep it out of his face.

"Try not to be rude, Tomas," Devin says. "And I suppose I should introduce you two. This here is my brother by marriage, Tomas Moore, Crynn's appointed member of the Wise. Tommy, this here is Robin, one of Londheim's Soulkeepers."

"My travels have been…interesting," you say, your gaze bouncing between the both of them. It surprises you to hear this Tommy fellow is a member of the Wise. Their organization is dedicated to history and record keeping. They were who you went to when you had a property dispute, needed a prediction on next year's weather, or someone's lineage traced back a few generations to settle a family argument. They were, almost exclusively, older men, and yet here was a fresh-faced youth barely in his twenties holding the title.

"Interesting how?" Tommy asks. "Did you encounter the spider-wolves? A firekin? Maybe something new, like a waterkin?"

You raise an eyebrow.

"Something…new?" you ask, as if the other things he referenced were perfectly common.

"Enough, Tommy," Devin says. "Please, sit with us, Robin. Tell us your story, and when you are ready, I shall tell you mine."

You begin with the ghostly version of Rachel and the many souls swirling within her. Then the black water, the loss of Elkwerth, and the tragic deaths of John and Daniel. You watch their reactions as you mention the black water's arrival, and by the haunting look in both their eyes, you know they share a similarly horrid tale. When you get to Wotri, though, Tommy in particular cannot contain himself.

"A wolf king?" he asks. "That's...that's so wonderful! Is he still with you? I'd like to meet him, and ask him so many questions."

"If I answer, then I tell the story out of order," you say. "So please, let me finish."

You continue with the spider-wolves, Wotri's growing size, and eventually the wolf king clearing out the dead city of Westwall. When you tell them of Wotri's departure, there is no hiding Tommy's disappointment. From there, you mention your arrival at Crynn, finding the path of the survivors, and hurrying to catch up with everyone.

"It's a familiar tale," Devin says when you finish. "And mine is similar, if you are willing to hear it. I, too, encountered the dead walking, and those spider-wolves, though I also met a woman named Lavender who commanded them."

It is surreal, hearing Devin recount the tale, and hard to believe even though you know he has no reason to lie. A woman who was part spider, part crystalline beauty commanded the spider-wolves that assaulted him on his departure from the mountain village of Dunwerth. Like a spider, she fed off him, but not of blood and organs. She drank his memories, and from them, learned of the Cradle.

"From what I can tell, there was a time when all these strange creatures and beings once lived among us," Devin explains. "And then something happened to put them all away. Into a slumber, as Lavender put it. She said centuries had passed while the 'dragon-sired' slept, and yes, dragon-sired, the same as Wotri called himself. But now all these strange, fabled beings…they're awake. And it seems like we're going to need to figure out how to live among them." Devin shook his head and laughed. "It's going swimmingly so far, I must say."

Tommy nudged him in the side.

"It's going better than you're implying," he says. "You get along with Puffy at least, right?"

"Puffy?" you ask. It's a strange name, and you expect him to reveal a pet cat or dog.

Devin leans closer toward the fire, staring into its center.

"I did not escape Lavender alone," he says. "I had help from another, if it is brave enough to introduce itself. If you're worried, Puffy, don't be. Robin is a fellow Soulkeeper, and worthy of your trust."

You have no idea who or what Devin might be talking about. You follow his gaze, and briefly wonder if the Soulkeeper might have lost his mind during his encounter with the creature known as Lavender…and then you see two eyes staring back at you from the heart of the fire.

They look like two little black circles of coal, and they hover within a swelling of flame that stands up on two elongated legs. From its circular body an arm protrudes out, yellow and burning, to wave 'hello' before shrinking back down to a tiny glowing yellow blob of fire. It then rolls underneath one of the burning logs, vanishing from your view.

Your mouth drops open, and you look to a thoroughly amused Devin and Tommy.

"Its name is Puffy," Devin says. "At least, that is the name it accepts, for its own is beyond the ability of human tongues."

"It's a firekin!" Tommy eagerly exclaims. "And it's

friendly, very friendly. It's why all those murderous and strange people were burned in the fields before Crynn. It set fire to the decayed grass to protect Devin. Now, it's not very friendly to *me*, I should add, but maybe it just has a thing against members of the Wise."

"Yes," Devin says dryly. "That is surely the reason."

You stare at the fire, trying to catch another glimpse of the little creature made of living flame.

"Firekin," you say, echoing what Tommy called it earlier. "Does that mean there are others? A...waterkin, perhaps, or airkin?"

"Puffy seemed insistent on the existence of waterkin," Devin says. "Beyond that, I cannot say. Communicating with it is difficult, given the lack of speech. Puffy is quite capable of spelling words, when it is so inclined, however. So far that is just not often."

The firekin pokes back up from the logs. A bit of smoke puffs up from the top of its head. Its arms, little thin tubes of liquid flame, press against its non-existent hips before it reaches out and begins rapidly spelling letters with such speed an after-image of them hovers in your vision.

IHEARU.

Devin laughs.

"Forgive us, we are only curious," he says.

"Indeed," you tell the fire. "I meant no offense, I swear."

Puffy settles back down on top of one of the logs, but its eyes remain visible, slanted and distrusting. A constant sizzle of white smoke rises from its forehead as it feeds upon the dry wood.

"As fascinating as this all is," you say, "what next is the future? The people of this caravan regard you as their leader."

"There's not much to the leading," Devin says. "I

encourage people where I may, and I keep us moving toward Londheim. Food and water are tight, but I think we can manage. Once there, we'll be safe."

"Are you certain?" you ask. "The world is changing. Is anywhere safe?"

"It is possible everywhere has changed," Tommy says. "But it might not all be for the worse. What shape is Londheim in? Who can say, until we get there ourselves."

"What few people have joined us on the road to Londheim have told us some strange tales," Devin says. "Talking foxes, enormous owls, living wind, rabbits who shape the ground…it's been a lot, and there's no making sense of any of it."

"But those stories are not the horrors we first encountered," you point out. "These tales…they are different from the destruction of the black water. They aren't ruined grass, mutated wolves, or the violent dead. Foxes? Owls? What if they're like Wotri? What if they're noble, and kind?" You feel almost naive for suggesting this, but you cannot deny the things you've experienced. "What if these changes, not all of them are the for the worse? What if this awakening world is one of magic and wonder?"

Devin leans over and squeezes your shoulder.

"I would say, like me, you have spent too much time in the mysterious wilds of the west," he says. "And I would also admit I pray to the Sisters with all my heart that you are right."

15

The next days pass in a paradoxical manner, both painfully slow, and yet also much too short. No amount of progress seems like enough as the caravan of refugees makes its way toward Londheim. It grows slower over time as more join you from the north and south, the number swelling well past a thousand.

They come carrying stories, each one more outlandish than the last. Made worse is how quickly they get retold, until you're hearing rumors of rumors. You swear a new arrival could say they saw a blue grasshopper and by the end of the day, the whole caravan would be abuzz about a six legged monstrosity that ate children, wielded swords, and sang as he butchered whole villages.

Even worse is the steady drain on food and water. You watch this sprawling caravan of survivors break into groups, family units and village remnants, and they share what they have amongst themselves. For the first two days, the mood is tired but good-natured, but as the food stores dwindle, and water grows scarce, the little factions grow more careful with their supplies. Each new family that arrives is immediately accosted with greeters, people eager to see what they have with them and, if it can be shared, that it be shared with their specific group alone.

It's a recipe for disaster, one that finally explodes like a broken flamestone on the third day.

"Robin!" a young girl shouts. You don't recognize her,

but she apparently recognizes you as she comes running. You're praying with a group of elderly men and women, for their travels have been harsher than most, and they are in constant fear of being left behind.

"Yes?" you ask.

The girl looks to be twelve or thirteen, and you only vaguely recognize her. Her green eyes are wide, her whole face twisted with panic.

"Please, you have to come, they're going to kill Ayric!"

You stand, and ensure your sword and pistol are tightly belted around your waist.

"Lead the way," you tell the girl, and follow.

You hear the ruckus before you ever see them. Angry shouts and accusations lob back and forth without pause. When closer, you see two distinct groups, each facing the other to clog the road. Some people go around, while those with blocked wagons or carts shout and holler angrily, adding to the cacophony.

There are swords and knives held at ready, the naked steel chilling your blood and hardening your expression.

"Enough!" you shout as you step between them. Your voice is thunder, and while the people do not quiet, they calm considerably. Ever since the Second Council of Nicus some three hundred years ago, Soulkeepers have been granted authority by the Crown to oversee trials where no judges have been appointed. It gave the Keeping Church power, but it also granted a sense of law to the lawlessness that had been growing throughout West Orismund as the westward spread reached its end and then contracted, with many villages steadily shrinking, and others abandoned entirely.

"Good, we have someone here who can put this wretched boy in his place," says a white-haired man holding a young boy by the arm. The kid has gone deathly pale. If you were to guess, he can't be more than ten years old. Two burly farmers hold hatchets at either side of him, and it is a grotesque sight.

"You look ready to execute a child," you say, meeting the older man's gaze and giving not an inch. "Release him. You are not the one in charge here."

"And you are?" he says, refusing to release the kid.

"You arguing with a Soulkeeper now, Brecht?" shouts a woman from the other group, her hair wrapped in a red bandanna. "Just no limit to how low you'll sink."

You look to each group as another avalanche of shouts and fruitless arguing resumes. You catch pieces of it, but nothing close to a clear understanding. Only one thing is clear: the old man, Brecht, claims to have caught the kid stealing from their camp.

"You," you say, and point at Brecht. "And you." This time to the woman who appears to be the loudest and fiercest of the other side. "Come with me, so we may talk. The rest of you, continue with your travels. We have not the time nor luxury of a delay."

"Leave?" one of the men with hatchets says. He grabs the kid from Brecht, wrenching his arm violently in doing so. "You think we'll scurry off while you protect this little shit from what he deserves? I don't care if you're a Soulkeeper, you—"

You draw your sword before he can finish the sentence and put it to his throat. Silence follows immediately, so that the ringing of your steel is all that accompanies your careful, calm words.

"Release him. Now."

The man lets go of the kid. His eyes are wide, and he's fuming, but against Soulkeeper steel, he backs down. There are a thousand stories of Soulkeeper skill, feats of impeccable aim with their pistols and holding off hordes of bandits with their swords. That reputation aids you now, as none are willing to challenge you, even if they have the numbers to do so.

"Go on, Cliff," Brecht says. "I'll catch up with you when this matter is settled."

The crowd starts to disperse, and while you don't sheathe your sword, you lay it casually over your lap as you kneel down before the boy. He's more mud than clean skin, his clothes torn and his face a little thin for his age. The travel is wearing on him, and you doubt he's had a full meal since the black water came.

"What is your name?" you ask him.

"Ayric," Brecht answers above you.

You slowly turn to look up at the man. You say nothing, only stare at him coldly until he takes a few uncomfortable steps backwards. You then look back to the boy and repeat your question.

"Ayric," he says.

"And I'm his mother, Olivia," says the woman you ordered to remain behind. "Thank the Sisters you arrived when you did. That," she pauses to point at Brecht, "*monster* was about to cut my boy's head off for a crime he never did."

You stand, and offer the boy your hand. He takes it and stands himself.

"Protecting your family don't make you a monster," Brecht argued. "And it may be harsh, but we're in a harsh world. I won't watch my family starve because someone else is willing to rob while the sun's still sleeping."

"Starve?" Olivia snaps. "You damn liars!"

"Better than a thief!"

"Enough!" you snap at the both of them. "Brecht, you insist the boy is a thief. Was he caught in the act?"

The old man puffs up a bit.

"Red handed, this morning. But don't be confused, it ain't just been this morning. Our stores have been irregular for the last few days, and when we finally hid a guard to watch, that's when we caught Ayric trying to pilfer our food."

You glance down at the boy, whose face is bright red. You suspect there's no lie here. The guilt is written plain as day upon him.

"The boy's young, and can't have taken much," you say, trying to calm the situation and bring in a bit of sense. "Yet when I arrived, you looked ready for murder."

"That's because of what the boy told us," Brecht says, and he sneers down at him. "Ain't that right?"

Your curiosity piqued, you cross your arms and face Ayric.

"And what was that?" you ask when the kid offers no explanation.

"That *she*," he points at Olivia, "put him up to it. He's following orders, and that's why we came to get what we were due."

You hold back a grimace. That complicates things immensely if true. It's one thing for a youngster to get a bit of greed in his heart. That's easily explained, and easily remedied. But if Ayric was stealing on orders of another family...

"What say you to that?" you ask Olivia.

She crosses her arms and glares at you.

"I say Brecht is a liar. Ain't that right, Ayric?"

The boy nods.

"I was helping my family," he says. "And I said so. I didn't mean they were making me. That's shit that Brecht made up in his own head."

You keep your face stone-masked as you listen. It's a plausible denial, but you can see Brecht fuming upon hearing it. You'd need a way to confirm Olivia's participation, but how?

"So you admit you stole several times, and not for yourself alone?" you ask Ayric. The boy glances once at his mother and then nods.

"Yeah," he says. "That's what I said."

You turn to Olivia.

"Which means your boy has been sharing food with others in your group," you say. "Did you not think to ask where he got it from?"

The woman's cheek twitches, and she hesitates to answer.

"We…I thought maybe he was helping others around the caravan," she says eventually. "That food was his payment."

It's a terrible lie, and everyone knows it. So the group was definitely aware the boy was stealing. Whether or not they were ordering him to is a different matter, but one you likely won't be able to confirm or deny. Still, if they were benefiting, even through ignorance, it adds a layer of guilt to those who should have known better, or asked questions so they could put a stop to it.

"See, she knew," Brecht insists. He points at the pair. "She's not stupid, and if she turned a blind eye to it, that don't make it right. If anything, she deserves some lashes, too."

"No lashes," you say, glaring at him. "And I saw your weapons when I arrived. You were preparing for far more than mere lashes."

You've heard enough. There's only so much wiggle room when the boy's admitted to the theft, and with his entire family benefiting, you decide the entire family must repay back the debt.

"Brecht, I want a full list of what was taken," you say. "And do not think to exaggerate in the slightest, you hear me? I'll be checking what you claim was taken with what Ayric admits, and with the others in both camps. Once I have it, I'll try to take what is equivalent from Olivia's camp and repay what was taken."

It sounds more than fair, which is why you're shocked

by Olivia's vehement reaction.

"You can't," she shouts, and she glares at a pleased Brecht. "You fucking bastard, you can't do this, we'll starve when you don't even *need* it, when you took what wasn't even *yours*."

That piques your curiosity. "What do you mean?"

"It means she's mad she was caught and looking for excuses," Brecht says.

You point a finger at him, a clear signal to shut his mouth, and then wait for an explanation.

"I mean me and Brecht are both from Verdt Vale," Olivia says. "And when the decision came to flee for Londheim, his family raided his local shop and claimed everything in it was his. But it wasn't. Most was owned by traders in Londheim, and Brecht only sells it for them. I said it should be shared among everyone, but he threatened blood if anyone tried to take it."

You listen with your face calm, but your mind is racing. Such a dispute is complicated, given a question of ownership. If it was a true consignment, then Brecht would also be responsible for paying back those merchants for the goods. Perhaps they would be lenient, given the arrival of the black water, or perhaps they will be ruthless and cold. You put it at a coin flip.

The main problem is that the issue would have effectively been settled before the people of Verdt Vale joined the current caravan. Does it truly excuse the theft?

Something else she said gnaws at you, and you turn to Brecht.

"Is it true, what she says?" you ask.

"Those supplies were entrusted for me to sell, and I hold responsibility for them still," Brecht says, straightening up. "And I intend to pay it all back, too, which is why every bit of theft is that much more I can't hand over when we arrive. It's coin out of my pocket, and food out of our bellies."

"You don't need any more damn food in your bellies, you pigs," Ayric says, surprising you with the outburst. The kid had been content to keep his head down and his mouth shut unless addressed. It does remind you of a point Olivia raised, and after glaring at the boy to let him know such an outburst is not acceptable, you focus back on Brecht.

"That's not what I meant," you say. "Olivia insists she'll starve, but that you are not in need. Londheim is another three days away. Do you have enough food and water for those under your care to reach it?"

A bit of his confidence falters.

"If we tighten our belts a little," he admits.

You feel ire growing in your belly.

"And is that before or after I have Olivia repay anything taken?"

He refuses to look you in the eye. "Before."

You turn to Olivia. "And you? How fare your stores as is?"

There's no hiding her shame.

"We've rationed the best we can, but we'll be out of food tomorrow morn," she says. "We've been talking about what to do, but it's hard, knowing we'll have to beg. Because that's all we can do. No newcomers with full pockets are going to join a camp that's clearly starving."

Survivors of the same village, split into two groups, one starving, and the other, carrying excess. Part of you wants to scream. Another part wants to order Brecht to hand over half his goods just to punish him for his greed, but you know that violence would be inevitable.

You cross your arms, and the rest fall silent as you think. Ayric needs punished, that seems clear. But can you let Olivia off the hook? And what blame falls on Brecht, that he would gleefully let others starve to take what he doesn't even need?

No choice is going to leave people happy. You fear no choice will avoid bloodshed. Whatever you do, you're going to have to stick with it, and enforce it with your blade and pistol if you must.

"Ayric has admitted theft," you say, beginning with the easiest part. "And I cannot let people think everyone's stores is fair game. Ayric, there's a group of elderly I've been helping on the road, and now you're going to be helping them, too. Sunrise to sunset, you'll be carrying what they cannot, as well as taking a turn pulling the cart transporting three of them. A word of complaint, and I will give you a far more odious task involving the latrine trenches we dig when we settle down. Is that clear?"

He nods, and you can tell he's relieved. You swallow. Now for the harder part.

"Brecht, I will still need that list of supplies taken," you tell him. "When we get to Londheim, I'll assess its value and have the local magistrate put it into record as an official debt in Olivia's name. Until then, nothing else shall be done, nor goods repaid."

"Londheim? That deters nothing! If they think they can just take and have it count later, they'll—"

You step close, your face in his, your glare silencing him.

"I will not sentence people to starve," you say. "The world has turned dangerous. People have lost homes, land, and livelihood, and despite it all, nearly everyone here has shared with their neighbor. That you have not condemns you in my eyes more harshly than Ayric's theft. As for the cost, you will have it repaid to you, once we are in safety, and the threat of starvation no longer hangs over all our heads. Have I made myself clear?"

He says nothing, only flushes red as he fumes in

silence.

"Have I made myself clear?" you ask again.

"Yes, Soulkeeper," he mutters. "I'll go and make myself that list. Just make sure no one comes crawling near my family and friends again. The next time we catch fingers in our belongings, we're cutting off hands."

He trudges off.

"Thank you," Olivia says, approaching you.

"If you were starving, you should have come to me or Devin," you tell her, unable to hold back your frustration. "And if you thought Brecht's people had more than they needed, again, you should have come to us. We could have bargained with him, promised Keeping Church funds, or pressured him to share with the entire caravan. Instead, you stole, and robbed my arguments of teeth. Too many within the caravan will sympathize with him against a thief, no matter the circumstances."

"Forgive me, Soulkeeper," Olivia says, and she lowers her head. "We were hungry."

"We are *all* hungry," you say, exasperated. "Have someone prepare a list of all you have, and how many mouths you must feed, and then send it to Devin. We'll figure out a way to redistribute a bit of food so your family does not suffer."

Olivia nods, and she grabs her son's hand.

"Thank you," she says. "From us both, thank you. We will."

And then she rushes off, to join her family. Now alone, you remove your hat, rub your eyes with your thumb and forefinger, and wonder if you made the right decision. You hope the promise of repayment is enough to placate Brecht and his group. It might. If it does, you've averted the crisis. If it doesn't…

Well.

It wouldn't be the first time there's blood on your hands. At least it will happen because you chose what you thought was right. Better that, then starved corpses of people you could have saved.

16

The next morning, you wake to the rumbling of an earthquake. You lurch to your feet in a panic, your head swiveling about. Everywhere, people scream. Some huddle in groups, others wail loudly in prayer to the Three Sisters. It's not the quaking that frightens people, but the remembrance. The black water. It began not long after a similar quake.

You stare west, at Alma's Crown, and imagine a flood of black water rushing out from within, this time past Crynn and to the fields beyond. You imagine it washing over these thousands of people, burying them in its otherworldly flow to turn them into pale, hairless things.

It doesn't feel right. It doesn't feel fair, that you would all struggle to go so far and then be swept up when safety was so close.

As much as you search the horizon, you see no sign of its flow. You wish that would make you feel better, but it does not. The quake soon ends, and what follows is a strange aura of sniffled tears and soft, comforting murmurs as people try to assuage the fears of those they love.

You walk for an hour, chatting with those who look like they need a smile, praying for those in distress, and focusing on the little things. You help tidy up bedrolls, pack up supplies, and put out cook fires, all so people may begin the day's trek toward Londheim. Life moves on. It always must.

A few hours into the day, Devin finds you amid the

crowd and pulls you aside.

"There you are," he says. "I was hoping you could tell me if I was losing my mind."

You shrug. "About?"

In answer, he points west. You turn, confused. Behind you is the long line of the second half of the refugee caravan. Beyond that, fields of grass, and in the far distance, the faint image of Alma's Crown, the mountains hazy and seemingly small at such a distance.

"What am I looking for?" you ask.

"There," Devin says, pointing. You try to follow his finger. "That mountain, right there."

And then you see it. Sure enough, among the tall, distant spires is a mountain that seems closer than the others. You frown. Much closer than the others...despite you leaving Alma's Crown behind before ever reaching Westwall.

"Devin," you say softly. "Are you implying a mountain just...appeared? A whole damn mountain?"

"Was it there this morning?" he asks.

"I...don't think so?" you say, but it wasn't like you were focusing your attention on the distant mountains. "You said Tommy is a local Wise. He should know all about the mountain range. I assume he says it is new?"

"You'd be correct."

You stand next to your fellow Soulkeeper and stare into the distance.

"What does it mean?" you ask, baffled.

Devin claps your shoulder, sharing in your bafflement.

"Your guess is as good as mine. Just...keep an eye on it, all right? And try not to tell anyone. More people will notice in time, but if we don't make a big deal out of it, I'm hoping no one panics."

"Panic, over a mountain?" you ask. "Why? How? I'm sorry, Devin, this doesn't really make any sense."

"Yeah," he says while walking away. "That's how things work now, I guess."

You continue your journey, but are not allowed an uneventful morning. Wailing reaches your ears, and you hurry toward it.

The source comes from the group of elderly you've been helping. The small wagon used to carry the three that lack the strength to walk has halted in the middle of the road, currently empty. Near one of the wheels lays a familiar young boy, Ayric.

"What happened?" you ask as you push onlookers aside. A burly man is attending Ayric, and he looks to you with tears in his eyes.

"Me and Ayric, we were pulling the cart," he says. "And then we were bumped, not much, but Ayric stumbled, and we had such momentum…"

"Who?" you ask, and look about.

But you already have your answer. Not far ahead, you see Brecht's group, several dozen survivors along with two carts of their own. You swallow down your rage. You have no proof, even if your gut already knows the entire story. Instead you lean closer to Ayric.

He's still breathing, and appears remarkably calm for having been momentarily crushed by the cart. His blue eyes peer at you, glazed. You think he might be in shock.

"My legs are cold," he says.

Before you can ask anything more, a loud wail pierces the morning. Olivia. She's come for her son. You stand and turn to face her.

"Is he..?" she asks, seeing you there.

"His back is broken," you say.

What calm she'd managed upon seeing you breaks, and sobbing, she rushes to her son, drops to her knees, and embraces him. Her tears wet his face, and absurdly, he is the one whispering calm words to her, insisting it was fine, he was fine, it was just an accident.

You walk away, unable to endure more.

Ayric rides the rest of the way to Londheim atop the wagon with the elderly.

*

Late that afternoon, the ground quakes again. The fear is less palpable this time, just a few surprised shouts and a lot of murmuring. You've gathered with Tommy and Devin to eat supper, and all three of you peer about when the quake ends. No one admits it, but all three of you are searching for signs of the black water and its possible approach.

The setting sun is harsh to your eyes when you look west, but you see nothing. No flowing shade of stars and darkness to overwhelm the world. What you do see, however, leaves you baffled.

The mountain, the one that seemed nearer than the others and appeared from nowhere…is now even closer.

"That's…that's not possible," Devin says when you point it out.

"I think we need to stop believing we know what is and is not impossible," Tommy says. He looks to you both. "What do we do? Do we flee? Try to push everyone to go faster?"

"How does one outrun a mountain?" you ask, meaning it as a joke more than anything serious.

Devin looks your way. His face is pale.

"We wake early with the dawn," he says. "And whatever that mountain is, and whatever makes it move, I pray we are in Londheim long before it comes close enough for us to find out."

17

It is only the sight of Londheim that keeps the panic at bay from the refugees flooding toward the grand city. Its stone architecture is unique among all of Orismund, and grants it a feeling of age some of the truly old cities in the east lack. A grand brick wall surrounds it, and you pray its protection will mean something to that which chases you.

"Robin!" you hear Devin shouting, drawing your attention from a man and wife you've been encouraging due to their son falling ill. You glance up to see the other Soulkeeper hurrying toward you from the front.

"Yeah?" you ask.

"Lawkeepers approach from the city," he says, and gestures that way with his thumb. "I'd like you with me in case matters turn ill."

"Turn ill?" you ask. "Why? Surely the mayor would never turn us away?"

"I pray not," Devin says. "But we're about to find out."

The two of you jog to the front, passing even those eager to reach the city, and ordering them to wait behind you if you must. The Lawkeepers march toward you in a group of four, and they too move with urgency.

"Do you want to do the talking, or should I?" Devin asks as you cross the remaining stretch of road.

"I've never gotten along well with Lawkeepers," you say.

"Fair enough. I'll talk for the both of us."

The four stop before you, their steel cuirasses and sallet helmets shining bright under the midday sun.

"You in charge?" one of them asks. He is bigger than the rest, and is not shy about the pike he carries.

"Soulkeeper Robin and I have been helping to keep the people calm," Devin says. "I'm not sure I'd say we are in charge, but they listen to us, and we can answer whatever questions you have."

The Lawkeeper shrugs. "Good enough for me. You fuck this up, then the Church will suffer for it too, so keep that in mind. My name's Troia, and I'll be the one breaking your refugees into groups."

"What for?" Devin asks.

"We've been preparing for your arrival since we saw you on the horizon. Multiple Churches have agreed to house people, and we're working with volunteers to open their homes as well. Before we do, though, every person is to be questioned about their trip here." Troia steps closer. "Most importantly, no one is to break from their group, or speak with the people of Londheim until after their questioning."

"Are we to be arrested?" you ask, surprised by the condition.

"View it as such if you'd like," the Lawkeeper says. "But Overseer Downing wants to avoid a panic, so you'll do what he says, or no one here comes inside the walls. Is that understood?"

It's clear to the both of you that there will be no arguing over this. Royal Overseers are elected every ten years by land owners to rule South and West Orismund in the Queen's stead, a concession reached at the end of the Three Year Secession. This means Royal Overseer Albert Downing holds supreme authority in matters in West Orismund, including Londheim's mayor. Only the Queen could directly overrule him, and any attempt to discuss the refugees with her would take weeks of travel by parcel.

"Why would our arrival cause a panic?" Devin asks, careful to keep his voice calm and pleasant.

In answer, Troia gestures to the thousands forming a long caravan upon the road, and then the mountain behind them.

"Don't pretend this is normal," the Lawkeeper says. "Now help us form groups numbering one hundred each. The gates to the city stay closed until we start seeing orderly arrivals. Cause too much commotion, or refuse, and we'll set up tents for you to stay outside the walls instead."

You glance behind you, to the following mountain.

"I fear outside is not safe," you say.

"All the more reason for you to behave," Troia says. With that, he marches past you, to begin forming the Royal Overseer's groups.

"There's not much we can do," Devin says, keeping his voice low as you watch the four Lawkeepers shout their orders to the rest of the caravan. "Hopefully it's only some bureaucratic nonsense."

"Avoiding panic," you say, thinking back on the Lawkeeper's words. "Not by our presence, but by what the people might say. The Overseer wants our silence. He knows of the oddities we've already encountered in the wild."

Devin nods, following your logic.

"That, or such oddities have also occurred within the city itself," he says.

You can't decide if that is a comforting thought or a disturbing one. Either way, you have no time to waste, not with a mountain giving chase.

"Come," you say. "Let's do our part. I won't feel better until we're safely inside those walls."

*

NIGHT OF WINGS AND SMOKE 127

For a long, painful hour, the vast majority of the refugees are piled together in groups before the gates of the city, awaiting entrance. Hundreds of Lawkeepers stand watch upon the walls, or wait just within the iron gates. It looks like the entire city's forces have been summoned for your arrival.

But, in time, Troia decides matters are to his liking and orders the gates opened. One hundred by one hundred, your group enters the city, hopefully putting an end to what has been an arduous journey for so many of you.

You walk the cramped, winding streets of the city, Lawkeepers forming a wall on either side. At some point you lose contact with Devin, leaving you to wander about your group of one hundred and offer words of comfort to lessen their nerves.

"Londheim is a city of plenty," you tell one nervous couple. "The Septen River's bounty alone will keep us all fed."

You're not entirely sure that's true, but better that than a panic.

What helps not at all is the rumble of the ground underneath you. It starts low at first, then grows in intensity.

"Keep moving," Lawkeepers shout, but your curiosity is overwhelming. Throughout the past days, the mountain has loomed closer and closer, traveling somehow in a way you cannot even guess. Now that the people are safe, you're ready to leave them be, and resume your other responsibilities. Plus, you're sure your Vikar, Forrest Raynard, would love to hear your story in full.

Come the third quake, you hear Londheim's people, cordoned off behind the Lawkeepers, begin shouting and calling for others to come look west.

You leave your group to join them, only for a Lawkeeper to immediately try to stop you.

"You haven't been questioned yet," the man says.

"I am a Soulkeeper of the Keeping Church," you say,

refusing to back down. "I will not be detained by a mere Lawkeeper of the city. If you dislike that fact, you are welcome to bring the matter of my refusal to Deakon Sevold."

The man pales slightly.

"I suppose no Soulkeeper's gonna be stirring up panic," he says, giving himself an excuse to let you leave. "Just, no stirring rumors, all right? I'll make sure the Church knows who's responsible."

"You do that," you say, and sprint past him. You need to reach the walls. You need to see what is happening with your own eyes. You've spent days with the mountain behind you, lurking, taunting you by its sheer presence. What could explain it? What could justify it? Nothing, and so it wore on you, crooked little fingers scraping along your mind. For good or ill, at last you will have an answer.

You race along the lively streets, weaving past people looking west and chatting with one another. The roads are cramped and winding, and made to feel almost claustrophobic with how high the stone spires and multi-story homes loom over them. The ground rumbles beneath your feet as you reach the wall and search for stairs. There, not far. A few soldiers are at the top, gazing out. You'll just have to hope they don't mind your joining them.

"Make way," you say as you reach the top of the stone steps and onto the ramparts. Two of them glance at you, see the triangle pendant hanging from your neck, and immediately relax.

"Happy to have a servant of Anwyn with us," one of the men says. "Because I think she's going to be taking the whole lot of us soon."

"Keep such comments to yourself," you say quietly as you step past him. "Of all precious things, hope is the last we can afford to lose this day."

He mumbles an apology, which you mostly ignore, for

your attention is upon the mountain.

From base to peak it looks about a third of a mile high, and twice as long in length. Its individual peaks are sharp, and while they seem covered with snow, something is wrong about the color and texture. It's as if they were painted that color. A hill is between you and it, covering your sight of the mountain's base. With each passing moment, you feel the ground rumble, tiny little quakes that reverberate up your legs.

"What could it be?" one of the soldiers beside you asks. His voice is calm, but his eyes are wide and his hands shaking. "It don't make sense."

"Nothing has lately," you mutter, mostly to yourself.

The mountain reaches the hill, and with a great shaking of earth and explosion of dirt, it pierces right through in a great black cloud. You clutch the wall of the rampart and watch with dread growing within your chest. The dust fades, and at last you can see the truth of the mountain that has followed you.

The mountain crawls. Six legs poke out from each side of it near the base, vaguely resembling a turtle's, only these are massive in size. Each of its claws is the size of a house, each leg, larger than any spire in all of Londheim. These legs slam into the earth, dig in their claws, and then drag the mountain along. The bulk of it carves a groove through the dirt, leaving a chasm behind that must be gigantic in size. At its front is a serpentine head, eyeless and smooth. Its scales are so dark it looks like it is made of onyx or obsidian. Leaking from its closed mouth, to drop down its chin and splash upon the earth, are streams of black water.

This is it, you think. *This thing, this crawling mountain, is what created the black water.*

Viciss, Wotri had named it. A being of another time, you can only surmise, now unleashed upon your world. The ground trembles with its every footstep. No hill or tree slows its progress straight toward the gates of Londheim.

Panic spreads throughout the soldiers as they grow more numerous along the western wall. Many pass out bows and crossbows, though you laugh at the thought of them being used against a creature of such size. What could arrows do to a thing whose very hide is the thick rock of a mountain? Still, you suppose it is something to do, a way to prepare to hold off the growing nerves.

The sound grows louder along with the shaking. The monstrous creation is so close, you can hear the ground churning. Its a thunderclap of breaking rock and scraping dirt, so loud and so deep you feel it in your teeth.

Shouts behind you momentarily steal your attention. Word of the mountain's approach has spread, and you see the telltale signs of panic. People shouting and running every which way, wanting to flee, but to where? You suspect the east gate on the opposite side of the city, and you are not surprised to see hints of smoke from that direction. A riot, perhaps?

"We…we can't fight it, can we?" the nearest soldier asks. He's looking at you for reassurance. You want to offer it to him, but it would sound hollow.

"Pray we must not fight it," you say. "Better peace than violence, especially against a foe we do not understand."

The soldier swallows hard and cradles his crossbow to his chest.

"I don't want to die today."

We may not have a choice, you think to yourself as you stare at the black water drooling from the thing's mouth. You imagine the devastation of Westwall and Elkwerth, inflicted upon a city the size of Londheim. Hundreds of thousands of people, all buried under a wave of black water shimmering with stars and foul magic, corrupting them, turning them into monsters…

Perhaps it would be better to die this day, than survive

amid that madness.

You wisely keep such comments to yourself.

Then without sign or reason, the living mountain comes to a halt. Its legs sink into the dirt and grow still. The rumble of its passage, nearly deafening by the end, suddenly ceases. The ensuing silence is shocking with its power and tenseness. You watch the head of it, and now only a half mile away, you can see clearly the grooves of its scales, and your breath catches at the sight of gigantic blue eyes along the top of its head, staring at the walls of Londheim.

Its mouth opens. Black water pours out to form a ruined stretch of grass beneath it, hundreds of yards long.

"No," you whisper. Crynn. Westwall. Elkwerth. It couldn't happen here. It cannot happen here.

Teeth the size of houses fill its mouth, white as alabaster and jutting like stalagmites and stalactites. It inhales, so long and deep you feel the wind of it blow across your skin.

And then it roars.

You clutch the wall to hold your balance as the force of the roar shakes the very firmaments of the city. Your ears ache, and you fear they will pop. The roar goes on and on, blasting through you, shaking your bones and robbing you of breath. Soldiers around you cry out, some falling to the ground, others fleeing the ramparts for the city below.

Its head turns to the north. A river of black water roars out from its mouth, traveling with silent, horrifying speed. The sun glistens of its surface like it were oil. The night sky swirls within its depths. All the lands north of Londheim are buried within it, the grass turning a now familiar pale, ashen shade. On and on goes the flow, traveling so far you cannot see its end. At last, the river ceases, and the monster slowly turns its head from north to south.

Another flood of black water, this time to the south. It's forming a line before Londheim, a strange demarcation to the west. The sight is staggering. To one direction, a line of foul rot. The other, green grass, and then the sparkling waters of the Septen River. When finished, it turns its gaze to Londheim, and opens its mouth.

This is it, you think. *We're isolated. We have nowhere else to go.*

You don't know if the water can climb the walls. You fear it won't matter.

The crawling mountain opens its throat once more. Out comes a third deluge of black water, silent in its passage as it rushes toward the western gate of the city. You imagine the destruction that will follow. Buildings crumbling, their supports unable to hold up their old stone. All food turning to rot. Men and women lashing at one another, their skin pale as the dead, their mouths sealed over with black blood. All who survived would be overwhelmed by the creatures that remained.

Soldiers scream. Some drop their weapons and run. You stand firm, determined to watch to the very end. You will not look away. You will stand strong, to the end of all things and the start of whatever lays ahead in the Sisters' arms.

Two hundred yards from Londheim's city gates, the water suddenly splits in half as if striking an invisible wall. It rolls north and south, forming two perfectly straight lines. Not a drop passes beyond. It flows on and on until reaching the edges of the city, where it fades away like smoke.

You have no time to ponder its meaning, for the ground is shaking, and you clutch at the rampart. What screams you hear dwindle as people realize their doom has not yet come. The mountain shudders, its legs curling and its massive weight settling down into the grass. Its eyes close. All is still. The mountain sleeps.

"Are we…we safe?" the nearby soldier asks. He's clutched his crossbow so tightly to his chest its handle has broken against his cuirass. His face is wet with tears.

You look upon the crawling mountain, the being Wotri named Viciss, the Dragon of Change. Your hands itch for your sword and pistol.

"I don't know."

18

The ruling seat of the Keeping Church in Londheim is at the Cathedral of the Sacred Mother. It is a gargantuan complex, surrounded by three walls, each one dedicated to one of the goddesses. You climb the steps toward Anwyn's Gate, through which is the Soulkeepers' Sanctuary. It's quieter here compared to the teeming mass of people at the main entrance of Alma's Greeting.

The people are frightened. They're looking for answers, and you don't blame them.

Two novices stand guard, and they nod at you and step aside upon recognizing your garb and the pendant hanging from your neck. You pass through the halls, the contents within a peculiar mixture. Some rooms are dedicated to study and learning, while others, the martial arts of battle. Libraries are next to armories. Such is the life of a Soulkeeper. The walls are decorated with scriptures from Anwyn's Mysteries carved into golden plaques, and the many paintings showcase their patron deity lovingly guiding the souls of the dead on from their bodies to the stars beyond. A few familiar faces recognize you in the hallway and call out greetings, and you politely greet them back while hurrying onward. There is only one man you wish to speak with right now.

Your Vikar's office is separated from the barracks by a long, carpeted hallway. At its end is a door laced with silver, and in its center, a triangle-shaped window. You hear voices arguing from the other side. After hesitating to knock, you decide not to bother. After the last few days, you've lost what little patience you have for etiquette.

"Who's interrupting now?" Vikar Forrest Raynard asks from his chair. He is Vikar of the Dusk, and in charge of all Soulkeepers in West Orismund. The tight black uniform is a comical sight on a body so full of muscle. A silver moon pendant hangs from his neck, a larger, more ornate version of the one you wear. There are two decorations on the plain gray walls. One is a portrait of Forrest's wife and children. The other is the enormous ax he'd wielded prior to becoming Vikar, when he had been known as one of the strongest, most headstrong Soulkeepers in all the church's history.

"Soulkeeper Robin," you say, though Forrest well knows your name. It's more for the other two in the room. One is a Faithkeeper you do not recognize, the other, a man in a fine suit you suspect was sent by the mayor, or perhaps the Royal Overseer. "And I've just arrived from Elkwerth."

"Elkwerth?" Forrest says, and after a second, you can tell he has mapped out the path you traveled. "Goddesses help me, the shit you must have seen." He turns to the others. "You two, out. Now. You have my answers. We in the Cathedral shall help Londheim in any way we can, but it won't be done in a rushed panic. Get the Faithkeepers to open up their churches, and get them counting numbers. Once we have those, we can figure out what we have to spare, and where."

The two men exit in a huff. Forrest glares at them as they leave, then bursts out of his chair the moment the door slams shut. He steps around his desk in a heartbeat and wraps you in an enormous hug.

"Robin, you bastard, it's so good to see you alive. I've been getting reports from every Soulkeeper who's returned from the wilds and the stories they tell me are horrifying."

"That's one way to put it," you say.

Forrest steps back, claps your shoulder hard enough to nearly knock you over, and then returns to his seat.

"All right, your turn to fill me in. I've had Devin explain the madness he saw at Dunwerth, and Lyssa's given me some details of what it was like when she traveled from the north in Pathok. I believe you were with Devin for some of it, right? What happened before then?"

So it sounds like Devin did not tell your story to your Vikar. You appreciate it greatly. So much of it already feels like a fever dream, and you are unsure just how your Vikar shall react to what you have experienced. Part of you wants to reveal everything, starting from your arrival at Elkwerth. Part of you fears if you describe encounters with talking wolf kings and the dead walking will have him believe you lost your mind.

Then again, a mountain did crawl to the fields beyond the city and spew black water.

"It started in Elkwerth," you begin. "With a dozen souls occupying a single body."

You tell Vikar Forrest everything. You spare no detail, not your terror at the events unfolding, nor the bizarre changes happening to the world around you. Forrest says little, but at the point you reach the encounter with the spider wolves, he interrupts you.

"Hold it up," he says, and reaches into his desk. From a drawer, he pulls out two glasses and a half-full bottle of Nelme bourbon. He fills both, and then offers you one.

"Gladly," you say, and down it greedily. The burn in your throat feels refreshingly simple, a pull back to the here and now. Forrest drains his own glass, refills it, and then settles back into his chair.

"All right then," he says, and tips the bottle toward you. "Go on."

He listens in silence to the tale of Wotri, King of Fang and Fur. He shakes his head at the destruction of Crynn, which you know he has already heard much more of from Devin. You continue until reaching Devin's band of refugees, what had once been a small group fleeing the village of Dunwerth now numbering in the hundreds.

"From there, I suspect Devin has told you everything useful," you finish.

Forrest leans onto his desk, his folded elbows atop it. A bit of fire enters his blue-green eyes.

"You are not to speak a word of this, do you understand?" he says. "Not to your friends, not to fellow Soulkeepers, no one."

"Is the truth now dangerous?" you ask.

Your Vikar gives you a hard look.

"That…Wotri…told you several things that either border on blasphemy, or sail right over the fucking line and then keep on going. Perhaps they're true. Perhaps they're lies, and you swallowed them because you were isolated and confused. I don't know which, but what I do know is that too many people in this city are already convinced that crawling mountain out there is the void-dragon come to usher in the age of Eschaton."

He leans toward you.

"In case you can't figure it out, that is *bad,* Robin. We have thousands of refugees we need to find beds and food for, a bizarre threat just outside our walls, and a populace very much in panic. If they think the world is about to end, our ability to keep the peace is finished."

"I understand," you say, and nod. "But I assume this is only a temporary decision? I will hold my tongue for now, but what I have seen and heard deserves to be discussed, even if to decide whether or not what Wotri says about dragons and such is to be rejected."

"I've been taking notes of what every Soulkeeper tells me," Forrest confirms. "The other Vikars are doing the same.

The mayor's collecting rumors from the refugees, too. We'll have a chat with Deakon Sevold soon enough, and decide what the church's official opinion will be involving all this…madness."

It's what you should have expected. Deakon Sevold is the highest ranking member of the Keeping Church in West Orismund. His word is law, and his decisions will be distributed by the three Vikars to the Soulkeepers, Mindkeepers, and Faithkeepers of their respective sacred divisions.

"Fair enough," you say, and stand. "Thanks for the drink, Vikar."

Forrest stands with you, and he opens his arms for another embrace.

"Thank you for the tale, and for surviving to tell it," he says. "Glad to have you back with us. We're going to need all the help we can get in the coming days…and nights."

He steps back and thuds the back of his hand against your shoulder.

"Starting tonight, actually. I've a job for you, Soulkeeper."

You try not to look disappointed. You have no home of your own in Londheim, and instead use the barracks in the Soulkeeper Sanctuary in the rare times you stay in the city. Right now, your bed is calling you with a voice loud enough to challenge the roar of the crawling mountain.

"And that is?" you ask.

"I'm assigning you a patrol," your Vikar says. "A request from the Royal Overseer himself. With how crazy everything is, he's flooding the streets with Lawkeepers, and requested Soulkeepers join their ranks. He thinks the people will feel safer that way."

Arguing would be pointless. Forrest is a stubborn man, as firm and straightforward as the enormous ax stashed behind him. If he's already agreed to the request, then you are absolutely going to be spending the night patrolling the streets.

"So be it," you say, resigning yourself to a long night before you get a chance to sleep on a padded mattress with proper pillows and blankets. "Where am I going, and who with?"

19

For four nights, you patrol the dark streets of Londheim. Your assigned district, the Quiet District, is one of the wealthiest in the city, a walled off section where merchants, money lenders, and business owners have staked their claims. Normally it would be an easy patrol, for many of them employ their own guards, but the mood of the city is dire. Panic and hunger are potent forces, and several times you catch thieves attempting to break into homes.

The cold and tedium wear on you, but you've learned to tolerate those as a Soulkeeper. What you're not used to, however, is the partner assigned to you: a soulless Lawkeeper named Ansell.

"You ready for another long and boring night?" you ask Ansell as you meet him at the entrance to Quiet District. He's standing rigid in his cuirass and light chain. A club is strapped to his belt. His dark hair is cut short, simple and efficient without care for style. Across his throat, marking him as one of the soulless, is a line of interlocked chain tattoos. The man stares at you, his expression blank.

"I am adequately prepared for my duties," he says.

"You always are," you mutter. "Anything interesting happen before I arrived?"

"I have seen nothing of note that I should act upon."

"Stellar."

The pair of you step through the gates into the district. Another Lawkeeper is there on the other side, and he waves at you before shutting the gates for the night. They rattle behind you with wood and metal as you begin your patrol. You walk in silence, wishing for conversation but knowing it will be fruitless.

"Keep an eye on the right," you say as you keep to the center of the street. "I'll watch left."

"I am capable of observing both sides of the street."

You grimace. One does not make small talk with the soulless.

"I'm sure you are, bud."

You've never felt comfortable around soulless. Church records claim they first appeared in the year 1382. They were rare at first, once in a generation, but over the past decades they have grown far more numerous, until there are over a thousand in Londheim alone. They are men and women without a soul granted to them by Alma at the moment of their birth. At first the church had executed them, considering them strange or horrid aberrations, but that thankfully changed after only a few decades.

Now, soulless are carefully trained and employed as servants, custodians, even Lawkeepers. Without a soul, they hold no desires of their own. They care little for inconveniences. If given orders, they obey, so long as they did not contradict already given orders. They are a strange, passive existence that unnerve you with their presence. Perhaps it is because the reason for their lack of souls has never been satisfyingly explained.

Some claim it is a curse, though cannot give a reason why Alma would do so. Some, pointing to the growing difficulty of reaping rituals, claim the Sisters have abandoned the Cradle. Neither possibility is a pleasant one.

"It seems like things have calmed down a bit," you say as you continue your patrol.

"We have yet to encounter anyone," Ansell says.

"I mean, compared to the last few nights. And in the city in general. People are settling in. They're starting to believe the crawling mountain won't kill us."

"Was there reason to believe it in the first place?"

You chuckle. "A giant living mountain crawls to our doorstep, roars, and bathes half the land in black water that corrupts all its touches? Yes. I think it was a valid possibility."

Ansell's head slowly swivels left to right, checking both sides of the street despite your request for each of you to focus on a particular side.

"Then it is still a possibility," he says. "You make assumptions based on inaction."

"Are you suddenly versed in the decisions of a mountain?" you ask, thinking surely you've got the soulless on that one.

"I am not," Ansell says. "Which is why my opinion is irrelevant."

"I'd like to think if it didn't kill us when it arrived, then it has no intention of doing so now," you argue.

Ansell pauses a moment to peer at a nearby mansion.

"Are you versed in the decisions of a mountain?" he asks you.

You're half tempted to lie, if only not to lose the argument.

"No," you grumble.

"Then your opinion is irrelevant." He snaps back to attention. "I thought I saw an intruder. It was just a cat. We resume."

You continue on, reminded yet again why no one holds small talk with soulless. No curiosity. No imagination. Try as you might, you can not even get Ansell to act surprised or intrigued by what the crawling mountain is, or what its arrival means. And should half the city drown in black water, Ansell would shed no tears. Grief? Sorrow? Robbed of them, like all else when Alma denied them their soul.

"Sure, we resume," you say, and your patrol continues.

A shadow passes overhead, large and fast, but when you glance up you see nothing.

"Did you see what that was?" you ask, scanning the stars.

"That?"

You gesture above you. "What caused that shadow."

He looks up, then back to the street. "No. Is a shadow relevant to our task?"

For once, it'd be nice if the soulless's basic questions didn't leave you feeling like a fool.

"Maybe," you say, and continue. Not a moment later you hear the deep cry of an owl. It's far from the hoots you'd tend to hear amid the pines out west, and much more like the screeches made when birds fight over territory with one another. You shudder at the sound. Ansell doesn't even flinch.

"Do you recognize that sound?" he asks.

"I think it was an owl," you say, glancing over your shoulder. It sounded like it was not too far away.

"Then we continue. Owls do not pose a risk of thievery."

"Says you. With how the world's gone crazy, maybe they do."

Ansell immediately halts in place and turns to face you. The sudden intensity has you take a step backwards.

"Am I to look for owls now?" he asks.

You clench your jaw. The Lawkeeper has been taught to accept orders from Soulkeepers, so long as they do not contradict a few core tenants. You cannot tell him to harm himself unless someone else's life is at risk. You cannot force him into deviant or sexual behavior. Most importantly of all, you cannot order him to kill.

Soulless who kill are executed, no matter the reason.

"No," you say. "I'm nervous, that's all. Forget it."

"I cannot voluntarily forget, but I shall disregard."

You wince. "Right."

The sound of breaking glass interrupts what counts as a conversation between you two. Both of you turn in search of the source. A dark home, protected by a fence of iron bars. Its gate is locked, the owners fled when the crawling mountain arrived. The noise came from within, one of the windows, you suspect.

"Follow me," you say, and jog to the locked fence. You could try to climb over, but the sharpened tips give you pause. When you stare at the place, near identical to its neighbors in size and style with sharp edges, slanted ceilings, and more stone than wood, you fail to see the cause of the broken glass.

"Are you certain the sound came from here?" Ansell asks.

"I thought so."

The Lawkeeper immediately departs from the locked gate and circles the fence. You shrug and follow. It's just a broken window, and you're not in the greatest of hurry to discover the cause. The fence turns sharply at the property edge and leads toward one of the tall stone walls that surrounds Quiet District. Ansell pauses halfway for you to catch up.

"That window," he says, and points. Sure enough, you see it, a side window of the house is broken. It's fully shattered, too, not just cracked or with a hole from a thrown rock. The implication to you is clear. This wasn't simple vandalism. Someone wanted to climb through.

The question was, how did they get over the fence?

You continue toward the stone wall, and it is there you find your answer. The construction of the fence appears to have been done quite some time ago, and it looks like it was never built properly flush with the wall. The final two poles are pushed inward and away from the wall to create a gap, not much, but you could see how someone of smaller stature might squeeze through.

A fully grown Soulkeeper and a Lawkeeper in armor? Not likely.

"I do not believe I can fit through there," Ansell says, as if reading your thoughts.

"Not even if you suck in your gut a little?" you ask.

You turn to grin at the Lawkeeper. A blank stare is your reward.

"No," he says. "Holding my breath or changing my posture will not affect the size of my cuirass."

You rap the cuirass with your knuckles so it produces a dull thud of metal.

"Never change, Ansell. Now give me a hand."

"How so?"

"I'm going over."

With the way the fence is leaning, its not quite so tall, and the slant makes it so you'll be able to brace your weight near the top without impaling yourself on the spikes. You lift a foot, and Ansell realizes what you want, squats low, and offers his hand. You step onto it, and with surprising strength, he vaults you upward. Your heel catches the cross bar, and rather than risking worse injury on the fence, you hop forward to continue your momentum.

The landing hurts, but not as much as it could have. The grass is soft and neatly trimmed. The owners should have paid whoever maintained their yard to also maintain the fence.

"I do not know how to follow you," Ansell says from the other side.

"Just wait at the front," you say, and cross the grass to the broken window. Already you can hear soft movements from within the house. Footsteps. You're careful not to make any noise as you eye the broken glass. Whoever climbed through made sure to break all of it along the bottom, presumably as to not cut themselves when climbing in. You appreciate it as you follow through. Your coat snags once on one of the upper pieces, but you twist your shoulder a bit to undo it.

The twisting, however, leads you to losing your balance, and you tumble ungracefully to the cold floor of the mansion. You clamor back your feet and hold your breath in the sudden silence.

You still hear noise farther in, a clang of wood and rattle of metal. Someone's looting the place. They do not appear to have heard your entrance.

You have no choice, you tell yourself as you draw your sword. You're not exactly keen on protecting the valuables of some wealthy merchant who fled the city days ago, but this is the task your Vikar assigned you. Weapon ready, you skulk through the halls. Bright spots on the walls mark where paintings have been removed. You see indents on carpet where furniture used to be. You suspect whoever was here has no intention of returning.

The home, while nice, is not particularly large, and it isn't long before you find the source of the noise in the kitchen. You carefully peek around the corner, wanting a better idea of what you're dealing with before you barge in with sword at ready.

Every drawer has been pulled out and dumped to the floor. Half the shelves are open. A scrawny kid moves through the kitchen like a whirlwind, grabbing silverware and dropping it into a growing pile he's formed using his shirt to carry. At best guess, he's ten years old, perhaps younger. You lean back around the corner and sigh.

This just got both easier, and harder.

"Hey," you say, and step around the corner.

The kid spins, and upon seeing you, freezes in place like a rabbit spotting a predator. He's got a ragged look to him. Not one of the refugees, you suspect, but someone who's lived in Londheim for a while. Someone who has not had a decent meal in weeks. A bit of silverware clatters to the floor, spilling out from the pocket he's made of his shirt.

"I...I live here," he says.

You don't bother to acknowledge such a terrible lie. Instead, you sheathe your sword and hold your hands out to either side in an attempt to calm him.

"You're not in too much trouble yet," you say. "Let's put all that stuff back and find out where you live, all right?"

The boy's eyes widen slightly, and you see him glance past you. A floorboard creaks. You have a single heartbeat's worth of time to realize your error before something heavy slams into your back. You gasp at the pain as you tumble forward, struggling to catch your balance. You slam into the side of a counter, roll across it, and spin about to face your assailant.

A man with a club stares at you from the entryway to the kitchen, his own pockets bulging from ill-gotten gains. He looks torn with indecision, you suspect between fleeing and attacking you further.

"Run, Hesh," he tells the kid, and then his mind made, he lifts his club and attacks. You reach for your sword, attempting to draw it, but he's too close. His club slams hard against your arm, and you bite back a scream as your elbow twists in ways it was not meant to. He rears back for another swing, and you abandon drawing the sword, especially with your sword arm half-numb from the hit.

Should never have sheathed it, you think as you brace yourself. When he swings, you twist your body so the blow strikes along your braced arm, lessening the impact. The second you feel the pain, you lunge out of your defensive posture, your fist striking his throat. The hit staggers him, and he coughs roughly when he attempts to breathe. Two more punches to the face leave him squinting and swinging his club blindly. It hits your arm, but not nearly as hard as before.

You flung your entire weight against him in retaliation. He's emaciated, that much is obvious by his wiry frame and the way his dirty clothes hang off his body. When you two collide, you easily flung him backwards. He stumbles, trips on a collapsed shelf, and then loses his balance. His head smacks the counter top on the way down, and you wince at the meaty sound it makes.

When he lands, blood pools beneath him. The man does not move.

A scream steals your attention. The child, Hesh. He's standing in the doorway. No words, no real thoughts, just horror at the sight before him. You meet his gaze, and a thousand empty, pointless words come to you. You didn't mean it. It was an accident. The pair should never have been robbing the home in the first place.

All of them pale against the anguish in this young boy's eyes.

"Enough," you say. It's the only word that comes to you.

Hesh releases his shirt. The silverware clatters to the floor. Amid its rattle, he sprints away. You glance once more at the body, wince, and then chase after. You need to identify the deceased man and report what happened to your Vikar. That boy is your best bet at finding out a name and a family. You doubt the kid will even be punished, not with the state the city is currently in. But it is entirely possible you just turned him into an orphan, and by the Sisters, at least you can ensure he won't starve.

You sprint after him, expecting him to return to the window. Your guess is correct, and he's able to wiggle through much faster than you given his size. He tumbles onto the grass, you right behind him as his shadow. You smash a bit more of the glass with your elbow and then climb after. He rushes the gap between the fence and the district wall, and you grimace. Ansell isn't there. You told him to await you at the front.

"Wait," you shout at him, as if he would listen. Hesh easily slips through, and once out, he stops once to look back at you. His eyes are wide with panic and red with tears.

"Please, don't run," you tell him as you approach. It is no surprise he does not listen. You killed someone close to him. His father? His uncle? A caretaker? You don't know, and won't know if he gets away. You're almost tempted to let him. Is there really any good going to come of this? The man may die unknown, but he wouldn't be the first life to pass nameless in the night. Anwyn would still take his soul come the reaping hour, and if not, well, there was a reason all graves are unmarked. No one should be judged for the Sisters delaying their ascension until the end of all things.

The boy runs. You chase. You're not sure you even know why, but you do. You'd hoped to find keys within the house to unlock the front gates, but it seems you'll need to make the climb after all.

The dead man did it, you tell yourself. *So can you.*

It's not as comforting as you thought it'd be. Instead you leap, grab the bars, and sling your legs halfway up, where the gap between the fence and the wall is a bit larger. It's a tight squeeze, and you halt momentarily with a painful hit to your chest, but in the end you make it through and collapse to the street on the other side. Hard stone is your welcome.

No time to deal with bruises. You push back to your feet, catch sight of Hesh hooking a right at the main road, and sprint after. Upon turning, you glance the other direction and shout at Ansell, patiently waiting at the front gate.

"With me!" you cry. He immediately sprints after, joining you in the chase.

Not two blocks down, you fear it won't be much of a chase after all. The lanterns are lit, a privilege you suspect only wealthy places like Quiet District and Windswept District still afford, but the night is dark and the sky full of clouds to grant the fleeing boy a multitude of shadows to hide within. You pass empty or darkened homes, the fleeing boy a faint visage in the distance, and then, not there at all.

You slow your run. Never should have let him get outside the fence. His chance of fleeing was too great now. Any alley you pass might have him hiding at the far end, and you lack the manpower for a proper search.

You stop completely and gaze upon the midnight district road.

"I'm sorry," you whisper, knowing he will not hear but pretending he might. "I truly am."

You turn back toward the home, and Ansell, still running to catch up. You make it only three steps before a bloodcurdling scream roots you in place. It's behind you, and so close you feel the fear and intensity of the scream in your teeth. Instinct spins you around, and you're sprinting again, straight into the next alley where the sound originated from.

The second you're within, you skid to a halt. The sight breaks your mind.

Hesh's body lays on the ground, and in two pieces. His chest is a mess of gore and broken bone. Innards splay out upon the stone, but not many. Not many, for they are within the black beak of an enormous white owl. The bird towers several feet over you, each glimmering yellow eye the size of your head. Its wings flutter as it gulps down its meal, rib bones and all.

"A small morsel," the gigantic owl says. His voice rumbles, deep and aged. He takes a single step toward you, his body lowering and his wings fanning out. The feathers nearly touch side to side in the dark alley. "I seek bigger prey."

You can't imagine what good a lone shot from your pistol will do against a bird of such size, nor is it even loaded. You draw your sword and hold it before you.

"I am no mouse to hunt," you say, wishing you sounded more threatening. You feel his eyes drawing you in. With each step, his claws scrape grooves into the cobblestone.

"Which is good," the owl says. "I seek humans for my feast, not mice."

How lucky for you, you think as the enormous bird flaps his wings once, the wind blasting over you. He rotates his lower body, rearing up, just to then lunge forward, his feet open and reaching. Time itself seems to slow as you see bits of gravel from the broken cobblestone falling from those enormous claws, each one the size of your forearm. You see the great display of his wings, white as snow and speckled with haphazard black spots. He keens, signaling the start of a new hunt, and the noise pierces your mind stronger than a blade. There is blood on his beak, and bones in his belly. Hesh. A child. Eaten.

Training, or perhaps instinct, carries you through the shock. Instead of slashing with your sword, you dive aside. Against that weight and momentum, you cannot hope to withstand. Wind blasts above you as the owl goes sailing past. One of the claws catches the loose, lower portion of your coat, and you feel it tug before ripping through the leather. You roll due to your own momentum and then bounce back up to your feet while, at the end of the alley, the owl skids to a halt. His head spins a full half-circle to stare at you as he awkwardly bobs his body to turn.

You assault him as fast as your legs can carry you, hoping to deny the owl any chance at recovering. You stab with your sword the moment you're in range, your waist bending and your arms fully extending to maximize the lunge. The owl hops backwards, and it lifts one of its legs up in defense. The claws snap closed, and though they fail to grab your arm and shoulder, they do shift the aim of the sword so it only scrapes across the hard, almost scaley feet. If you draw blood, you cannot see it in the night.

The owl lands from its hop, fans its wings, and buffets wind toward you to halt your chase.

"I am Yont, champion of the Queen of the Winged," he says, the force of the wind so strong you have to brace your legs to remain standing. Charging him is completely impossible. "You are but a meal to me, little Soulkeeper. Your sword is the biting fang of the serpents who break in half between my beak."

"First I'm a mouse, now I'm a serpent," you say, preparing your sword. "Care to make up your mind on which animal?"

His wings halt, and in the sudden pause, you stagger.

"You are and forever will be human," says Yont. "That is your irrevocable sin."

He charges you, this time with his head low and his beak open and leading. The long crook of it forces him to turn his head sideways, his beak far better for snatching prey from above than in such a charge. You hesitate a heart-beat of time, judging his speed, his angle, and then dash again to the side. Your sword swings, aided by your movements. The blade smacks across the beak and then slides along its side toward his eye. You hit the wall before you can see the results, and you roll along it twice due to your momentum.

Yont's furious shriek confirms the injury before he even turns toward you. His left eye is squeezed shut, and a bit of blue blood trickles down to stain the white feathers surrounding his beak. You lift your sword as your pulse races. He's trapped you against the wall, and he knows it. His wings spread wide, and his beak snaps with strength great enough to shatter steel.

"You will suffer, Soulkeeper," he says. "The quick death, denied. I will feast, and while I feast, you will watch. You will witness your own innards pulled out of you, made food for your betters."

He shrieks again, wordless, thunderous in volume and shockingly high pitched for how deep his voice normally is. As you wince against the volume, you notice Ansell at the entrance to the alley.

Standing there. Not moving. His head is tilted slightly to one side, so that he almost looks like a confused puppy. He's readied his club but shows no intention of using it.

"Ansell!" you shout. Yont spins his head about, following your gaze.

"Is it a threat?" Ansell asks. "I was not taught owls are threats."

Yont spins his head back around and then dives at you with his claws leading. You shift your weight at the last moment, narrowly dodging. The claws slam into the wall, crashing into the wood of the nearby home and easily piercing through. Pinned between his legs, you lift your sword as his beak comes snapping down, its edge diving straight for his throat. The owl practically swallows the blade, and you see another spray of blood as your sword slices across Yont's tongue. The pain has him rear back his head, earning you another moment's reprieve.

"Yes!" you scream at Ansell. "It is a fucking threat!"

Another snap of the beak, much too fast for how giant he is. You position your sword in the way a second time, and this time he purposefully bites at it. His beak closes about it like a steel trap, and with almost comical ease, he rips it from your grasp, twists his head, and flings it further into the alley. Panic pushes you to move while his head is turned. You can't stay trapped here, waiting for him to rip you apart. You duck and roll between his legs. His tail feathers brush against you, and you hear the owl cry as he spins to chase.

The moment you come up to your feet, your mind scrambling for ideas, you see Ansell leap in from behind Yont. The owl turns, hearing his approach at the last second, and is rewarded with a direct smack into his wounded eye from Ansell's club. Whatever damage you inflicted does not compare to the gross 'pop' you hear as blood showers across the owl's face. Yont twists his head and slams the top of his beak into the Lawkeeper as he lands, sending him tumbling your way.

You're weaponless, and Ansell's club, still so meager against the furious owl.

Well. Not completely weaponless.

"How dare you?" Yont screams as he turns your way, one eye weeping blue blood, the other wide as the moon and shining yellow. It is at that eye you aim your pistol upon drawing it from your hip holster.

"You've lost one eye, Yont," you say. "And if you don't leave now, I'm putting a lead shot straight through the other."

Except you haven't loaded it with lead shot. You pray the owl is unaware of that fact. He stares at you, the sight of such hatred shocking on an animal of nature, but then he spreads his wings.

"We are not done, Soulkeeper," he says. "My Queen is but the first to come to your wretched city. Others will follow. The centuries did not absolve you of the crimes you committed against us."

"So I hear," you say, keeping your aim perfectly centered on Yont's good eye. "Now get fucking lost."

Yont takes to the sky, lifting higher and higher until he is but a large black shadow spread across the midnight field.

Moments later he is gone, soaring north, and hopefully out from Londheim altogether. Ansell watches the owl depart, then turns to you.

"You were incorrect," he suddenly says.

You spin to face him, rage and laughter mixing together in your tired mind.

"I'm *what?*" you ask.

"Incorrect," the soulless Lawkeeper says, as if you failed to hear him the first time. "You said I should not watch out for owls."

The last of your rage bleeds out into exhaustion. You retrieve your sword, sheathe it, and then holster your pistol.

"Lesson learned," you say. "I suppose we resume our patrols, and yes, Ansell, this time keep your eye on the goddess-damned sky."

20

"Is something wrong?" you ask Vikar Forrest as you step into his office.

"Wrong?" he asks as he leans back in his chair. "I could spend all day answering that question with things that are wrong. But safe to say, you mean why I summoned you?" He lifts a letter off his desk with two fingers, waves it at you, and then plops it back down. "I've a job for you, and it means leaving Londheim."

"Leave?" you ask. Memories of your trek to the city flash through your mind, and a tightness bands about your chest. "Why would I leave? I'm needed here. The city isn't safe."

"No shit, it isn't safe," Forrest says. "I'm half-tempted to drag my own ax out for nightly patrols. But you're one of the few Soulkeepers under my care who has no family, so if I have to pick someone to leave for a bit, well, that's why I'm picking you."

You bristle but do not argue. It's true you have no family here. You were orphaned as a child, and brought into the Cathedral of the Sacred Mother to serve as a novice. Over time, your hard work was rewarded with a choice of which sacred division to enter: Mind, Faith, or Soul. A life preaching to the masses as a Faithkeeper did not appeal to you, nor did spending hours each day writing sermons or studying scripture as a Mindkeeper. You chose the life of adventure, or at least, as it was told to you as a child, and entered the

Soulkeeper Sanctuary.

"If you decide I'm the best choice, then I'll accept," you tell Forrest. "Even if I think my talents would be better served here. The night is dangerous. It has been since the owls arrived."

"Owls," says your Vikar. "Crawling mountains, void take me, I've even been hearing rumors of gargoyles and murderous foxes. But we Soulkeepers serve all of West Orismund, not just Londheim. I've sent Devin to Oakenwall to investigate disappearances there, and Moore down south to see if the black water reached the Triona River. You're not getting singled out, all right? We're stretched thin, but we have to keep our priorities."

He stands and crosses his arm over his barrel chest. He might be twenty years your senior, but you're not certain you could take him in a fight. Perhaps it would be best if he did carry through with his rant and take that ax out on patrol.

"A shipment of flamestone from Roros never arrived," he finally explains. "And given the sudden threats we face, our need of flamestone has grown immensely. This was a task requested by Royal Overseer Downing himself, but one I agreed with in taking. We need to make sure Roros is safe. The flow of Flamestone cannot be stopped."

"So I go north to make sure the black water didn't reach that far?" you ask.

"Among other tasks," he says. "You're not going alone. Lyssa will be coming with you, so you can rely on her pistols keep you safe. Mayor Becher will also be sending a small escort. The flow of flamestone from Roros cannot be interrupted, not if we're to defend ourselves fully. Should our walls be breached, we'll need more than our swords."

"Of course," you say. You're happy Lyssa will be coming with you, at least. Lyssa Amenson is, despite her fiery temperament (or perhaps because of it), one of the finest

Soulkeepers you know. She's also a far better shot with her two pistols than you are with one.

"Two Soulkeepers," you say. You eye the letter on Forrest's desk. "Are you certain we have heard no word from the town? All this caution is due to an absence of a single shipment?"

Forrest swallows as if his mouth were suddenly full of stones.

"I've told you all you need to know," he says. "Prepare for travel. You have a duty to perform, Soulkeeper."

You let the matter drop. If your Vikar does not wish to discuss it, nothing short of a miracle will pry his lips open.

"Very well," you say. "When do we leave?"

Forrest crumples the letter between his enormous fists.

"Sorry, Robin," he says. "I hope you can pack quickly, because you're to be gone by the hour."

*

You find everyone waiting for you at the west gate. It's a small group, no horse, cart, or wagon among you. Just foot traffic, it seems. Of the group, Lyssa is the first to spot you.

"Hey there, Robin," she says. A smile lights up her slender face. Her auburn hair is pulled back into a bun and then covered with a tricorn hat similar to yours, only with five raven feathers tucked into its band. A pair of short swords are sheathed at her hips, and beside them, a brace of pistols.

"I'm sorry you got roped into this," you say, and then smile back. "But if someone has to come with me, I'm glad it's you. I could have much worse for company."

"Did you request Forrest for me specifically?" she asks, and then winks. "If you needed company, Robin, there's far easier ways to get it."

You wink back at her. Lyssa has always been

shameless when it comes to her flirting. Shameless, and most definitely willing to share a bed with a fellow Soulkeeper. Given the loneliness of the road, and the difficulty of having any sort of family given the constant travel, such pairings were common, if still expected to be kept quiet and hidden from the public.

"Forrest picked, not me," you say.

"Oh, Forrest, of course. Terrible matchmaker, him. I suppose I should lower my expectations."

You laugh, and you purposefully brush her shoulder with your own as you walk past to investigate the rest of your group. There's three others also waiting. One is a short man in a fine suit, his chin sporting a bushy red beard. You sense a politician of some sort, or perhaps a coin counter to look over Roros's supplies. He is not properly dressed for travel. With him is a tall and clean-shaven manservant loaded with enough packs to care for three people. Beside him...

"No," you say. "Someone tell me this is a prank."

"Why do you wish someone to tell you that?" asks soulless guard Ansell.

"I see you've met already," Lyssa says, joining you. She gestures to the shortest of the three. "Robin, this is our assigned auditor, William Breech." William nods at you. Auditor. That fits your guess.

"And his manservant, Whistler."

"Well met," says the tall man. His voice is deep and confident. He may be a servant, but he is used to others obeying his commands. In charge of the manse, perhaps?

"And it seems you already know Ansell," Lyssa finishes.

"We've met," you say, and grin fiercely at the soulless man.

"Four times," Ansell says.

"I'm glad you've been counting." You shift your pack

more comfortably onto your shoulders. "Shall we be off?"

"We would have left already if not for you," William says. "So if you're ready, then we all are."

You shift your grin William's way, all teeth.

"Forgive me for keeping you waiting," you say, already deciding if push comes to shove, it will be the auditor who first gets eaten by owls. "Onward to Roros, and may the Sisters watch over our travels."

Together, you exit the western gate and follow the road north at the split. To your left stretches the line of corrupted grass, formed by the crawling mountain's black water. On and on it goes, as far as your eye can see. Behind it, the mountain looms, quiet and still, but most decidedly alive.

Lyssa catches you staring at it as you walk, and she nudges your side.

"Ever seen anything crazier?" she asks.

You laugh.

"Actually, Lyssa, let me tell you a story about the King of Fur and Fanged…"

21

That first day's travel is uneventful. You spend much of it telling stories of the black water's arrival, and the oddities that both preceded and followed in its wake. To your relief, the line of black water ends several miles north of Londheim, the barrier line gone. Beyond is the pale grass you're well familiar with.

"It's a border line, it has to be," Lyssa says at its end. "The mountain has claimed all lands west of Londheim."

"Then what of Roros?" you ask.

"Stop with this nonsense," William says, overhearing the both of you. He walks at the head of the group, and behind him, his manservant carrying the multiple packs. "A mountain cannot claim anything. This land belongs to West Orismund, and has for hundreds of years."

Where now is my kingdom? Why now are the nights silenced, and my pack, gone to me?

"Perhaps," you mutter, Wotri's words echoing in your ears.

Come nightfall, you have Ansell gather wood for a fire and then light it with a bit of oil. You camp just shy of the road, where the grass provides softness atop the earth. The eastern side, you all decide without saying anything. Despite the end of the black water's corruption, it is hard to shake the feeling that the west belongs to the new beings that have awakened.

"Shall we set up watch?" Lyssa asks.

"Of course we set a watch," William says. "The nights haven't been safe for years, and that was before all…this happened. Whistler can take first watch. He doesn't need much sleep."

"I can endure all night if need be," the other man says. "Though I will be an unpleasant conversationalist come morning."

You glance at the multiple packs he's been carrying, supplies for both him and William.

"Perhaps you could, but you also need to rest those muscles of yours," you say. "I'll take first watch."

The auditor shrugs.

"Volunteer if you wish. You could also make the soulless stand guard for most of the night, now that I think about it. It won't matter if he's tired come the next day."

Your cheek twitches. A soulless ordered to stand guard throughout the night will indeed follow that order. A few scholars even suggest soulless need less sleep than normal humans, but you find that doubtful. Ansell would grow tired, haggard, and his already unique decision making become that much more compromised.

"I'll keep it in mind," you say. "Second watch, perhaps."

William snaps his fingers at Whistler.

"A drink," he says, and his manservant digs through his packs to withdraw a wineskin. The auditor removes its cap and takes a long drought.

"If you insist," he says, coughing a little. "But the soulless is here to help us, so you may as well use the help."

"As I said," you repeat, your teeth clenched. "I'll keep it in mind."

*

It's hard returning to your feet after the many miles you've walked, but you trudge to the road and begin a lazy pacing, ensuring you look both north and south on your little loop. The silence is nice, and the stars beautiful. The solitude, however, does not last long.

"Shouldn't you be sleeping?" you ask Lyssa as she joins you on your patrol.

"Probably," she says. Her hands rest casually on her pistols. "But I'm still a bit wired from the travel. How's a bit of company sound while the late hours pass?"

"It depends," you say. "Will it interfere with my keeping watch?"

She lightly smacks your arm with the back of her hand. "Not that kind of company."

You cease your pacing, exaggerating the pain of her hit.

"So cruel," you say despite grinning at her.

Lyssa winks. "It's what I'm best at."

The two of you resume your little walking path, looping back and forth along the road adjacent to your camp. You smothered the fire as to not make the camp visible for miles, but a few embers remain, a faint sign of where Ansell, William, and Whistler currently rest.

Lyssa pauses after a few minutes, her arms crossed over her chest as she stares west.

"With how normal everything looks, you'd be forgiven for thinking nothing has changed," she says. She laughs and shakes her head. "I swear, those first few days feel like they were a dream."

"Wotri said it was the opposite for him," you say. "As if he had woken from a dream."

"A strange thought. Are these creatures our dreams, now made real? Or did they dream while we lived and built and spread, and now they've awoken to find the world having moved on without them? All these rumors we hear, they often match the stories and faery tales our parents told."

"Faery tales," you say. "There's an idea. Do you think faeries are real?"

She shrugs. "Whose to say? And which kind? The ones that kidnap our babies and eat those foolish enough to disturb their mushroom circles, or the ones who are kind, lead lost children out of forests, and make young those who are old and infirm?"

"Hopefully the latter."

The smile does not last long on Lyssa's lips.

"We know so little, Devin. So little. It's going to cost us, the learning. I fear monsters now live in the shadows, things that would never bear the name 'human'."

You remember the crown upon Wotri's head, and the way the forest blossomed from the breath of his howl.

"Monsters," you say. "They cannot all be mon—"

"Get down!"

Lyssa grabs your shoulder and pulls, hard. You drop with her to the grass, the two of you landing on your stomachs. You swallow down an instinct to ask her the reason for the alarm, trusting her instead. Besides, it does not take long to have your answer. Her eyes are locked to the sky, and you follow her gaze.

Shadows overwhelm the skies to the north, burying the stars behind a cavalcade of feathers. Enormous owls, dozens of them soaring southward. Your throat tightens. Toward Londheim, to besiege it as they do every night.

Are you up there, Yont? you think, watching the shadows approach. You're careful to lay still, and you pray to the Sisters that their keen eyesight does not notice your forms among the grass, nor the faint embers of your campfire. If a whole flock of the enormous owls descends upon you, nothing will stop them. You'd be torn to shreds, all of you, and the fear keeps you frozen.

Just keep flying, you think as their shadows pass over

you. Beside you, Lyssa draws her brace of pistols.

"There's too many," you whisper, fearing she aims to take shots at the owls as they fly overhead.

"People in Londheim will die," she whispers back.

"Us dying *here* does not save them *there*."

Ordinarily you might fear they'd overhear you, given the quiet of the night, but they are overhead now, and the sound of their wings is a torrent. Goddesses help you, they're all so enormous, and so strong. You feel exposed, and you fear the bedrolls nearby will be easy to spot by creatures with such fine eyesight, even amid the dark of night.

Keep your eye on Londheim, you think. *Keep focused on your prey. We're not here. We're not below.*

Lyssa watches them pass, and once they are gone, she rolls onto her back so she can continue tracking their passage south. You breathe a sigh of relief, and the muscles in your shoulders and neck finally unclench. After a long pause, Lyssa finally jams her pistols back into their holsters.

"We need to bury our campfire," she says, standing. "And no one else goes on watch. We need everyone laying low."

"Why?" you ask, thinking the danger passed.

Lyssa shakes her head and points toward Londheim.

"Because just before dawn, all those owls are going to be coming *back*, and I don't want us to be their morning snack."

*

You wake the other three, and after explaining the situation, you get to work. You shovel dirt over your fire until no smoke or embers remain, then set about camouflaging your sleeping arrangements. There isn't much you can do, but you do it anyway, relocating everyone's bedrolls so they're more spaced out and placed where the grass is tallest. You smear a bit of dirt over the tops of blankets, and then hide everyone's belongings in another batch of tall grass, careful to ensure no bits of metal buckles or buttons are exposed to reflect the starlight.

That done, you lay down for the night, your hands behind your head, and stare up at the stars. Worry squirms unwelcome in your gut, but there will be no removing it until morning. The owls will return. How many of their beaks and claws will be wet with the blood of the innocent?

'Monsters', Lyssa called them. The memories of Wotri's crown battles with memories of entrails hanging from Yont's beak within your mind. Can there be reconciliation? Or are some evil, and some kind?

And I fear, little Soulkeeper, that those days of war will soon be upon us again.

You shudder.

Will there ever be peace? you wonder. *Can there be peace, with a being that would unleash something so vile as the black water upon us?*

You don't know, and that lack of knowledge keeps you wide awake, watching the stars and waiting. Waiting.

Sleep comes, light and dreamless. When you next open your eyes, you do not remember closing them. The stars remain, but they are faint, the first hints of the rising sun casting its crimson glow to the western horizon.

You hear the beat of wings before the shadows blot out the stars. The owls pass overhead, and you lay there, perfectly still. Watching. Waiting. All it'd take was one single owl to break from the flock, a lone shadow to curl back and around, curious as to what those strange shapes amid the grass could be. A single cry to alert the rest would spell your doom. You would die, you know for certain, all of you ripped apart with beaks strong enough to crush steel and stone.

"Why do you hate us so?" you whisper, but there is no answer, only the passage of the owls. None depart from the rest. Together, the flock continues its flight north.

North, the same direction as Roros. The words of your Vikar echo in your mind.

A shipment of flamestone from Roros never arrived.

You close your eyes, but no sleep is coming, for you are plagued with waking nightmares of what you might find when you arrive at your destination.

First Elkwerth. Then Westwall. Would Roros be next?

No more, you pray to the Sisters. *No more broken villages. No more streets choked with corpses that walk. Keep them safe. Keep them well, if it is within your power.*

Within your power, a phrase so strange to you, one you had never uttered before. You are the Sisters' children, safe within their Cradle. They are the shapers of the world, the givers of your souls, and your caretakers in the great hereafter. Nothing is beyond them.

Yet Wotri had insisted differently.

Our father. His name. I know his name.

Perhaps humanity are the children of the Sisters, as are the beasts of nature and vermin of the earth, but these grand owls, talking wolves, and living fire belong not to the Sisters, but to others. To Viciss, as Wotri named his father. To the bringers of black water.

You watch the dawn sweep away the stars, bringing in a new day, and you pray, futilely, that it bring comfort with it.

22

Smoke on the horizon tells you that your day will not be uneventful. Your tired and cranky group continues their passage north. All the while, the sign of fire lingers ahead of you, a gray mark upon the sky.

"There's a lot of explanations for that, none of them good," Lyssa says beside you as you walk.

"The owls aren't known to use fire," you say.

"But they could have toppled a building with a lit cook fire," she argues back. It's a fair enough point, though you still pray she is wrong nonetheless.

"It could also just be abandoned."

Lyssa shrugs. "We'll find out soon enough."

The road gently curves further east, bringing the smoke closer, as well as the distant shadow of Alma's Crown. On the way, you encounter your first explanation of what is happening, though hardly what you expected.

Several dozen families approach from ahead. They look haggard, and nearly all are carrying bags and sacks of their sole possessions, without carts or horses to aid them. Your gut sinks. These were people forced to flee in a hurry.

When seeing your group, a younger man sprints ahead of the rest, running full speed to close the distance.

"Attack!" he screams at you, his words occasionally stalled by his gasping for air. "We're under attack! Stay…stay away from the village!"

You gesture to the others, putting a halt to your group.

The young man staggers to a stop before you and then leans over, his hands on his knees as he recovers his breath.

"Your name," you say. You keep your voice calm and controlled, to better counteract his obvious panic. "Start with your name, son."

"Gant," he says, and he jabs a finger toward the village in the distance. It looks to be a quarter mile off the road, with a lightly foot-trodden path leading toward it through fields of tilled soil. "Sorry, I just...I don't know how safe we are since the monsters arrived."

"Monsters?" William asks, the red-haired man sliding closer beside you. You glare at him for the interference.

"Well..." Gant's face turns a bit red. "They're kind of human, only...rabbits."

You thought you were used to the strangeness of the current world. Apparently not.

"Rabbits?" you ask.

"Yes, rabbits, and they tower over all of us," Gant insists. "They showed up this morning, all of them wielding spears, and ordered us to abandon our village if we wished to live."

"We don't have time for this rubbish," William says. "We are on a task deemed of the utmost importance by both Mayor Becher *and* Vikar Forrest. Some small farming village overrun by...by over-sized rabbits is not our concern."

"You wouldn't call them that if you saw them!" Gant shouts back at him. He takes a step closer, and you stand between them, your hand on his chest to keep the agitated young man at bay.

"Careful now," you say, and rest your other hand on the hilt of your sword. Instead of arguing, his eyes widen. He's staring at your moon and triangle pendant, signifying your dedication to Anwyn. A glance at Lyssa, and his jaw drops.

"You...you're both Soulkeepers," he says.

"We are," Lyssa says, a hard edge entering her voice. Her arms cross. "And why does that matter?"

Gant points back to the distant village.

"We fled, but not all of us. Some chose to stay behind, whipped up by the village elder's son, Reuben. They barricaded themselves in the elder's home and kept daring the…the rabbit people to do their best to make them leave."

You bite down a curse. What did the fools think would happen? An army would arrive out nowhere to rescue them? Half of West Orismund was ruined by the black water, with tens of thousands of refugees fleeing east, to both Londheim and beyond.

"There's no real fighters among us," Gant continues. "But you two…you're Soulkeepers. You can save them."

You exchange a glance with Lyssa.

"We should help if we can," she says. "I'm not scared of some over-sized rabbits."

"And Roros?" you ask.

The woman shrugs. "I don't know, Robin. My gut says whatever's happened in Roros is already done and settled, for good or ill. At least here, we can help people."

When you give it thought, you find yourself agreeing. Roros is protected by a stone wall and a contingent of soldiers. Anything that could threaten the city would be a threat beyond your own influence. On the other hand, it could be under siege, and needing reinforcements sent from Londheim. Even more pressing was their proximity to the Helwoads. They might be enduring nightly attacks just like Londheim.

"We'll help," you say, and at Gant's rising excitement, you shoot a glare. "But not to retake your village. We go in, convince Reuben and his foolish friends to leave, and then get out, all without bloodshed."

"And don't wait up for them, either," Lyssa tells Gant.

"Have your people make way to Londheim, and to safety. If Reuben's bunch are as young and foolhardy as I suspect, they should have no problem catching up."

Before either of you can leave, William hurries over to block your way.

"I did not approve of this," he says.

"I don't remember you being in charge," you respond.

He starts to bluster and fume. "You were to escort me, not—"

"Tell you what," Lyssa says, interrupting him. "We'll put it to a vote, and no, servants and soulless don't get one. All in favor of helping the idiots who locked themselves up in an abandoned village, raise your hand."

You and Lyssa both lift your hands. William glares, his face nearly as red as his beard.

"So be it," he says. "Whistler and Ansell are coming with me, and we won't be waiting for you. I'll just pray the soulless Lawkeeper is enough to keep me safe."

Between him and his giant-sized manservant, you think William will be just fine, but you do not argue the point.

"All right then," you tell Lyssa. "Let's go meet some rabbits."

*

Only a few of the homes are aflame, a sight that gives you some meager optimism. If these rabbit-people weren't torching everything in sight, it showed potential restraint. The lack of scouts or guards puts you on edge, and you scan the area looking for your first sign of the creatures Gant described. Despite nearing the village, you see no signs of them, not at first.

The problem was, you were searching the ground, not the sky.

The rabbit-woman slams to the ground before you with a thunderous rumble of the earth. Air blasts around her, swirling strong enough that the impact knocks both you and Lyssa back a step. Her spear leads the way, strangely carved so it resembles more a plow, so that it carves a groove in the earth with its v-shaped top as her momentum carries her closer toward you.

"Halt," she says, as if you both weren't already shocked still.

Now one of them is before you, you regret all amusement you showed poor Gant at his predicament. The woman stands a good foot taller than you, her body lean and well-muscled. Her face is long and rounded, definitely resembling that of a rabbit, and with a similarly flat nose. Her marbled eyes glare at you with naked distrust. She wears stitched leather armor, intricately woven and carefully oiled so it makes hardly a noise with her movements. That which is not hidden by armor or leather reveals a soft white fur. Her ears, so long they hang down past her waist, are both pierced and then connected together with five iron loops.

With a crack of stone, she rips her spear free.

"Why are you here?" she asks. Her voice is surprisingly soft. "Do you come as heroes, Soulkeepers?"

Interesting. Neither of you have removed the pendants hanging from your necks. So these human-rabbits or rabbit-people or however you should refer to them are familiar enough with the Keeping Church to recognize the symbol of Anwyn?

You suspect that means she understands the danger of your pistols. Whether that is good or bad, you have not yet decided.

"We are more fools than heroes," Lyssa says, taking lead. "We come only to spare the lives of even bigger fools who refused to leave this village when you arrived with your threats."

"Our threats?" she asks. "They are not threats. They

are orders, given to those who live on lands stolen from us by your Sisters. What was once ours is now ours again."

Her words match up with how Wotri spoke of the past, and of the return of the slumbering creatures. At some point, these magical beings must have lived in these lands, but how long ago was that? And how do they somehow remember it still?

"I'm not here to argue," you say. "Only prevent bloodshed. Might we have your name, if only so we know with whom we speak?"

She pauses. "Sylvi," she says.

"Well, Sylvi," you say, "I am Robin, and the lovely lady with me is named Lyssa. Now that we're familiar with one another, how about we work to avoid any further bloodshed?"

"Blood has already been shed, human," Sylvi says. "But the fools still live, if that is what you wonder. If you can bring them out, then come, and give wisdom to the fools."

You take one step, only to halt when her spear blocks your path. The speed with which she moves is frightening.

"Keep your swords sheathed and your pistols holstered," she says. "Ready your weapons for any reasons and my windleapers shall paint their spears with your blood."

Windleapers? You suspect it an honorific, like knight or Soulkeeper, and it feels very much literal. When Sylvi turns to lead you into the village, you glance upward, and sure enough, you see another of these rabbit-people hovering in the sky. The space below their feet is blurry and swirling, as if they stand upon a cloud of hardened air.

That rabbit-person's spear is drawn, and you shudder when imagining the damage it could cause with all the energy of a fall from such height poured into it.

"How should we refer to you?" you ask as you walk, finding 'rabbit-people' clumsy, even in reference within your mind.

"Did I not give you my name?" Sylvi asks.

You try not to get flustered. "Yes, but I more meant…me and Lyssa, we're humans. How should we refer to—"

"Lapinkin," she interrupts. "Dragons help me, I forgot how awful you humans are with your names. Lapinkin, and nothing else." She glances over her shoulder, a glare on her furry face. "Not rabbits, and most certainly not any variation of bunnies. Is that clear?"

"Crystalline," Lyssa answers for the both of you.

Two more lapinkin greet you at the village's edge, both wearing rustic leather armor. Their ears are similarly clipped together with rings behind their heads, so that they almost resemble long hair. Each has only three rings holding their ears together instead of Sylvi's five, and you wonder if there is significance to the number. A ranking, perhaps.

"We were ordered to banish the humans," one of the two says. He sneers, a disconcerting sight on a face so fuzzy and long. "Yet you bring two with you, Sylvi. The Warrenchief will be displeased."

"The Warrenchief will care only for the results, Tapet," she says. "The Soulkeepers are here to escort the remaining humans out."

"Soulkeepers?" Tapet slams the butt of his spear to the ground. The muscles beneath his calico fur tense. "You bring the champions of the Sisters here, willingly?"

Your first urge is to defend yourself, but you decide Sylvi is more than capable. You do not understand the politics at play, but you suspect the Warrenchief is a rank above Sylvi's, and the one giving the orders to these windleapers.

"The less blood we shed, the easier it will be for the humans to accept the borders of our new lands," she says, closing the gap between her and Tapet so that her chest presses against his in a direct challenge.

"Then you forgot the stubbornness of humanity," Tapet argues back. "They will accept us only when they fear us."

"Fear will lead to war."

Tapet stood tall, matching Sylvi height for height, glare for glare. "Then let there be war."

Their noses touch, their glares stretching, and you fear a fight will break out. Both lapinkin are clutching their spears tightly, and if Sylvi loses, you have a feeling you and Lyssa will be the next to face his ire.

"We were told we may speak with those we remained, and convince them to leave unharmed," you say, your voice knifing through the tension. "Will you hold to your words, lapinkin?"

The pair separate. Tapet attaches his spear to his back via little metal hooks.

"One chance," he says. "And then the tumult takes the building, and any foolish enough to remain within."

Wind gathers beneath him in a swirl, and then Tapet leaps into the sky with an audible gust. He soars higher and higher, the pull of the world meaning nothing to him, until he is beside the other lapinkin you spotted keeping guard on your approach to the village.

"Follow me," Sylvi says, attaching her own spear to her back.

"Thank you," you say. She surprises you with a glare of her own.

"I do this not for you, but by order of my Warrenchief," she says. "Violence is the last measure, not the first. I pray you remember that."

She leads you further into the village, following a footworn path that splits the thatched-roof homes. You fall back a step, hoping the enormous size of the lapinkin's ears does not mean she can overhear you.

"Imagine facing an army of them," you whisper, and glance toward the two lapinkin hovering above you.

Lyssa shrugs and pats her pistols. "Lead shot goes up as well as forward."

You realize 'home' is probably inaccurate to describe the building you're brought to. It clearly doubles as a sort of gathering hall, square and tall and with uneven shingles nailed to its roof. Thick tan curtains are drawn over the open-air windows. The door is shut, and likely barred from within. Three more lapinkin stand near the entrance, casually leaning on their spears and chatting with one another. They startle at your approach, though you can only guess as to the reason. Because of your swords and pistols? Your rank as Soulkeepers? Or just the very nature of your humanity?

"They're in there," Sylvi says, needlessly gesturing to the home. "Make it quick."

You exchange a look with Lyssa.

"This was your idea," she says. Her hands casually rest on the handles of her pistols. "Go be the charismatic one."

Feeling the eyes of both Lyssa and the lapinkin upon you, you approach the front door, then veer aside to one of the windows. You have no desire to hold a conversation through a closed door, and besides, you see the faintest hint of a face peering from behind the curtains. Reuben, perhaps, or one of his daft friends?

"Not a step closer," you hear someone within order, and then to your shock, a pistol pokes out from underneath the curtain. You halt a few feet shy of the window, your mind racing. Damn it, you expected them to have only a few small swords. Firearms are expensive, and the flamestones required to enable them highly regulated. The village's proximity to Roros must mean they've bought some flamestone smuggled out by the miners there.

"Brave of you to point a pistol at a Soulkeeper," you

say. "I pray it is not loaded with shot and flamestone?"

"Of course it is," the voice behind the curtain says.

Your face hardens. "Then your finger best not be on that trigger, or the lapinkin will be the least of your worries."

After a moment, the pistol retreats back behind the curtain.

"Sorry, we thought you were some kind of trick. Hey, Legrand, let him in!"

The door opens to your left, just a crack. You glare once more at the window and then push your way inside.

True to Gant's word, there are three of them in there. Two are big men, barrel-chested and with forearms like tree trunks from their hard work in the fields. The third man with the pistol is smaller, his trousers and shirt more familiar to the style of Londheim than the suspenders favored by the fieldhands. His eyes are little black coals, his blond beard neatly trimmed. You safely assume him to be Reuben.

"You're a Soulkeeper," he says, and nods at your Anwyn pendant.

"I am. Soulkeeper Robin."

"Well I'm Reuben. This big man to my left here is Legrand, the other, Goff. We're the last defense our village has against these monsters."

"Not anymore, right?" Goff asks. "You're a Soulkeeper. You've come to help us?"

You cross your arms. "To help you leave. I'm not here to fight a hopeless battle."

"Hopeless?" Reuben arcs an eyebrow. "There's eight of them over-sized rabbits out there, just eight. Even with just the four of us…"

"Five," Legrand interrupts. "There's another Soulkeeper out there with the rabbits."

"Five." Reuben lifts his pistol. It's finely polished. Clearly a family heirloom. "So five of us in total, three of us with pistols, against a bunch of rabbits that wield only spears. No, Robin, I ain't leaving. If you two Soulkeepers aren't cowards, we got this easy. I say we go hunting."

You clench your jaw, your mind racing. You remember Sylvi's speed, and the way the many lapinkin so casually leap about. You're confident in your aim, and doubly so of Lyssa's, but these foes would be no easy marks. Worse, you've never fought one in battle, which means you'd be fighting in ignorance of the capabilities of your opponents. That way leads to injury and death.

"If you hunt, you hunt alone," you say. "I gave my word. I came here in peace."

"Peace?" Legrand steps closer to tower over you. A long scar covers the fieldhand's left cheek and much of his nose, which has been broken at least once and not allowed to heal properly.

"Legrand…" Reuben starts, but the big man holds a hand in front of him, silencing him.

"Peace," Legrand repeats. "You come here in peace? Well, those creatures out there didn't give a shit about peace when they landed out of the damned sky. They threatened us in our fields, our streets, and our homes. *Our* homes, Soulkeeper. Homes we built, fields we plowed, this village we bled and sweat and broke our backs for. We ain't leaving, you hear me? They want it, they can spill blood to take it."

You take a step back and reassess. You'd assumed Reuben was the one in charge after what Gant described, but though the smaller man might wield the pistol, he is not who convinced the others to remain.

Worse, LeGrand's words are damn appealing, even to you.

"Listen," you say, deciding to use the most blunt, honest truth to counter Legrand's passion. "I don't know what those lapinkin can do. I don't know how they fight. I have seen them move, and they are fast, and they are strong. Perhaps we can win, but even if we do, there are going to be casualties."

"Then let there be casualties," Reuben says. "If we can fight, and take those eight…"

"But it won't be just those eight!" you insist. "Many of them have referred to a Warrenchief giving them orders. That means there are others, don't you understand? Maybe we can defeat those eight here, today, but what happens when two or three dozen more arrive, and Lyssa and I aren't here to protect you?"

You step closer to Legrand, deciding he's the one you must truly convince. Your eyes bore into his, which are a surprisingly soft baby blue.

"What happens when they return, this time seeking to avenge their dead? You three may be willing to give up your lives, but what of everyone else in your village?"

This time, Legrand has no words for you. Reuben shuffles in place nervously. The other man, Goff, puts a hand on Legrand's shoulder. By their looks, and the shared color of their dirty blond hair, you suspect them brothers.

"He's talking sense," Goff says. "Even if we fight them off, no one's coming back. They're headed to Londheim, just like they've wanted to ever since this all started. These creatures are just the reason they been waiting for. If not these lapinkin, it'll be another threat."

"Londheim will never be home," Legrand says.

"Anywhere new can become home," his brother insists. "So long as we don't die in the old one."

Legrand looks to the sword in his hand.

"Home," he says, then looks to you. "You'll escort us out?"

You nod. "That's why I am here."

Legrand sheathes his sword. "Fine. Just keep your

sword and pistol ready until we're safely out."

You let out a slow sight of relief. It seems you've talked some sense into the three after all.

"Follow me," you say. "We'll get you to the rest of your village in no time."

You turn, push the door open, and exit. The three men follow you out, squinting against the light of the sun. Lyssa stands at ready, her hands still on her pistol handles. Her eyebrow arcs, asking the question she will not voice, and you nod in the affirmative.

All around her are six lapinkin, with Sylvi at the front. She points at Reuben, her distaste plain to see.

"Still he brandishes his pistol," she says.

You glare over your shoulder. Reuben slowly lowers his pistol so it is pointed to the ground.

"I don't trust the lot of you," he says. "But if you keep your word, and let us leave, you have nothing to fear."

One of the lapinkin beside Sylvi starts to argue, but the leading windleaper silences him with a movement of her hand.

"Leave," she says. "And do not return. Humanity's time in the west comes to an end. These lands belong to the dragon-sired, and you are no longer welcome within our home."

The four of you march through the center of their number, all but Legrand, who stops just shy of Sylvi. His voice is cold, his face an emotionless mask.

"Home," he says, "is where our blood is."

He's fast for a man his size. Legrand pivots on his heel. His sword remains sheathed, but he has a knife in his hand, drawn from somewhere, or hidden, you don't know, you didn't think to search him. His thrust is aimed straight for Sylvi's throat, but though Legrand may be quick, the lapinkin faster. Sylvi has but a moment to cry out before a gray-furred lapinkin beside her shoves her out of the way. The knife slides across his throat, catches, punches deep.

Blood seeps across gray fur.

"No!" you scream, but it is a meaningless protest.

Spears draw. You reach for your sword. Legrand yanks back his knife for a second thrust, but is never given the chance. An explosion of gore marks Tapet's arrival, blasting down from the sky with the fury of a meteor. His spear strikes the big man in the chest and then punctures straight through to erupt out his back. The tip hits the ground, its strange groove carving into the earth to slow Tapet's momentum. Together, he and Legrand drag several feet forward, his corpse flailing, his death rattle stolen by the spear that tore apart his lungs.

"You would dare!" Tapet howls, tearing his weapon free and shaking bits of dirt and intestines off it.

"Legrand!" shouts Goff, sprinting for his brother's body. He makes it a single step before a spear punches through the back of his skull. Reuben collapses to his knees, horrified by the sight and his eyes wide at the lapinkin around him, readying their weapons. You are almost certain they will kill him.

Your instincts scream warning before you can interrupt. One of the lapinkin to your side, you see his spear at ready, and you pivot, your sword up to block. Your foe is fast, the thrust deadly, but you parry it aside and then shove the shaft of the spear further out of position.

The lapinkin is exposed now, and for the briefest moment you decide whether to push for the kill. That delay is all the lapinkin needs. He releases the spear with his left hand and pushes his palm toward you. A gust of wind blasts out from its center, with such force you have to brace yourself just to remain standing. Attacking is out of the question. During the reprieve, the lapinkin retreats three steps and lifts his spear, though in a far more defensive position.

The sound of an erupting flamestone thunders through the empty village. The lapinkin who killed Goff collapses, a weeping hole in his forehead. Smoke rises from one of Lyssa's pistols, but not the one that is now aimed straight at Sylvi's heart.

"Another step from any of you and she dies," Lyssa says, her voice cold as winter.

"You think we will let you live?" Tapet snaps, his spear at ready. Beside him, two lapinkin press their spears to Reuben's back, ready to kill at a moment's notice.

"Silence, Tapet," Sylvi says. She stands tall, unafraid of Lyssa's pistol. "You claimed to come in peace, Soulkeepers. Why should we let you live for breaking such a promise?"

"Self-defense, love," Lyssa says. "You broke your promise, too."

"That wretch got what he deserved for murdering Uyana," Tapet argues, refusing to listen to his apparent leader. "I took the life of a murderer."

"Perhaps," Lyssa argues. She gestures toward Goff with her empty pistol. "Care to tell me what his crime was?"

"You dare compare—"

"Enough!" Sylvi shouts, and clips her spear to her back. There is no disguising her rage, but who it is aimed at, you are unsure. She points a finger your way. "Be gone. Now."

Tapet simmers, but he seems unwilling to argue with his leader. Instead he grabs Reuben by the shoulder and flings him toward you.

"Do not think this matter settled," he says to you.

"I'll keep it in mind," you say, grabbing Reuben by the arm to steady him. You turn your attention back to Sylvi. "What of the bodies? The reaping ritual must be performed."

"Your Sisters wake," she says in answer. "They will have no need of your ritual. I will burn them in a pyre afterward, along with our own dead, if it will give you peace enough to leave our lands."

It is, and you express as much. You exit the village, flanked by lapinkin until you reach the main road. Then they soar back into the sky in great leaps, leaving you alone. Reuben remains silent the entire walk, and with their departure, he wipes his brow and starts to stammer some weak excuse.

"Goff and Legrand," you say, interrupting him. "Did they have families? Mothers, fathers, aunts, uncles, and the like?"

Reuben bites his lip and then nods. You point south, to the distant speck that is the rest of the village making their way toward Londheim.

"Then save your words for them. They are of no use to me."

You offer the young man no other goodbye. You have your own group to catch up with. Lyssa trudges alongside you, carefully unloading her other pistol of its flamestone and returning it to its assigned pouch.

"Robin..." she says, sensing your displeasure. "They were defending their home. We'd do the same if Londheim were under attack."

Home is where our blood is.

"Perhaps," you say, and leave it at that.

23

You catch up with relative ease. William greets you with cold silence, while Ansell shows not the slightest concern nor curiosity at your departure. Only Whistler acknowledges your return.

"I pray matters went well?" he asks.

"Well enough," you say, which is all you feel like elaborating on. The rest of the day passes uneventfully, and though you try not to, your eye keeps drifting west, scanning the sky for windleapers. Thankfully, you see none.

Your group eats dinner early, for you wish to have the cookfire doused long before nightfall. You choose your sleeping arrangements far more carefully, too, purposefully trudging a quarter mile offroad to camp beneath a small copse of trees growing around a pond at the bottom of two slender hills. Your hope is the cover will keep you hidden from the owls should they return again that night.

Wired from your travels, you elect to take first watch. As before, Lyssa joins you. Together, you sit with your backs against the same tree trunk, your gazes upon the northern horizon.

"You couldn't have known," she says after a long silence. "You talked all three into leaving their sad little fort. There was no reason to think any would choose violence after that."

"Perhaps," you say, resting your chin on your palm. "But I should have considered it. You didn't hear Legrand talk. He was so adamant, so proud...I should have realized he would not listen to me so easily."

Lyssa elbows your side. "Hey. Stop it. You know what we call Soulkeepers who second guess their every decision?"

You faintly smile. It's a common joke among your order. "Ex-Soulkeepers."

"Exactly. Now don't let this go to your head, Robin, but I think you're a pretty good Soulkeeper, so I'd like you to stay as one, which means accepting you aren't in control of every situation. Legrand wanted to die in a blaze of glory defending his home. He got what he wanted. Those lapinkin attacked a village and forced everyone out, so they're not innocent, either. The only person I pity is Goff, but that's how things go. The fanatics and the warmongers never die alone."

You nod softly, but your attention is elsewhere. The reaping hour is close, very close, and you cannot shake Sylvi's words.

Your Sisters wake. They will have no need of your ritual.

"There it is," you say, and point. Two faint beams of light shine above the distant village, their blue only barely visible against the backdrop of the night. A moment later, you see twin flashes, Goff's and Legrand's souls leaping up to the sky to join the great flow in the hereafter.

The reaping hour passes. The creeping sensation releases its grip on your neck, and the hair on your arms relax. Slowly, you let out a breath you did not know you were holding.

"What does it mean?" Lyssa asks, and you know what she questions. Why now did the souls leap to the heavens on their own, without the need of Soulkeepers and their accompanying rituals?

"The Sisters wake," you say. "Have they been sleeping? Imprisoned?"

"I mean for us," she says, glancing at you. She yanks

out the pins holding her bun in place so that her auburn hair falls across half her face. A shake of her head and it smooths out, though she has to run her fingers through it to remove a few gnarls. "Without the reaping ritual, what purpose do we even serve?"

"We still aid the living," you argue.

"Perhaps." Her fingers continue their little rhythm through her hair. "But we aid them with our swords and our pistols. Sure, we have our prayers, but the Faithkeepers are far better at giving sermons and tending to people's hearts. I fear what we ourselves may become." She leans against you, shoulder to shoulder. Her voice quiets. "I fear that, in this new world we find ourselves in, we will be weapons, and nothing more."

You wrap an arm around Lyssa, and after a moment, she slides closer so her hip and leg are touching yours. Her head rests upon your shoulder. The proximity is welcome, the touch of her, the offered warmth, pleasant to you in more ways than one.

"There they are," she says, her voice strangely calm despite her words. "The bloodthirsty fucks."

The sky darkens with the shapes of owls making their way toward Londheim. You two remain perfectly still underneath the tree as they fly overhead. Within moments they are gone, and the sound of their wings, a distant rhythm.

Lyssa sighs. Her fingers idly brush the top of your shirt, the tips occasionally touching your skin.

"Today has not been a good day," she says. "How about we make sure tonight goes better?"

Your heart skips a beat. You grin at her, deciding to play coy.

"Now what could that mean?" you ask.

Lyssa climbs onto your lap while facing you, her legs straddling your hips. Her head tilts to one side, her lips curling into a smile.

"I forgot how beautiful you are in the moonlight," she says, her arms casually draping around your neck. Your own hands slip around her waist, pulling her closer.

"We should keep watch," you say as her right hand reaches for the drawstrings of your trousers.

"Indeed, we should."

"There might be more dangers than the owls."

"Might be."

The drawstring goes slack. Her hand slips lower.

You do not keep watch.

24

The next few days are all a similar slog, long walks that met few travelers. Those you do encounter are families fleeing to Londheim, and they tell strange yet similar stories. Either their villages were accosted by giant owls, whose claws ripped apart their homes and sent them running, or more weirdly, they encountered what they described as deer-people. Tall and strong, walking on two legs instead of four, and with arms and hands like a human's instead of hoofed. No reference to the lapinkin, which you cannot decide whether is good or bad.

"This world is getting weirder," Lyssa mutters to you after the third story of these deer people arriving with clubs and hammers and demanding the people vacate under the threat of violence.

"At least these deer-people haven't killed anyone," you say. The same could not be said for the damn owls. You spend far more time during the day preparing for their passage, with the lone man or woman on watch covering the blankets of the rest with grass to aid with the camouflage since finding tree cover has grown difficult on your approach toward the mountains. Whatever campfire your group builds is doused with dirt long before the arrival of the stars.

Each time, you watch the flight overhead, fearful to be spotted and dreading the chaos they will inflict upon Londheim. *Why such a campaign of terror?* you wonder, but there is no one to ask, and you certainly have no desire to flag them down for an attempt at conversation.

At last, the final day of travel comes. Roros nears, and you steel yourself for the arrival. Of all the scattered families you've encountered, none have come from the distant town nestled against the far northeastern stretch of Alma's Crown. You pray that is a good sign, even if it feels hopeless. Not far to the east of Roros is the sprawling forest known as the Helwoads, and after watching the giant owls' flight for several nights, you're almost certain that forest is their home.

At midday, you first see its walls. Roros is the only place in all the world where flamestone is mined, and as such, it is heavily defended compared to most far flung mining towns. Tall stone walls form a protective U around the southern half, sealing in the town nestled against the towering spires of Alma's Crown. To your shock, you see the faintest movement of soldiers patrolling atop those walls.

"The town," you say, overwhelmed by the relief you feel. "It's…it's safe."

"Was there reason to believe it was not?" Ansell asks beside you.

"A hundred reasons," you say. "Most of them wearing feathers."

But sure enough, there are additional signs of life. Smoke lifts above the walls from chimneys. The city gates are open, and as you near, you see people working the fields that fill the miles beyond those walls, preparing them for the spring planting.

"Roros is well-defended, protected by a guard stationed by Queen Woadthyn herself," William says, overhearing your surprise. "You give far too much credit to these owls, Soulkeeper. They may be large, but we wield sword and flamestone, and our armies are more than enough to keep us safe behind our walls."

Lyssa slips beside you, her fingers nervously drumming the handles of her pistols. Her voice drops low so

William will not overhear.

"Don't get me wrong, I'm thrilled people are safe," she says. "But walls don't mean shit to those owls. We've seen their numbers flying overhead. Londheim has enough soldiers and Soulkeepers to protect her, but Roros? We should be arriving at a ghost town."

"Maybe the owls have a reason to spare it?" you say. "Or perhaps a reason to hate Londheim more?"

Lyssa shakes her head. "They've attacked each and every night, with no respite. All other nearby villages have been destroyed as well, their occupants chased south into Londheim. For Roros to be left alone, here at their doorstep? I'm not buying it."

You find yourself agreeing, which leads to the obvious question, one you yourself have no answer for. "Why then were they spared?"

The other Soulkeeper shrugs. "I don't know, but that doesn't mean I'm wrong. Keep your eyes and ears open, my friend. Something is amiss."

You earn a few stares from those in the fields, but you are left alone until your group arrives at the gates. They are open a crack, the enormous wood slabs bolted together with steel that tower over you thrice your height. A pair of soldiers stand guard at the entrance. Above them, you see two more keeping watch. All four brandish pistols, a luxury afforded to the place that supplies the Cradle with flamestone.

With William sent with the authority of West Orismund's Royal Overseer, and you and Lyssa carrying the weight of the church, you do not expect any problems passing any sort of inspection.

You are wrong.

"Could…could you repeat that?" William asks the nearby guard that has halted your group.

The young guard speaks again, and though you hear

him clearly, your mind aches.

His speech. It is gibberish. You understand not a single word.

"Is this a joke?" Lyssa asks.

"I don't know," you say, your bafflement growing. The first guard steps back, confused and worried. He calls over the other gate guard, and when they converse, you again hear them speak in a vaguely familiar and yet indecipherable language.

"Listen, I am an auditor sent to represent Royal Overseer Downing," William says, and he pulls out a letter from an inside pocket of his coat. The first guard grabs it, frowns, and then hands it to the other. He barks something, harsh and angry. One of the guards on the wall shouts something back. His pistol is drawn and loaded. Again, their words mean nothing to you.

Ansell taps you on the shoulder, stealing your attention.

"I fear I may be unwell," he says.

"No, it's not just you," you tell him. "We're all hearing nonsense, like they're talking a different language."

"Oh." The soulless guard looks to where William is still gesturing and pointing angrily at the letter. "Why would they learn a different language? The Oris tongue is sufficient."

"No one just learns a different language," Lyssa says, eying the two armed soldiers on the walls. "Impostors, perhaps? Creatures in disguise?"

You glance at the fields, and then what traffic you can see further inside the city.

"That'd be a lot of impostors," you say. "And based on the looks on those guards' faces, it seems they think *we* are the impostors."

"Us?" Lyssa asks. "They're the ones talking in…whatever language they're speaking."

Ansell tilts his head. "If they did not learn a new language, how do they speak in a new language?"

William retreats a few steps as the gate guard with the letter draws his pistol and starts shouting something.

"Good question," you say, and haven't the slightest clue.

*

Hours later, you camp outside the walls of Roros. The guards refuse you entry, but for whatever reason, they do not chase you off completely. You suspect it is the official seal upon the letter from Albert Downing keeping you safe.

"This is absurd," William says as he hunches before your campfire. "Something or someone has bedeviled our tongues, but why would they think us to be anything than who we say we are?"

"Perhaps they think we're monsters that stole the skin we're wearing," Lyssa says, and despite the exhaustion of the road, she grins. "I heard a few stories like that growing up, and this world has changed plenty since the black water came."

Ansell sits up sharply. "Are there creatures that wear the skin of others?"

You shoot a half-hearted glare at Lyssa.

"No," you say, as if explaining things to a child. "There are not. It is only a story."

"Good." Ansell relaxes. "I am to follow William's orders, and if not his, those of a Soulkeeper. If another is wearing your skin, your orders are no longer valid. I would need to check."

"Check?" you ask. "How?"

"By looking underneath your skin."

You don't know how the soulless planned on doing that, nor do you want to know.

"No removing anyone's skin," you say. "Consider that a very, very strict order."

"Should we set up watch?" Whistler asks. The manservant sits beside a pot positioned over the fire, stirring its contents. That pot contains most of your remaining rations. The expectation was to resupply in Roros. You imagine trying to haggle with a shopkeeper without understanding them and grimace.

"We're in the shadow of the town's walls," Lyssa says. "If we're not safe here, we're not safe anywhere."

A scowl mars Whistler's handsome face. "If you will forgive me for saying, but I feel neither comfortable nor safe here. It is like the air is wrong."

You know exactly what he means. Your head has ached ever since arriving at the town, and you cannot shake this feeling of...wrongness that permeates the area. The problem is, you have no explanation for it beyond the oddity of speech.

"We'll try again tomorrow morning," William says, sitting up. "And I'll make enough of a stink that they send the overseer instead of just the mayor. If they still reject us, at least I can return to Londheim knowing I did everything I could."

A town of Roros's size would normally only have a mayor, but given their importance, as well as the funds and protection offered by the Queen herself, it is run by an appointed overseer of the crown. You aren't sure his or her name, a fact that annoys you in retrospect. You would normally be apprised of such details before a mission. That you weren't spoke to the haste, and slipshod nature, of the request Forrest foisted upon you and Lyssa.

"Something strange is going on," you tell everyone once your dinner is ready. "So please, all of you, remain calm, collected, and do not lose your temper with the guards until we figure out what."

"Losing my temper is the only reason I was able to speak with the mayor," William says. His voice lowers. "Not that it did much good."

"Aye, and losing your temper again may end with your body full of lead shot. The guards are scared of us, and if our speech sounds to them like theirs does to us, they're right to be scared. Do nothing to provoke them. Worst case, we head back to Londheim with a strange story and a guess as to why they haven't shipped more flamestone."

"What if it's the same in Londheim?" Lyssa asks.

You arc an eyebrow. "What do you mean?"

She shrugs. "I don't know. What if it is *us* that is different? What if we upset some strange creature, or those lapinkin, or we slept in a faery ring and didn't know it so we're now suffering some sort of curse?"

"My mother told me stories of faery rings when I was a child," Whistler helpfully adds. "To have garbled speech would be a kindness compared to what usually happened to those who trespassed."

You groan and rub your eyes with your thumb and forefinger.

"Please, make me a new promise," you say. "From now on, no conjecture based on old stories and faery tales, at least until I *see* a goddess-damned faery, all right? The world is changed, yes, but it hasn't changed *that* much."

"Yet," Lyssa says, and she winks back at you, unaffected by your glare. "There's always time for more strangeness in the world, Robin, whether we want it or not."

*

The night is deep, yet your eyes open, your mind fully alert. The air feels abnormally heavy, as if you are breathing in honey. You keep still underneath your blanket. If the arrival of an intruder awoke you, perhaps your waking can go unnoticed. Yet you hear no one. Slowly you sit up and look about. The land just beyond the wall is flat but for the fields, currently barren from the receding winter. You see nothing, no intruders or…

No. That isn't right. A sharp pain knifes through your forehead. Yes, you *do* see something. Nearby, you see the shadowed outline of a man facing Roros. He is naked from the waist up, and his skin is an unnatural shade of gray. That he could be so close to your camp without anyone noticing…

This is foolish, you think to yourself, but you withdraw your blanket and stand. Strangeness has been afoot ever since arriving here. Whoever this is, you suspect he is not human.

Please, help me out here, Sisters, you pray as you approach. *We're all fumbling in the dark.*

The half-naked man lifts his arms, his gaze not leaving the town despite your arrival. Again you feel a sharp pain in your head, and the image of the man blurs.

No. Not a man. His skin is not gray, for he is a creature of stone. He is fully naked, and below his waist are four legs, not two, with each leg pointed a different cardinal direction. Though one face looks upon Roros, this creature bears a second face, the eyes of both closed. His muscled arms slowly shift back and forth. At first you think him scarred, then merely tattooed as you near, but no, neither is correct.

There are words carved upon him, you realize. Thousands upon thousands of words covering every single inch of his body.

"Protect the divine," he suddenly speaks, his voice as deep as the stone he looks carved from. "Preserve the divine."

He suddenly leans to the right, and with the lean, the words across him burn as if filled with molten lava. It is an awesome spectacle, this four-legged, two-faced man erupting with crimson light.

And then you see another such man, several dozen feet to the west, in the direction this nearby creature leaned. The words burn alive, and then you see another, and another, a full line of them, dozens surrounding the walled town of

Roros. All of them speak as one, and you feel their words like a rumble in your belly.

"The divine is eternal. Let there be no barriers. Let there be no walls. All as one, one shared amongst all."

They speak again, this time not in unison. You watch the nearest man sway, and you hear him speak, not sentences, but single words. One after another, flowing like rapids. Across his skin, the carved words flare with faint light like fireflies, and you know for certain that they match that which the strange creature speaks.

Minutes pass. You feel rooted in place as the words wash over you. Thousands upon thousands, each one firm and satisfying to your ears. They bathe over you, lulling you not into sleep, but a calmness that is almost pleasant.

The wrongness of the air fades away. The ache in your mind recedes. When you look upon Roros, it no longer feels like an open wound.

One by one, these strange creatures lower their arms.

"The divine is preserved," they say. "The divine is protected."

The divine...

You bear no doubt as to what these beings are. Language. These creatures, the words carved upon them...they're keepers of language. This midnight ritual...have they performed it upon you before? Perhaps on all of Londheim? You never once considered the oddity that you could understand Wotri, or that the lapinkin also shared the Oris tongue. A *human* tongue, one by no rights they should be able to speak after the supposed centuries that have passed since they once lived.

No barriers. No walls. All as one.

The eyes of the nearest face open and turn your way. You freeze in place, your blood running cold. You feel a deep, instinctual understanding that you have broken some sort of unknown law of the world.

"Why do you not sleep?" he asks.

Your throat binds in a knot, and you have to swallow before you can answer.

"Couldn't," you say, feeling foolish and simple even as you answer.

The creature takes two steps toward you. Though his weight must be tremendous, being a creature of stone a good foot taller than you, his passage is as quiet as the stars.

"None should bear witness," he says. "There is risk."

"There is danger," says another. You spin to see a second of the creatures approaching from behind you. "Our touch is gentle, yet the waking mind may break at the change."

You look to the rest of your party, sleeping soundly by the dwindling remains of your fire. Too soundly. Lyssa, at the least, should have awoken from the sound of their speech.

"You…you're why we couldn't understand the people in Roros," you say.

"Their language, mangled," says a third, suddenly to your left.

"Their divine, bloodied and wronged," says a fourth.

You're boxed in. The men, carved of stone and words, surround you on all sides.

"We have protected the divine," they say in unison. "We have preserved the divine."

"I'm sorry," you say. "Forgive me, I meant no offense. I only wished to see. To understand."

The first pauses. His face, it lacks hair, and where should be pores, are merely letters forming the thousands of words that make up his being. His eyes shimmer a frightening blue. His lips pull back into a smile. He has no teeth, no tongue, only darkness within.

"We are blessed by Gloam," he says. "And twice now you hear our words. Gloam's blessing shall be upon you as well, human. He will hear your words when you speak them. He will grant you power, if you are wise to him."

"Words?" you ask. "What words? Whose words? Who is Gloam?"

Those blue eyes pull you in. Your body turns light as air. You feel like you're falling.

"The Dragon of Thought. The Dragon of Heresy. Two names, you gave him. Two names, I return to you."

You want to ask what he means, but all you see is a blue wider than the ocean. The night fades from you. A thousand words rattle within your mind, orderless and wild, and you sink down, down, down within them.

*

You wake from the most restful sleep you've had in ages. The sun is bright, and all around you, the rest of your party prepares for the day.

"Finally up, eh?" Lyssa asks beside you. She's munching on a hard biscuit wrapped in a small cloth. "You were snoring like a horse."

You sit up. It feels like your mind itches. Images hover around you, half-faded as if from a dream.

"Gloam," you say, the word coming to your tongue of its own accord.

"Gloam?" she asks. "What's that?"

You wish you knew. You mutter it again, and feel a spark, feel its significance, but nothing else comes to mind. Why would you become fascinated with a lone, nonsense word?

"Nothing," you say, realizing Lyssa is still looking at you. "Got a spare biscuit left?"

"No," she says, and tears in half the one she's eating. She tosses it onto your lap. "But you can have that. Once we're inside the town, I'm planning on buying something that isn't dry as a bone."

NIGHT OF WINGS AND SMOKE

Once everyone is ready, your group returns to the town gates, which have opened with the morning sun. Apprehension builds inside you as you approach, but you cannot nail down why. You're nervous, and unsettled. Is it because of the guards?

The gate guard waves at you as you near, and then dips his head in respect.

"I was told to offer our dearest sympathies for forcing you to spend another night out in the rough," he says. "But given the dangers of the changing world, and the importance of flamestone, Overseer Hezar wanted time to confirm the authenticity of your orders."

You stand there, shocked and confused, and yet no one else seems flustered in the slightest.

"Perfectly understandable," William says. "Albert will be pleased to know you are taking proper precautions to protect West Orismund's most valuable resource."

But the guards...they shouldn't be understandable, you think. Should they? And your stay outside the walls, it wasn't to verify your identities, it was...it was...

"Nonsense," you say, jabbing Lyssa's side with your elbow. You keep your voice low so the guard does not overhear. "Shouldn't they be talking nonsense?"

The other Soulkeeper gives you a confused look.

"He was a little rude about it, but I don't think a few precautions count as 'nonsense'," she says. "And as much as I wanted a warm meal and an even warmer bed, one more night under the stars wasn't going to kill anybody." She smirks. "Well, maybe it could, but it'd be the owls to blame."

You shake your head. No, you're certain, you...you tried to speak but they said...what? What did they say?

You pour over the memories, but in all of them, you remember hearing the guards voices clearly, ordering you to remain outside while they verified William's documents.

There was no misunderstanding. No confusion. No garbled speech.

"Forget it," you say, and scratch your head. "I guess I needed sleep more than I thought."

Lyssa grins at you. "A few nights with me, and already you're tired out and needing a rest?"

You grin right back. "Fuck you, Lyssa."

"You have, twice."

Whistler clears his throat, and you realize he is behind you, and heard every word.

"If we are prepared," he says, and gestures to where William is following another guard's escort. "Overseer Hezar is waiting for us."

25

Roros is a strange place, not quite a city but much bigger than any other town you've visited. The mining of flamestone dominates all aspects of its community. You pass craft stalls for wagoners and cart-makers for the handling the flamestone shipments. Multiple seamstresses and their apprentices fill an entire street, making clothes for the miners as well as the soft pouches flamestone is packed and shipped in. With the wealth of the trade comes additional luxuries, stalls of fine wine and ale the most common…though you notice how empty most shelves appear to be as you walk the open market.

"How goes the trade?" you ask the guard guiding you to the Overseer's home.

"Poorly," the guard says. "Food shipments from the east come rarely, if ever, and we've given up entirely on expecting anything from the west beyond what we grow in our own fields."

Not surprising. You've long suspected whatever is happening here, with the awakening of creatures long thought impossible, is happening all across the Cradle. Hopefully those in the east have not had to deal with something as stark and awful as the black water.

"Even among hardships, trade will continue," you say, trying to cheer up the man's dour attitude. "For good or ill, there will ever be a need of flamestone."

"Perhaps," he says, his mood seemingly growing

worse. "This way, if you could. We are almost there."

You turn down one of the roads that ends at a modest but finely crafted home. Two stories, its rooftop slanted and well-shingled. The Overseer's house, without a doubt. The guard leads the five of you to the front door, knocks twice, and then steps aside. Almost immediately the door flings open, and a middle-aged man in a fine suit steps forward, his hair neatly combed and his mustache spread wide with his smile.

"Welcome, welcome, come in," he says. "I am Roros's appointed Overseer, Clifford Hezar."

William leads the way. You pass through a small parlor and into a grand dining room, where six steaming cups of tea wait on little plates. It seems you were expected.

"The soulless has no need of any," William says, taking a seat. "Besides, six is too much of a crowd. Whistler, you and Ansell wait in the front parlor."

"Of course," Whistler says, dipping his head. He smiles slightly. "Might I bring the tea with me? I would hate for any poured cups to go to waste."

William shrugs to show his lack of care. You take a seat beside Lyssa, who scoops up the cup intended for Ansell.

"Don't worry," she says, setting it beside her own. "I'll make sure Ansell's doesn't go to waste, either."

"May the Sisters watch over us and bless us," Clifford says as he takes his seat beside William, opposite you and Lyssa. You sip the tea as the standard introductions circle around. It's a little bitter, but you can taste a hint of honey and cream, which is nice.

"Two representatives of the Keeping Church, sent as escort?" Clifford asks after your introduction. "You must be valued highly, Mr. William."

"The value is not in myself," William says. "But in the flamestone Roros provides. Flamestone that, as I am sure you are aware of, has not been shipped to Londheim for some time."

Clifford's smile does not fade, but he leans forward, his gaze intensifying and his voice hardening.

"Indeed I am, and it is a shame the messenger I sent to the city did not safely arrive. I suspect the dangers of the road are to blame. It used to be that the occasional bandit was the worst of our concerns. No longer."

You sip a bit more of the tea, taking stock of Clifford. He's charismatic enough, and he wears his wealth well, so you are not surprised he convinced the Royal Overseer in Londheim for his appointment. His kindness and welcoming attitude are practiced and forced, but that is to be expected of politicians. The excuse about a messenger was too ready, though, too eager. Perfectly reasonable as it sounds, you can't shake the feeling he's lying...but why?

"I am sorry to hear this," William says. "Well, I am here now, and speak with the authority of Overseer Albert himself. Would you share with us the message you meant to impart?"

You can't help but notice how much nicer William is with Clifford than any of you on your trip. Is it the wealth? The power? Or just an act, a two person play the politicians both expertly know their parts?

Clifford sets down his tea, crosses his hands before him, and smiles.

"I fear you will not believe me, and I warned my messenger the same. I am sorry to say, all mining of flamestone is currently halted due to the monster in the tunnels."

You arc an eyebrow. "Monster?"

"Indeed, a monster. It appeared not a day after we first heard reports of the black water and its devastation on the lands to the southwest."

By the look on his face, the Overseer is prepared for an argument as to the monster's existence, but isolated in the north as he is, you suspect he has little news of the crawling mountain that arrived at the gates of Londheim, let alone any of the surreal encounters you've endured since the arrival of the black water.

"Have you any idea the nature or build of this monster?" you ask.

"I've heard many conflicting stories," Clifford says. He shrugs his shoulders. "Some claim it is made of teeth and eyes, and that is all. Others have described it as a snake, yet lacking in scales. It is large, it is fast, and it is strong. Most importantly of all, it has begun attacking anyone who sets foot inside the mines."

"You have soldiers and pistols," Lyssa interrupts. "Have you tried killing the thing?"

"I assure you, we have made attempts, but the tunnels are confusing even to those who have grown up working their depths. The groups either found nothing, or were ambushed, suffering terrible losses without inflicting any apparent damage to the creature." He lowers his eyes. "Two men were…eaten, before the rest retreated, may Anwyn guide their souls."

"Eaten," you say.

Lyssa nudges you with her elbow.

"Aren't you glad Vikar Forrest nominated you for this job?" she asks, grinning with morbid humor.

"You're here with me, too, you know," you shoot back.

"I'm not worried. No one eats me without my permission, Robin. You should know that."

William leans forward, his practiced smile growing.

"Well, I have good news for you, Overseer. Our esteemed Royal Overseer predicted such a possibility. Not the manner of the beast, of course, but that the flamestone might be endangered by something newly awakened in these strange times. Hence why I come with not one but two Soulkeepers. With their skills in blade and pistol, I suspect your troubles will soon be over."

Clifford smiles right back.

"That would be just excellent. Once you two are ready, I can grant you an escort of soldiers, as well as brave miners who know the tunnels and can guide you into its deepest depths."

You want to argue, but know there is little point. This is why your Vikar sent you and Lyssa, and you're beginning to suspect this was why he was cagey about the reason. You rise from your seat and push away the rest of your tea.

"We should find a place to stay before we head out," you say. "Have you an inn or a tavern with rooms you would recommend?"

"Nonsense," Clifford says. "I shall not have members of the Keeping Church holed up in the upper rooms of a tavern like common travelers. You shall be staying here, all of you. I have already prepared you your rooms." He smiles at you and Lyssa. "And I suspect you will feel quite at home with the decorations."

A clap of his hands, and a handsome servant enters from a side door. He bows low in his prim suit.

"If you are ready," he says, and gestures behind him. "I shall show you the way."

*

The room is cozy and well-furnished. A small stone statue of the goddess, Lyra, rests upon the bedside table, her head bowed and her hands locked in prayer. It is far from the only sign of faith in the Sisters you've seen in the home, but when you set your traveling pack down and turn about, you find a much more impressive one.

The entire wall beside the door is covered with an elaborate, and no doubt expensive, painting of the Three Sisters. It's a scene often recreated by artists, simply referred to as the Three Suns. On the left is Alma, a woman in white with pale skin and golden hair. The sun rises with the dawn behind her, illuminating her with its rays. She holds a dove in hands extended toward the next Sister, Lyra. Lyra is shown accepting the dove lovingly, its white feathers a sharp contrast to her dark skin and even darker dress. Her long black hair spills out across the grass at her feet, the strands seemingly dozens of feet long. A second sun is above her, high in the sky to represent the midday.

The third Sister, Anwyn, stands beside Lyra, patiently waiting with her hands outstretched to next receive the dove. Her skin is clear, almost translucent, and the painter represented her as such with faint strokes of color that almost resemble smoke. Unlike the other two, she stands naked, her head shaved and her face hidden behind a perfectly smooth porcelain mask. Behind her is a third sun, this one deep red as it sets behind the rolling hills.

Someone is trying too hard, you think as you admire the painting. Despite Clifford's constant invocations of the Sisters, you suspect much of it is an act. Not an uncommon tactic, sadly, but if Clifford knows the people of Roros are faithful then he will pantomime the same faith, if not attempt to go above and beyond the norm. Yet to your ears, accustomed to the prayers of the broken and beloved, his reference to Anwyn bore no familiarity, and no love.

Or perhaps you just don't like Clifford, and want to make up a reason for it.

A knock on the door stirs you from your thoughts. You open it to find Lyssa waiting on the other side.

"I'm armed and ready," she says, patting her brace of pistols holstered at her hips. "Want to go kill a mysterious teeth monster?"

You hide a shudder at the many images your mind conjures to represent such a threat.

"Sisters help me, I am."

26

"Is this all of you?" you ask as you arrive at the group waiting at the entrance to the mines.

"Were you hoping for an army?" Lyssa asks in return. The group is composed of six soldiers, along with two men in thick, worn shirts and trousers, both hopelessly stained with dust. Unlike the soldiers, who wield swords, one carries a hatchet, and the other, a sharpened knife. Standing awkwardly to the side of them, club in hand, waits Ansel. All nine carry little hand lanterns.

"I only jest," you say, not wanting to insult the squad you've been given. You nod at the soulless man. "How's it going, Ansell?"

"I have been instructed to avoid being eaten, and strike things that try to eat me," he says, perfectly flat and bored as if such concerns were normal.

"Good plan," you say, turning to the others, and noting their armaments. "Where are your rifles?"

"Flamestone arms are forbidden inside the mines," one of the soldiers tells you. "Safety reasons."

"We're about to fight a monster made of teeth," you say. "Surely that's the more dangerous threat?"

"It's the flamestone," one of the two regulars says. He's got a rugged, handsome look to him, his hair dark and his mustache long enough to curl down below his chin. "If you think being eaten is bad, imagine a whole tunnel collapsing on top of you because of an errant shot. Maybe you die quick, maybe you die of thirst over several days while we try to dig you out."

"And who are you?" you ask.

The man dips his head to show you respect.

"Liam, ma'am. Been working these mines since I was old enough to hold a pickax. That's why I'm coming with you, to guide you through. The whole place can be a maze once you get in deep enough."

You pat your holstered pistol.

"Well, Liam, I think being eaten is still worse, so I'm bringing this along." You lift a hand when he starts to protest. "But, I'll keep it as a last resort, fair enough?"

Liam hardly looks happy about it, but he also carries no authority, and knows it. He shrugs.

"All right, but if you start a chain eruption, it's on your head, not mine. I just pray I'm not caught in the thick of it."

"That's enough," one of the soldiers snaps. He offers his hand to you. "Henli Fairbough at your service, Soulkeeper. I hope the stories I heard growing up about the fighting prowess of Soulkeepers were not exaggerated."

"Oh, I'm sure they were exaggerated," Lyssa interrupts. "But we're still pretty damn good. Have you fought this thing before?"

"Once," Henli says. "And despite what Liam may try to tell you, we even had our rifles. The thing surprised us at an intersection, but we did fire a volley off. Didn't even break its skin."

"Its skin?" you ask.

"Skin, hide, armor, whatever you want to call it. Its brown, its thick, and it sure as shit didn't bleed when we shot it. That's all I can tell you. It killed six of us before we could reload, and the first fool to rush at it with his sword was swallowed whole."

You stare at the soldier.

"Whole," you say dully.

Henli offers you one of the lanterns he's holding. "Did I stutter?"

I'm going to kill you for this, Forrest, you think as you reluctantly accept the lantern.

Lyssa lifts her own lantern at you and shoots you a wink. "Makes you miss the owls of Londheim, don't it?"

Without ceremony, the eleven of you enter the wide tunnel of Roros's flamestone mines. The initial entrance has been heavily worked and expanded, with wood supports built every few feet. A small rail runs through the center, and you glance inside one of its thick iron carts. Empty.

"We don't know where the monster is staying, but it's been consistently attacking the deeper portions of the mine," Henli says, walking beside you with his lantern raised. As the entrance recedes, the darkness quickly grows. "Problem is, those deeper portions are where our flamestone resides, and where our miners must go."

You know little of flamestone mining, and you glance at the walls, curious. Much of the stone is chipped at odd angles, as if someone carved away at it with an ax or knife. The stone is not uniform, for across much of it you see a darker substance, much of it broken into thin chunks. More of it litter the ground, and it crunches beneath your boot.

There's little chatter among the soldiers as you walk. The ground generally slopes downward, and with each passing minute, you feel a growing awareness of the mountain above you. The walls narrow in, and eventually you reach the end of the laid down mine cart track. Liam leads the way, and as your nerves start to fray, you decide to join him at point.

"Do you know where you're taking us?" you ask.

There is little that's polite about the look he gives you.

"I know these mines better than you know your own ass, Soulkeeper."

"I'm not sure I'm all that familiar with my ass, miner. It's behind me."

"It's a pretty good ass, Robin," Lyssa pipes up. You didn't realize she was listening in. "Happens when you spend so much time hiking and traveling like we do."

You're glad for the dim light to hide your slight blush.

"Ignore her," you say as you trudge deeper and deeper into the tunnels. "I more meant if you had a specific destination in mind."

"The monster seems to hate it the deeper we go," he says. "So I'm taking us to our newest dig. It'll be dangerous fighting there, with the highest chance of a chain eruption, so I'll again repeat my desire that you keep your pistol holstered."

"What do you mean by a chain eruption?" you ask.

"You see this?" he asks, touching the broken black substance that litters the wall. "We call it the coating. Flamestones are usually caked in the stuff, which is good, because it means we can safely extract it. We chip around it until it flakes off, and then we transport it out of the mine where our flamestone chippers can do their own delicate work."

With a bit of effort, he pulls a chunk of coating from the wall. It reminds you of stripping tree bark from a pine.

"As you can see, it's pretty brittle," he says. "Which means if you strike it hard enough, there's a chance you punch right through and hit the flamestone pellets underneath. Do that, and you can rupture the pellet." He looks to you with a smirk. "You've plenty of experience with that pistol of yours, I'd wager. You know well the danger of carelessly breaking a flamestone."

"I do," you say. "A ruptured flamestone is loud and a bit hot, but generally the only worry is a bit of burns, or maybe losing a finger. You're talking about bringing down entire tunnels."

Liam pauses at an intersection, glances at you, and then grins.

"Right," he says. "One flamestone might do that, but what happens when an erupting flamestone breaks the ones near it, which then break its neighbors, and so on?" He turns right and pauses not a few steps later to raise his lantern. "What happens when you're not breaking just one, but thousands?"

Your mouth drops as you step into the cavern. It's about three times your height to the top, and every single inch of the walls is a deep black. Here the coating is unbroken, allowing you to see the little bumps of the flamestone pellets trapped underneath. They ripple along the walls, thousands upon thousands.

"Has it happened before?" you ask softly.

"Aye," Liam says. "Not often, but living in Roros, we all hear the stories. The ground'll shake, and even people in town will hear the eruption. Tunnels collapse, not just the ones with the fire, either. Each time, it takes weeks to clear out the rubble, because you got to do it slowly. Never know when you're hauling out that much stone and broken coating whether there's flamestone still uncracked from the initial explosion. If you're trapped inside when it happens, well…" He shrugs. "We hear those stories, too. About what men and women do to each other to survive when food and water runs out."

You decide you don't want to think about those stories, not when you can feel the omnipresent weight of the mountain all around you.

"Should I watch where I step?" you ask, for the flamestone coating covers not only the walls but the ground as well.

"Unless you got spikes on your heels, you'll be fine," Liam says. "It takes a lot to pierce unbroken coating.

Just…don't go testing it with your sword, or stars forbid, go shooting it with your pistol."

It's meager comfort, but after watching him calmly walk atop the coating, you follow…but that confidence doesn't prevent you from wincing slightly the first time you set your boot upon the bumpy black surface.

Twice you pass through intersecting tunnels, but Liam does not hesitate. At one point, you enter a surprisingly spacious cavern. Within are chairs and a table, plus some barrels of lantern oil and a crate in the corner with changes of clothes. A rest area, you presume, for miners unwilling to make the trek all the way back to sunshine.

Lyssa slides up beside you as you pass through the cavern.

"Have you any sort of plan?" she asks softly.

"My plan is to stab the monster with my sword," you say. "Beyond that, it's going to be mostly improvisation."

Lyssa glances over her shoulder. "I fear we might regret this, Robin. You and I aren't trained for this, and we can't even freely use our pistols."

Of course, Lyssa's pistols. She's a crack shot with the pair, but for now, she's stuck wielding her two short swords. You smile and put on a brave front.

"We'll make do," you say. "The Sisters will keep us safe."

"I'm not sure the Sisters can find us this far down below the earth," she says, then winks to let you know she's not as upset as she sounds.

"Hold," Liam says. The rest of the group pauses at his command, though not without comment.

"What is the matter?" Henli asks, pushing up to the front.

"Something's wrong," Liam says, and he glances at the other miner for confirmation. The red-haired man had been keeping to the rear of the group, to ensure no one fell behind or got lost.

"It's the stone," he says. "Come feel it."

Liam does, his face paling in the dim light.

"Vibrations," he says, and steps back. He rubs his fingers against his shirt as if distressed by what he touched. "The whole mountain is rumbling."

"An earthquake?" Lyssa asks.

"No," the other miner says, placing his hand on the opposite side of the tunnel. "It's even worse over…"

The wall cracks, then collapses completely from tremendous force. Screams mix with the thunderous noise of breaking stone, together forming a cacophony painful in its volume. You stagger, clutching your lantern in a death grip between your fingers. Liam knocks into you, and you catch him to prevent his fall while you stare in horror at the damage before you. Two of the soldiers plus the red-haired miner are already dead, crushed beneath the stone. The others lift their swords and shout, for the monster has arrived.

Its enormous, you think, staring at the thing lit by the lamplight. It mostly resembles a worm, at least in rough shape. If it has eyes, you do not see them. Its entire front is simply an enormous, circular, gaping mouth. Rows upon rows of teeth gleam a pale white down its throat. What you can see of its sides are scaled like a serpent, and colored a deep, dark brown. Behind it is a newly revealed tunnel, one you suspect has been carved by the monster.

Don't get eaten, you think, and then leap aside, bringing Liam with you as the creature lunges out of the tunnel, blasting aside the rubble. It scoops the three corpses into its mouth, along with broken chunks of stone and black coating. Without care of your presence, without fear of your swords, it begins to chew.

The sound of the *crunching* and *cracking* scrapes along

your spine like nails.

No one makes a move. No one is brave enough. The only one to remain in front is Ansell, who stands before the gigantic worm with his head tilted to one side.

It swallows. Its mouth opens. Blood and saliva drip along its circling teeth.

Cursing every one of the three Sisters for bringing you here, you lunge at Ansell, bodying him with your shoulder and flinging him out of the way. Together you tumble further into the tunnel as, behind you, the monster slams its non-existent face into the wall, separating you from the rest of the group. You hear its teeth scrape the stone and shudder to imagine yourself pinned there by them.

You pull out of the roll and disentangle yourself from Ansell, who looks surprisingly alert and energetic.

"Was that creature trying to eat me?" he asks.

"Yes," you say, for there isn't much else to add.

"I see." Ansell lifts his club. "Then we must attack."

Despite its tremendous size and weight, Ansell charges straight at the worm. From the other side, you hear a clang of swords, and you can only pray Lyssa and the soldiers are assaulting the creature, too. It turns their way, so its brown-scaled back is facing Ansell upon his arrival. He leaps into the air, his arm extending and his back curling to throw tremendous power into his strike.

The club hits the scales, cracks down the middle, and goes flying from Ansell's grip. The monster, with the most dismissive movement, flicks a tiny segment of its long body to knock Ansell aside. He trips, dropping his lantern as he rolls back toward you.

The soulless is back on his feet in seconds, a bit of blood dripping from his nose and a cut across his forehead.

"A club is insufficient," he says, with a tone so calm it is maddening down there in the deep dark.

You push through your shock. If your group is to survive, that monster has to die. You hand Ansell your lantern, grip your sword in both hands, and charge in.

Given the scales that cover its body, you suspect any blunt or slashing attack will fail, so you pull the sword back for a thrust. If you can slip your sword underneath one of the scales while the creature's attention is turned away from you…

It's dark, and moving, but your aim is true. You jam the tip of your sword against the creature's side, shift the angle, and then slam it underneath a scale. It slides deeper until hitting resistance, which only encourages you to pour additional strength into the thrust. It slows, stops, and then punches through. Black blood gushes across your hands. The thing lets out a horrific screech as you rip your sword free. You retreat before its sudden thrashing can knock you aside, and you join Ansell and Liam in the light of their held lanterns.

The creature turns your way, its mouth open, exposing the horror of its many, many teeth.

"We have its attention," Ansell says.

You draw your pistol and aim straight down the thing's gullet as a sickly sweet warm air washes over you from its exhalation. You cock the hammer, swallow your fear, and pull the trigger.

The noise is deafening in the tunnel, but even more deafening is the high-pitch shriek the worm lets out. It pulls back, closes its mouth, and then coils tightly. You recognize that movement, that shape. It's of a snake preparing to attack.

The way forward is blocked. There is only one other way to go.

"Run!" you shout, grabbing Ansell by the wrist. You sprint despite knowing deep down in your gut it is foolhardy to do so. You don't know these tunnels, and the light of your lantern is so limited you can only see a few feet ahead of you, but you have to run. You have to try.

To stand and fight that monster in a tunnel with no place to avoid its teeth means a quick, certain death.

You hear shuffling behind you as you sprint. You feel more warmth upon you. Twin eruptions of flamestone alert you to Lyssa firing her own pistols, and you suspect they are of little use against the monster's scales. You sprint faster, but your speed, it is not enough. You will be caught.

"Wait, here!" Liam shouts, and you feel his hand latch onto your coat and tug hard enough to spin you about. You see the frightened Liam, and behind him, the looming circle of teeth and scales. You haven't reloaded your pistol, and despite the pathetic difference in size, you reach for your sword.

It will stop nothing. The teeth close in. You hear the rumble of grinding rock and groaning innards.

"I said here," Liam shouts again, and slams right into you. You tumble aside, bracing for impact against the wall…only there is no impact. Suddenly you're falling. You have but a half-second to flail before you strike the ground. Your head and back hit stone, and your entire vision blooms red and yellow from the sudden pain.

From up above, you hear Liam shouting.

"Move!"

You can't see, and you don't know where you are, but the urgency in the man's voice is motivation enough. You roll to your left, still expecting a wall of some sort, but instead only hard, uneven ground awaits you. You stop when Liam lands, his lantern wobbling in his hand. In its light, you see Ansell leaning against the nearby stone wall, looking bruised and out of sorts.

Above you, you hear a loud slam, followed by the strange screech of the monster.

"Where are we?" you ask.

Liam brushes himself off and lifts his lantern. You

appear to have fallen down a small shaft of some sort. Ropes hang from a pulley higher up, and nearby lay large buckets latched to the ropes. As painful as it was to land on solid stone, you count yourself lucky to have missed the buckets.

"We don't carve the tunnels, only follow where they lead," Liam explains, still staring upward. "Sometimes getting back and forth from the later sections can take ten, twenty minutes, even if the tunnels are close, or in this case, stacked on top of each other. So we built some shafts and pulleys to funnel supplies."

You join him in looking up. It's much too small for the monster to fit through. A bitter relief. By the sound of it, you're now even deeper within the mine, and now ignorant to the fate of your group.

Please, keep Lyssa safe, you pray to Lyra, hoping she can hear you.

"I appear to be bleeding," Ansell says beside you. You pick up the soulless's dropped lantern and hand it back to him. In its light, you can see he's added another cut from the fall, this time along his forearm. Blood drips across his mouth from his bloody, swollen nose. You suspect you don't look much better, and when you brush the back of your head, you feel the warm stickiness of fresh blood.

"You'll live," you tell him.

"I was not questioning that fact," Ansell replies. "Should I?"

You turn away from the opening at the top of the shaft. "Right now? Probably."

Liam pulls you close, and he lets out a soft hiss.

"We don't know how well that thing hears," he says, his voice a whisper.

Instead of arguing, you nod. A wise enough idea.

"Do you know the way out?" you whisper back instead.

Liam bites his lower lip, then slowly exhales.

"Yeah," he says. "But its a long trek out. We do it slowly, and we do it quietly. What say you?"

You draw your sword, determined to fight to the death even if you're caught.

"I say lead the way."

27

You're almost tempted to take your boots off, it's so difficult to walk in perfect silence upon the hard stone. Urging Ansell to walk quietly accomplishes nothing, either. He was trained to be a guard. He doesn't know how to be stealthy.

"How much farther?" you whisper.

Liam pauses at another junction. There's blood across the walls, and you see discarded tools in both directions. A grim discovery. You suspect this was where the miners were first attacked when the monster appeared.

There's no bones. No bodies. It takes little imagination to guess why.

"Not far," Liam whispers back. He's trying hard not to look at the blood. "Not…not far."

You feel the vibrations long before you see the creature. Liam freezes, uncertain, but you know you cannot afford such a luxury. You drop to your knees, your hands on the ground, and listen. One shot at this. One hope.

To your left. The vibrations, the noise, the approach; it's from the tunnel to your left.

"Coming that way," you say, jumping back to your feet.

"Then we hide there," Liam says, pointing to a space not far from the intersection. It's another of the little alcoves with chairs and tables for the workers to rest. The three of you rush to it, and though you fear the noise, you quickly, and gently as possible, overturn the table so the three of you can hide behind it.

"The lanterns," Liam says, and you know you should douse them, but you also want to know the direction the creature travels.

Trying not to panic, you hurdle over the table, set your lantern down near the intersection, and then flee back.

You are just to the other side of the table when the creature arrives. It slowly crawls along the tunnel. The fit is a snug one, and leaves you with little doubt that these tunnels were dug by the monster long before humanity arrived to excavate the flamestone.

You watch, morbidly fascinated by its movements. So far as you can tell, it has no appendages, instead propelling itself with twisting undulations akin to a worm. A very, very big worm.

And then the tail end of it opens up, disturbingly similar to a sphincter. Your stomach tightens as black goo blasts out of it, splattering across the walls and floor of the tunnel. You can smell it even from here, the odor a strange mixture of sulfur and feces. You turn away from it to catch your breath.

"Lovely," you mutter. The monster has moved on ahead, down one of the tunnels, leaving only the black goo in its wake. When you turn back to it, you notice the goo is not smooth, but filled with little bumps or pellets. The similarity is undeniable, and it drops your mouth open.

"The flamestone," you say. "The coating. It's…it's this thing's excrement."

Liam looks ill.

"Our work," he says. "Our whole town's purpose, it's digging up that thing's shit?"

You glance down at the pouch of flamestone carefully tied to your buckle and realize you'll never be able to view it the same again.

"Self-defense," you say. "Nature's full of weird things like that, right? Lizards that shoot blood from their eyes, snakes spitting venom, and birds attacking other birds with vomit."

You look once more at the black pool blocking the floor. The coating the miners would normally chip through is currently a liquid, and you wonder how long until it hardens. Days? Years? Centuries?

"This thing lived here once," you say. "Right here, in these tunnels, before everything changed. Before the monsters and creatures were banished, it lived here, and then we came and found what remained."

"It's shit," Liam says, still refusing to let that go.

"It's hardened, dangerous shit," you say, torn between laughing and crying. "And now that shit pool is blocking our way to safety."

Liam clenches and unclenches his fists, and then sighs.

"I'm going to go take a look."

He slowly approaches the freshly applied excrement and then kneels before the nearest portion. After a moment, he touches one of the flamestone pellets with his fingers and gives it a squeeze. That done, he steps back and wipes his hand on his trousers.

"Well?" you ask.

"The pellets are still hard," he says. "But they're not protected by the coating like they would be when we normally excavate it."

"Can we walk on it?" you ask, getting to the important part.

"Safely?" he says, shaking his head. "No. A good stomp with a heel will crack one. But if you walk carefully, and keep your weight on your toes, I think we'll be fine."

You gesture toward Ansell.

"You hear all that?" you ask.

"I heard," he says, and stares at you blankly. You hold back a sigh. Right. Soulless.

"That means stay light on your feet," you repeat. "Put as little weight on the flamestones as possible, got that?"

"I understand. Make little noise, remain light on my feet, and attack whatever seeks to eat me."

Good enough, you think.

"All right, Liam, get us out of here," you whisper.

During your Soulkeeper training, you spent many weeks learning the ins and outs of your pistol, how its mechanics work, and how to properly clean it. On your very first day, you were harshly instructed on taking proper care of your flamestone, not to drop them, treat them carelessly, or try anything monumentally stupid such as hitting one with a hammer.

You never asked if it was safe to step on one. You wish you had as you slowly walk across the black, goopy floor. You feel them like pebbles underneath your feet. Solid, so far, but one crack, one eruption, and there's a chance you end up missing some toes.

Liam looks no more comfortable ahead of you, but he keeps his mouth shut and leads you through the winding maze of caverns. Several times you pass turns that, given the gentle slope of the stone, you'd think led to the surface, but Liam keeps on going. You have no choice but to trust his judgment.

After about ten minutes he approaches another junction. In one direction is an unlit cavern. After a glance inside, he freezes in place. Before you can ask what is wrong, he steps away and presses his back to the nearby stone.

"I think," he whispers, "we found its lair."

Perhaps it's bravery, perhaps it's foolishness, but you must see for yourself.

The cavern is clearly unnatural, its walls worked and

carved. The walls are about twice your height, and at one point were covered with flamestone before the miners excavated it. Scaffolds remain built along various sections of the cavern's sides, allowing access to the higher portions of the wall. Lying still beside one such platform is the enormous worm creature. It is still, its sides softly rising and falling from unheard inhalations. If you were to guess, the thing is currently sleeping off its most recent meal.

You pull back and use your coat to block the light of your lantern from reaching inside the cavern. Ansell stands there, patiently waiting, while Liam fidgets and constantly glances over your shoulder.

"We always wondered what formed this cavern," Liam says. "I guess now we know. What do we do?"

You brave another look inside. The miners of Roros had clearly removed most of the flamestone, but you see numerous freshly spread pools coating most of the floor. Seeing one of the scaffolds, you get an idea. It's an awful idea, but it's an idea.

"I'm going to climb up there," you say, pointing to the scaffold. "And then I'm going to kill the damn thing."

Liam pales. "Are you certain?"

"No, but I also lack any better ideas."

"We could just leave."

You frown. Perhaps, but your mission was to restore the flow of flamestone to Londheim. Until the monster is dead, that won't happen. And even from a selfish perspective, you can't be certain it won't awaken as you finish your trek back to the surface. Should it stir, and sense the vibrations of your movements, or perhaps hear the noises of your passage, well…you doubt there will be a convenient shaft to dive through a second time.

"I have my duty," you say as you load your pistol.

After one last prayer to the Sisters, you enter the

cavern. It isn't far to your chosen scaffold, but it feels like a thousand miles as you slowly tiptoe across the recently layered excrement. The coating sticks to your boots, and it feels like it's trying to tug them off your feet. You grit your teeth and press on.

At the scaffolding's ladder, you pause and look to the sleeping monster. At least, you think it's sleeping. You wouldn't consider yourself an expert on worms, let alone magical ones recently revived after the arrival of the black water. You put your hands on the ladder, hold your breath, and climb the first rung.

The wood groans from your weight. You freeze as the worm shudders a moment, then remains still.

Just sleep, you think. *For the love of Anwyn, just sleep.*

You climb the rest of the way, flinching at every creak and groan of the boards. Once up top, you slowly shuffle your way to the ledge. Below you sleeps the monster, curled into itself almost like a kitten. You set your lantern down so its light remains cast across the thing's body. That done, you holster your pistol despite it currently being loaded (your instructor would certainly have words over *that* decision), and draw your sword to hold in both hands.

It's just a bug, an enormous, over-sized bug. There can be no pity or mercy for such a thing. Not when the lives of your friends are at risk.

I'm sorry, you think, and leap on top of the thing. You expected it to be firm beneath you when you land, and are surprised by the give, an almost soft feeling beneath your feet despite the scales. The creature rumbles slowly, unaware of the danger it is in.

No waiting. No delay. You can only pray that, if it possesses a brain, it's in the same place as any other creature. With a single smooth motion you slide the sword underneath the scales of the portion just above the teeth and then jam it in deep. The flesh gives, and the sword sinks in all the way to the hilt. Blood and gore flow across your gloves.

The creature shrieks. It is loud, it is horrid, and it is clearly in pain.

What it is not, however, is dead.

Its body pulsates beneath you, and it spins once, catapulting you over its side and to the ground. Your shoulder absorbs the bulk of your weight, and you cry out at the sharp pain. The motion slams it against the scaffolding, snapping several of its supports. Your lantern falls, and it breaks upon hitting the ground, the little oil that remained within catching fire.

The creature turns toward you. In the burning light, it is truly a monster of shadow and teeth, exactly as described. Another shake, and your sword dislodges from its head, strikes one of the cavern walls, and lands beyond the light of your broken lantern.

You lift your pistol and aim at its open mouth. You may die, but by the Sisters, you're going down fighting.

"Hey hey hey!" Liam screams to get both yours and the creature's attention. "Robin, take the shot!"

And then he throws over two dozen thick, goopy flamestones straight at the monster's gaping mouth.

You shift the aim of your pistol, track the densest portion of the group, and then fire.

The blast of your shot has but a half-second to echo before the thunderous response. Your aim is true, and the first of the flamestones erupts, breaking the others and causing a chain reaction. The monster shrieks as the impact tears teeth free from its flesh. Fire washes across the interior of its mouth. It twists and flails, and though you try to dodge, you are much too slow. It batters you aside, and you roll across the stone, adding more bruises to your growing collection.

You lift your empty pistol as you stand. There's no

time to reload, and you lack your sword. Defenseless, you stare into the gaping maw of the furious, wounded monster of Roros's mountain. It's bleeding heavily, perhaps fatally, but that won't matter. It senses you, smells you, hears you, however it tracks these things, and it will defend its lair to its final moments.

You brace your legs to dodge despite knowing it hopeless. The monster rears up. The remainder of its teeth quiver as its mouth opens.

Since he is no longer carrying his lantern, you have no way to see Ansell until he is directly beneath the creature. Cast in the light of your discarded lantern, he is but a shadow with a sword. Mimicking your own attack, he slides it against the grain of the scales, into what would best be called the worm's 'throat'. It shudders as the sword sinks in deep, so deep Ansell's arms vanish into the scales.

One last screech, and it topples aside with a heavy thud and thankfully, blessedly, lays still.

"I used your sword since I lacked a proper weapon," Ansell says. He rips the sword out, black blood splashing across his hands and trousers. Now freed, he flips it and offers you the handle. "You may have it back now."

You grab the slick hilt, torn between laughter and offering gratitude to the soulless who would care not a lick about it.

"Thanks," you say, deciding to at least make the effort.

Ansell looks back to the creature's corpse. "I fulfilled my request. It cannot eat me. What now?"

"What now?" Liam says. "Now we get ourselves to fresh air and share the good news! The damn thing is dead!"

While you cannot muster Liam's enthusiasm, you certainly agree with the sentiment.

"To fresh air," you say, and honestly, you cannot think of anything you want more than that.

28

Lyssa and a trio of soldiers are waiting for you at the entrance, and there is no hiding their relief upon seeing you.

"I thought for sure you were dead," Lyssa says, wrapping you in a hug. You gingerly return it, careful not to touch her clothes with your gloves given the mess that is on them.

"Did you kill the monster?" Henli asks.

You grin at the guard.

"That we did," you say, and you laugh. "That we goddess-damned did."

*

Your next stop is Clifford's estate. You feel a little bad trudging into his nice and tidy home covered in monster excrement, and after a silent glare from one of the servants, you remove your boots and stash them by the front door. Clifford is quick to greet you upon your arrival.

"I've already heard rumors," he says, clasping Lyssa's hands in greeting. "Is it true? Have you slain the beast?"

"Not a beast, but a worm," Lyssa says. She nods your way. "And Robin did indeed kill the thing."

"To be fair, Ansell scored the final blow," you say. "And that was only after one of your miners helped weaken it with a timely volley of flamestone."

Clifford looks in shock. He wipes his forehead, then smiles wide.

"Well," he says. "Well, well, well, I cannot believe it. I must confess, I feared the two of you would perish, but you Soulkeepers have lived up to your vaunted reputations. Is there anything I can do to repay you for what you have done for our town?"

Normally you are instructed to turn down any rewards for performing your duty as a Soulkeeper, but not this time.

"Yes," you say, and lift your arms so the mess upon your clothes is obvious. "Ready me the hottest bath possible and a change of clothes so I can scrub myself, dress in something clean, and have my first good night's rest in days."

Clifford claps his hands.

"Of course," he says, and nods toward the young servant standing patiently in the doorway. "You shall have all that and more!"

*

You dream.

The world is black around you, but somehow still brightly lit. You are in your bed, asleep, surely you are asleep, yet your eyes are open. The world is barren. Though no roof is above you, only darkness, the comforting sound of steady rain upon the rooftop fills your ears.

You try to move. Nothing happens. Your blanket weighs a thousand pounds.

You try to speak, but your mouth will not open.

Gloam.

The word floats over you, sparking with energy.

Gloam.

No one is speaking it, certainly not you, but you hear it in your own voice. Again, and again, that word. That name. It is familiar to you, achingly so, yet you cannot remember why. It has no meaning. It has no purpose.

Gloam.

And then the fireflies arrive. They swirl from

underneath your bed, hundreds of them, zipping about in disturbing silence. You hear no buzz of their wings despite knowing that, in such a number, they should rival the patter of the rain. They swirl together, first a grand circle, then into a funnel. Their abdomens blink with lights, a yellow so deep and warm it resembles gold.

Legere tavrum.

It is not spoken by you, you know that, you feel it. Your lips are closed, your tongue still, but yet it is your voice that thunders in the darkness. The words should be nonsense to you, absolute nonsense, but there is a meaning underneath the syllables that feels perfectly natural.

Lightning arcs through the fireflies, sparking with life as you repeat the words.

Gloam legere tavrum.

The darkness parts. You see a door. Your door, from the outside of your room. A hand, hesitating beside the handle. Shaking. Nervous. Another hand, holding a pistol loaded with lead shot and flamestone.

Murder.

Gloam legere tavrum.

The fireflies coalesce, black forms melding, becoming a shape resembling a human figure. Gold bursts all about its body, lightning arcing silent and fierce among the light.

Murder.

Gloam. The being's name is Gloam, and it has given you its blessing.

Gloam, grant me thought.

MURDER.

The darkness parts.

Your eyes are open.

You are alone in your room, accompanied only by the sound of the rain. It is dark. Quiet. Still.

You hear the turning of your doorknob.

Your sword is at the foot of your bed, your pistol, unloaded and holstered in your belt hanging from a hook by the door. Despite the pounding of your pulse, you lay still, head tilted slightly and your eyes open but the tiniest sliver. You remember the nervousness of the individual, their hesitation. They don't want to do this. They'll be slow. They'll be cautious.

The door opens, creaking but a little. You recognize him immediately. It's the young servant who first guided you to your room. He holds no candle or lantern. He's fumbling in the dark, denied even moonlight through the window due to the rain. He takes step after tiny step toward your bed, his pistol held in both hands. He's getting close. Doesn't trust his aim.

You wait until he is halfway to your bed to speak.

"Lower your weapon, son."

He freezes in place. The gun vibrates in the air. If he pulls the trigger now, you suspect he has a coin flip's chance of actually hitting you. He says nothing, too shocked, too uncertain. This wasn't his idea. Someone put him up to this, and it doesn't take much to guess who.

"I said lower your weapon."

The pistol dips slightly, and then panic takes over. He lifts it back up, his legs bracing and his hands tightening. Your instincts, though, are faster. Even in this dim light, you recognize that moment when a man or woman walks past an edge, knowing there is no going back.

You lunge forward, your hand closing about the pistol. Your thumb wedges between the hammer and the chamber, preventing the spike from dropping in and puncturing the flamestone. You hold it there, the front of the pistol pressed to your chest, and meet the young man's eyes. They're wide with fear, and his mouth drops open as he pulls harder on the trigger.

"Careful," you say. The elbow of your free arm strikes him in the forehead, rocking him back a pace. His eyes cross, and the grip of his pistol loosens so that you can pry it from his grasp. You re-cock the hammer and then hold the weapon so it aims toward the ceiling.

"You could hurt someone with this."

He turns to flee, but you lower the pistol so it aims at his back.

"One squeeze of the trigger," you say, "and you won't set foot outside that door. Turn around, now. We need to have a chat."

The servant obeys. His hands are shaking, and he holds them at his sides. Sweat has soaked the collar of his suit. He's so young, so boyish in his features, you'd be surprised if he is older than sixteen. Sixteen, and sent to murder a Soulkeeper in her bed.

"Three questions," you say. "First, your name?"

"Durvin."

"All right, Durvin, question two. Who put you up to this?"

He swallows as if shards of glass are wedged in his throat. "Overseer Hezar."

Not a surprise. You'd already suspected Clifford the culprit.

"Question three. Why?"

Durvin shakes his head.

"I don't know." His eyes bulge as you lift the pistol so its aim is directly at his forehead. "I swear, he didn't tell me. He only said it was for the good of all of Roros. Don't kill me, please ma'am, don't kill me. I don't want to die."

"Neither do I," you say, pulling back the hammer halfway so it reopens the chamber. You tilt the pistol toward the ground and pat it against your leg so both flamestone and lead shot come sliding out. They silently hit the carpeted floor, bounce once, and roll to a stop. You toss the disarmed weapon onto your bed and retrieve your sword instead.

The tip of your sword presses against his breastbone.

"Let's go find Clifford, shall we?"

Together, you step outside to the hallway lit with several evenly-spaced candelabras hanging from the walls. You glance at the door next to yours. Lyssa's room.

"Is she..?" you ask. Durvin somehow pales even more at your hard expression.

"No, you, you were the first," he insists.

"Lucky you," you say and shove him. "Lead the way."

The servant takes you to the stairs, and together you climb to the second floor. To your immediate right is another door, the light of a warm fire flickering through the crack underneath it.

"In there," Durvin says, careful to keep his voice at a whisper. Smart lad. Sort of.

"Well," you whisper back. "Go in and say hello."

The servant looks ready to pass out, he's so frightened and confused. You gesture at the door, and then for some encouragement, nudge him with the hilt of your sword.

As he opens it, you slip to the side, hiding yourself from view.

Clifford's voice immediately calls out.

"Durvin! I heard no shots. Is the matter settled?"

Good enough for you. You shove Durvin aside so he tumbles out of the room and enter yourself. It's a lavishly decorated study, complete with a stocked bookshelf, a padded recliner, and a roaring hearth. Roros's Overseer stands beside the fire, dressed in a crimson bed robe and holding a half-full glass of wine.

The moment Clifford sees you, he drops the glass and dives for an end table beside the chair. There's a pistol resting atop it, and you suspect it is already loaded. You sprint after him, using the reach of your sword to your advantage. One thrust, and you strike the pistol, using the tip to shove it off the table and to the carpet. Clifford's reaching hands fumble, grabbing blade instead of a pistol grip. Blood splashes across the table and chair as he cuts himself upon your blade.

One kick, and you tumble the end table over. It lands atop the already fallen pistol, striking it hard enough the cocked hammer dislodges, striking the flamestone. It fires, lodging a ball of lead shot into the nearby wall. The roar of the pistol in your ears, you loop your sword about, ending its motion at Clifford's throat. He straightens up, anger burning in his bloodshot eyes.

"You damned fool," he says, clutching his bleeding hand to his chest.

"Perhaps," you say. "But I'd rather be a fool than a coward attempting to murder sleeping guests in my own home."

You strike him across the face with the hilt of your sword. More blood spurts across his bed robe, this time from his split lip.

"You couldn't even do it yourself," you say. "You sent a child, instead."

Clifford straightens himself, and he grimaces at the blood on his robe. After a shrug, he grabs its collar and presses it to his lip. Throughout it all, his glare does not break.

"Judge me all you want, but I'm not the one who just murdered every single man, woman, and child in this town."

You arc an eyebrow. "That's certainly a claim."

"It's no claim." He sneers at you. "Even the Sisters will judge you a fool after we are all dead."

The door opens, and a half-dressed Lyssa enters. She's armed only with a dagger, which is currently pressed to Durvin's throat.

"I heard a pistol shot," she says. "You all right,

Robin?"

"Perfectly fine," you say.

"Good." She pushes Durvin a little. "Care to explain what in Anwyn's name is going on?"

You grin at her. "That's what I'm here for myself, actually. Clifford tried to have Durvin shoot me in my sleep. He insists it is for the good of Roros, though as for how or why, well…"

Clifford stands tall and proud despite his bleeding fingers and the clumping bits of blood that are drying in his mustache.

"You may be fools," he says, "but you can surely understand that our town cannot withstand the anger of the owls, not when we are so close to the Helwoads. I made a deal with their Queen, one that would spare our lives and buy me some time to figure out an alternate solution."

A deal…

"The flamestone," you say, making an educated guess. "You agreed to ship no flamestone."

"The monster was my excuse," Clifford says, nodding in affirmative. "Arondel called it a lyndwyrm, the thing that created the flamestone." He shakes his head. "And now you've killed it. You damned fools, you killed it. Arondel said she'd know, and now she does."

"Arondel," you say, the name vaguely familiar to you. "Who is she?"

Clifford meets your gaze. "The Queen of the Winged. And when she turns her eye from Londheim to here, our whole town is doomed."

"Such pessimism," Lyssa says, and she shoves Durvin further in. "I'd like to think we humans still have a fighting chance."

"What is all this commotion?" William asks, his manservant right behind him. It seems you've made enough noise to wake the entire house. The auditor turns pale the moment he sees a bleeding Clifford standing beside the hearth. "Overseer? Are you injured?"

"Yes, he's injured," you say. "He tried to have me executed to hide how he made a deal with the owls to prevent flamestone shipments from reaching Londheim."

The chubby man's face goes from pale to a furious shade of red. "You would betray us to the beasts?"

Clifford stands tall, unbowed even now.

"I did as the Sisters command of us," he says. "I protected those I could, consequences be damned."

"Yeah, so noble," Lyssa says. "The question is, what do we do with his noble ass?"

"First, we lock him up in a room somewhere before he causes any more trouble," you say.

"Allow me," Whistler says from the door. He bows his enormous frame. "I can ensure the Overseer receives proper attention to his injuries."

You're happy to let Whistler handle the man. Having him not around will clear your head. Once the Overseer is gone, William scans the room, finds the half open bottle Clifford had been drinking, and grabs it for himself.

"This needs to be carefully done," he says after a long gulp. "Roros's mayor should be the first to learn, and if possible, we let him take over any sort of trial or punishment for Clifford. Proving him behind the attempt on your life will be tricky, though it helps we have the word of a Soulkeeper on our side."

"And a witness," Lyssa says, nudging a quiet and moping Durvin.

William glances at the servant. "You made the attempt, and at Clifford's request?"

Durvin hesitates, then nods.

"He said I would be saving the whole town if I did it,"

he says. "I'd be a hero. It wasn't my idea, I promise. I didn't want to do it."

"Get him in a room next to Clifford's," William says. "And make sure neither leaves."

"Gladly," Lyssa says. A single glare, and the young servant follows the other Soulkeeper out.

William finishes the rest of the bottle and then lets out a small gasp.

"Thought the wine would be better than that," he says, and sets the bottle down. His gaze settles on you, his expression hardening. "This will be tricky, Robin. I sense Clifford was well-liked here, and given the sea of changes around us, people crave stability. Even with witnesses and the truth, it may not be enough."

You shake your head. "It will have to be. If he's telling the truth, and I think he is, the owls will attack in retaliation for what we've done."

The man sucks in a breath through his teeth. "Fuck."

You can't help but laugh. "Yeah."

William stands up straight and claps his hands.

"Well, that is a task for tomorrow, I'd say. I will handle the political consequences, and lean heavily on your reputations as Soulkeepers. As for you..." His eyes narrow. "Can you organize the town's defense to make sure we don't die to a bunch of overgrown birds?"

Your opinion of the man rises ever so slightly. With a task at hand, even one arriving unexpected in the middle of the night, he seems almost eager to take charge.

"Can do," you say. "But first, I'm going back to bed. Tomorrow's going to be a long night."

Lyssa finds you halfway there, returning alone.

"Where you headed?" she asks.

"To bed," you answer. "Why? Planning to join me?"

She smirks slightly.

"Sorry, not tonight. Not in the mood." She leans against the wall, her arms crossed over her chest. "The Overseer did a piss poor job picking assassins. Hopefully that means he's not used to underhanded dealings here in Roros. Durvin looked ready to piss himself when Whistler tossed him in the same room as Clifford."

"I'm glad for his poor decision making," you say, and grin at her despite how tired you feel.

Lyssa chuckles. "Still, it doesn't take too much skill to shoot a sleeping man. How did you avoid taking a lead shot to the head?"

You start to answer, something flippant, but then half-remembered memories wash over you. Your dreams…you remember a voice in your dreams.

"It was the strangest thing," you say, deciding Lyssa's dealt with enough strangeness she'll be open to believing more. "I think I was warned about his coming in a dream."

"Warned?" she asks, her expression carefully neutral. "By who? One of the Sisters?"

"I don't know," you say, shaking your head. "It's hazy, but I remember a lone word being shouted over and over, and in my own voice. 'Murder'."

Lyssa rubs her eyes with her thumb and forefinger. "Robin, please, promise me something, all right?"

"What's that?"

She grins at you. "If you start hearing voices in your head telling you to murder, please, for all our sakes, *do not listen to them.*"

29

The town is abuzz with movement and fright. Too much uncertainty in too short a time. You walk the small market, without any desire to purchase but just to clear your head after your poor sleep. You hear rumors of Clifford's arrest. Some are frightened. Some are angry. Most, however, are just confused.

There is little room for talk of the arrested Overseer, though, since all are aware of the coming fury of the owls.

"There you are," Lyssa says, spotting you from afar. She pushes past a couple men huddled together that block the center of the road, then tips her hat toward you with her free hand. The other is holding a half-eaten roll of bread smothered with butter. She glances you up and down, not bothering to hide her inspection.

"Have you eaten yet?" she asks.

You shake your head. In response, she tears her remaining roll in half and offers it to you.

"Eat," she says.

"Are you my mother now?" you ask, but accept the portion.

"Only in my nightmares," she says, stuffing her own half into her mouth. "Now come on, Henli is waiting for us."

*

To your surprise, Henli Fairbough is guard captain of the town, and the one in charge of preparing its defenses. At least, he should be, but it sounds like he's been more than happy to pass that responsibility off to you and Lyssa. You find him at a firing range set up alongside the far eastern wall.

Thirty men and women are with him, taking turns shooting at hay bales set up at varying distances with wood targets bound to their fronts.

To your surprise, they're all using rifles instead of pistols. The roars of their cracking flamestone form a steady, booming chorus.

"I thought rifles were the purview of the Kept Lands only," you say as Henli sees you and approaches.

"They are, but Queen Woadthyn ensures we have the means to protect ourselves," Henli says, and offers his hand. "First the mines, now the outer walls. It seems you'll be responsible for protecting us once again."

"At least we'll be in open air this time," you say, clasping his wrist and shaking it. "And to be clear, we have no authority over you in governing these defenses."

"I am aware," Henli says. He shifts a bit awkwardly on his feet. "But I am also aware of how little I understand our foes. I am also not the one who faced off against the monster beneath the mountain. That was you. If you're brave enough to challenge that beast, then you can lead my men in their first battle."

You grimace. He's right, of course. This will not be any normal guard duty, nor a skirmish against a few bandits with more courage than sense. This will be a war, and against a foe not the slightest bit inconvenienced by Roros's impressive walls.

"Did the owls ever attack prior to making their secret agreement?" Lyssa asks as the three of you distance yourselves from the practicing squad, not only to lessen the impact of the noise but to ensure the soldiers cannot overhear your discussion.

"They did, once," Henli says. He grimaces. "It was brutal. We weren't prepared for it, as you can imagine. We'd only heard rumors of the black water and the crawling mountain. Had no idea the town was even in danger, or that the world was changing so much."

He gestures toward the front gate in the distance, its top barely visible above the rooftops.

"On a normal night patrol, we have maybe two people up there, and another two walking the east and west walls. Keeping an eye out for bandits and smuggling, that's it, some fools trying to sneak stolen flamestone outside with some ropes or ladders. So when the owls attacked, numbering in the dozens?" He shuddered. "They ripped the men apart, Robin. Picked them up and tore them to ribbons while flying over the town. We…we had to clean them from the rooftops, come morning."

You suppress your own shudder at a vivid memory of Yont's attack screech.

"It was no wonder Clifford made a deal to prevent another attack," you say.

Lyssa glares in response.

"And in doing so, sold out the rest of us across the entire Cradle," she says. "Fuck him. He should have fought. If he sent word to Londheim, we could have arrived with far more soldiers than just us two Soulkeepers."

You have no desire to argue the point. Just because you understand why Clifford did it does not mean you agree, nor that you would have done the same in his position.

"So you have the thirty or so soldiers here," you say, gesturing behind you to the group at the firing range. "Where's the rest of your army?"

Henli takes in a long breath. "You're looking at them, Soulkeeper."

You exchange a glance with Lyssa. "Just you thirty?"

"I told you, we deal only with smugglers and bandits," Henli says. "We have our walls and our rifles. Who would dare challenge either?"

You hold back a retort. It isn't Henli's fault. No one could have predicted an army would arrive, and from the sky, no less.

"All right, then," you say, your mind racing. There has to be more you can do. "What of those who aren't trained with rifles? Are there any miners with experience firing a pistol, any experience at all, even if just from hunting or target games?"

Henli shrugs. "It's a big town. I would not be surprised if there are a few."

"Then put a call out to them. We want every single person capable of pulling a trigger without shooting their foot off. And that's just the start."

You stare at the distant walls and frown. There are still valid reasons to guard them. From up on high, the defenders would have clear shots at the owls during their approach. The problem was, once the attack began, and the distance between them closed, the shooters would have nowhere to flee. The killing potential would be higher on both sides.

"We need to protect those with rifles," you say, thinking aloud. "I've seen your miners. They're strong. Ask for volunteers, and then arm them with swords, pickaxes, even clubs if we must."

"I can press people into service," Henli says. "We need not rely on volunteers."

You shake your head.

"No. Tell everyone the town, and all its people, are in danger, and you need those brave enough to defend it to come forth. The last thing we need are frightened and bitter people breaking lines and causing a panic."

"Fair enough," Henli says, though you can tell he doesn't quite agree. "But where do I station them?"

"I'd say put them with the riflemen," Lyssa says, looking to you for your opinion. "The owls will dive on whoever is shooting at them. Perhaps we can form a wall of muscle to hold them back."

It's certainly a thought, one you share, but you also remember how large and terrifying Yont was when you faced him in Londheim. Should the owls come diving at full speed, you wonder if anything short of a stone wall could stop them.

"I don't think we abandon the walls," you say, the battle plan coming together in your mind. "We keep our riflemen mostly together, maybe five squads of six, and set them equally distant along the wall. Shore up those numbers with anyone else who has a pistol. Then give them a melee escort of however many volunteers we can muster."

"The town itself will be undefended if everyone's on the walls," Henli pointed out. "Are you sure we shouldn't have some armed guards patrolling the streets?"

"Bunching everyone together will make it easy for the owls to focus on them, too," Lyssa adds.

You nod, aware of both facts.

"We cannot match the speed of the owls," you tell them. "If they choose to attack the homes and slaughter innocents, no patrol on the ground will matter. They'd be too few and too slow to prevent anything, not when the owls can simply take flight and attack elsewhere."

You point to the walls.

"I *want* their attention up high. Anyone without firearms will be hard pressed to force the owls into a fight unless we can bring the owls to them, which is exactly what the squads of riflemen will do."

"Better they attack our defenders than those in hiding," Lyssa says, reluctantly agreeing.

"And if the owls try to ignore them, then our riflemen can fire at will. We'll fill the sky with lead if we must."

"The fight will be brutal," Henli says. "Perhaps that is for the best. But you raise a point I have not dwelt on. Those unable to fight. Where should they go?"

"Their homes won't be safe," you say. "Have everyone prepare supplies and then retreat into the mines. It'll be cramped, but I can't imagine any owl being eager to go within, if they even fit."

Henli nods, his face hardening, a professional mask to hide all his insecurities.

"It will be done," he says. "If only we had more time."

"It's possible we do," Lyssa says. "Clifford said the owls would know if we killed the lyndwyrm, but there's always a chance he was deceived. And it may take time for them to discover its death, however they manage it."

"Do we send a runner to Londheim asking for aid then?" Henli asked. "Perhaps if the owls delay long enough, we may receive reinforcements."

It's the smart thing to do, even if you think it won't matter.

"Go ahead," you say. "But make sure it's someone good at hiding, not shooting. We can't afford a single loss."

Henli bows his head, then gestures behind him, to the shooting range.

"I've a lot to do, so if you'll excuse me, I need to get started."

You wave him off, leaving you and Lyssa standing near the wall. It's weirdly quiet, broken only by the firing of the distant rifles. Each one makes you flinch.

"You've seen the numbers the owls send at Londheim," Lyssa says softly now the two of you are alone.

"And they've certainly suffered casualties because of it," you say. "Perhaps their numbers will be fewer when they come here."

"Or perhaps they will swarm over us, tear us apart, and crunch on our bones."

You grin at Lyssa, and she grins right back.

"So cheery," you say.

"I can't help it, comes naturally when facing your own death. So what part will you play in all this, Soulkeeper?"

You think the plan over in your mind and decide where best you would fit.

"Both my sword and pistol can keep one of the firing squads alive," you say. "I'll be on the wall."

Lyssa pats the twin pistols buckled at her hips.

"Good plan. I'll be up there as well, eager to teach those owls the sky isn't so safe as they'd like to believe. I suppose that's settled, then. What now? Join the target practice? Help with recruitment? See if the fools that show up with swords and clubs actually know how to swing them?"

You bite your lower lip. "There's only so much you can teach in a day, but when the fighting starts, I'd like to trust those with me at least know how to properly hold a sword."

"All right then, it's a plan," Lyssa says, and she smacks you across the breastbone. "And as good as one we could hope for in this hopeless situation. Chin up, Robin. We're not dying tonight. Not even close."

"I take it that's *your* plan?" you ask, grinning.

Lyssa flashes her teeth.

"Plan? No, not a plan. That's a goddess-damned *promise*."

30

When you join your squad atop the wall at sunset, you are pleasantly surprised by one of the men brought in to protect the riflemen.

"I take it the giant worm wasn't enough fun for you?" you ask Liam.

The man stands there awkwardly, a large ax in hand.

"This is my home," he says. "I'm going to defend it."

You appreciate his confidence. It's why you wanted only those willing to volunteer to come to the city's defense. There's more of them than you hoped for, thankfully. Nearly each squad of riflemen has a good ten to fifteen additional men and women armed with whatever weaponry is available to them.

"I'm glad to have you with me," you tell him. "And just like last time, we're going to survive the dark and come out the victor."

"I pray you are right," Liam says. "But once, just once, it'd be nice not having to worry about something eating me."

You laugh, and thump him on the chest with the back of your hand. Your performance isn't only for him, but the others with him. They're nervous. They have every right to be.

"Hold tight to your ax, and should anything try, teach them why they never should have brought their appetite to Roros."

The hours pass. The stars slowly light up the night. It's an agonizing wait, standing atop the wall with the rest of your assigned squad. You're along the eastern curve of the wall, specifically so you have the clearest view of the distant Helwoads.

"There you are," you whisper. Great shadows from the east. The forest is their home, as you suspected. You begin giving orders to those with you, calm instructions to load their rifles. With the height of the wall, your group will have a decent shot on them when they come diving.

Your greatest element, though, is surprise. While the owls might suspect the city will be ready for an attack, there is no guarantee of it. More importantly, they will not know where the defenses have been prepared. Perhaps their keen eyes will spot the little groups scattered all throughout the walls, perhaps not. The curse of not fully knowing your enemy.

"Stay strong, stay confident," you tell them. "And do not fire until I give the signal."

Every single group has been given similar commands. Hold the shots until the last moment, when the owls will be much too close for the shooter to miss, and the owl, to close to dodge. The opening salvo will be the most brutal, and the most important. If their enemy's numbers can be thinned immediately, the remaining fight might actually go humanity's way.

More shadows, blotting the moon and the stars.

There's so many, you think. Forty, maybe fifty of the enormous creatures. Enough to tear the town to shreds, if left unchecked. You close your eyes and whisper a prayer to the Sisters.

Be with us, and keep us safe. Remember your children, if you love us still.

The first of the owls comes diving toward your group. You track its progress with your pistol, but you keep from pressing the trigger. The rifles of those with you will have better aim at long range, and greater impact. The order is yours to give, and you wait, and wait, as the silhouette nears.

"Now!"

Smoke and flame erupt as flamestone ruptures in multiple rifles. A hail of lead shot streaks through the air, peppering the owl's body. You hear it screech, and you see its angle shift. It's going to crash into your group.

"Hold strong!" you shout to those guarding the riflemen as the silence of the city is broken with the roar of rifles and the piercing cry of the owls. You can't afford to break now.

The owl slams into those guarding the riflemen, and the giant bird is nowhere near as dead as you'd hoped. It thrashes through the first two who try to halt it, then rolls sideways, a wing catching underneath. You hear the snap of bone, and it sends trembles through your stomach.

Can't focus on that now. The owl is before you, enormous and wild and in pain. Your sword is ready, but you decide it unnecessary. It needs put down, immediately, so the rest of your group can focus on the sky.

With one smooth motion, you lift your pistol, aim for the bird's eye, and pull the trigger.

The lead shot flies true. The bird, already injured, seizes momentarily and then lies still.

"Load, load, load and fire," you shout to the riflemen who are watching the slain bird. Some of them are frightened. Others are in shock. You scramble toward them, for this was but one of many. Two more are diving, and they're so close now, much too close. You ready your sword and find yourself beside Liam and his ax.

"Stand with me," you tell him as the owls arrive.

The giant birds arrive in tandem, and they do not slow their approach in the slightest. The initial impact is an explosion of blood and feathers, defenders trying and failing to halt the momentum and paying for it with their lives. The owls grab at your group with their talons, each scooping a man up and carrying them back into the air, all while enduring the frantic strikes of the defenders, including a swipe of your own sword that removes one of the talons. You hear the captured men's screams as their bones are crushed and their bodies dropped to die.

Rifles fire at the pair of owls, your group readying lead shot as fast as they can. The surviving melee defenders watch the two birds circle back around for another pass, and if any of the rifle shots are true, they are not enough to bring them down.

"Lift your weapons," you scream at them, your own sword high. "For your home, for your loved ones, stand tall!"

To their credit, these untrained, unprofessional defenders do as you ask. There is no fleeing this battle. There is only the fight to the death. They tremble, afraid but holding their ground as the owls blast into them in a shower of blood and gore.

There is no staying out of the chaos now. You dash into the thick of it, your instincts guiding your movements through the thrashing of limbs and swiping of talons. Your sword cuts through feathers, failing to score anything significant, but the nearby owl is forced to turn your way. Those with you leap at it from the sides during the distraction, beating at it with swords and axes. One of them retreats coated in blood, some its own, some of Roros's defenders. Another remains grounded, beaten and broken. It is your sword that scores the final blow, putting the owl out of its misery.

"Hold strong," you say, shouting to regroup. The melee defenders quickly gather, following your orders as you reposition them on the wall.

Another pass, just as brutal as before. You helm the

center of the defense, and it is only pure dumb luck that you do not lose your head to the snapping beak of an owl. It instead crunches down on the shoulder of the man beside you, who jostled you at the last moment in an attempt to save you. You wish you could thank him. You wish you could save him. The owl tears him in half at the waist, and all you can do is bury your sword into the owl's stomach so it forces another retreat. By the way it sags, struggling to maintain flight, you suspect a slow death awaits it. The fury of your riflemen deny it that, a trio of shots cracking across its back so it plummets to the ground. Its body collapses on the roof of a tiny shop, and within the wreckage, it lays still.

You dare a glance at the rest of the city. Several of your rifle squads are down, or at least, broken down so the people have separated to fight in scattered numbers. Others continue firing, steadily thinning the owls' numbers.

Maybe we have a chance, you think, and immediately decide you should never feel optimism again. It is clearly a curse.

The owls have not come alone.

You see them all at once, twenty lapinkin soaring over the city wall. They hover in place, the air below their feet swirling like a maelstrom, and then they dive. Their spears are sharp and jagged. Their aim, impeccable. They focus on what few defenders remain on the walls, and there is no chance you command enough to hold them off.

You lift your sword. You have to try.

One of the lapinkin slams down in the center of your group, impaling a poor man through the chest and dragging his corpse several feet along the stone before scraping to a halt. You charge at him, determined to help, but then the lapinkin spins toward you, his gloved hand spreading open.

Wind blasts out of his palm, as if you are walking into the heart of a tornado. You struggle, the muscles in your legs straining, but then your feet no longer touch stone. You're flying backward.

The fall down is very, very long.

"Robin!" Liam shouts, lunging toward the side of the rampart with his arm extended. Your fall halts as he grabs hold of your wrist. Your momentum continues, swinging you so you slam into the wall. The contact is painful, but nothing like if you'd continued on to the ground.

You reach up, grabbing his wrist with your other hand. His face is red from the strain. You want to climb, but then your eyes widen. The lapinkin. You can see him coming for Liam.

"Let me go," you shout at him.

What few defenders remain charge at the lapinkin, holding firm despite the growing number of casualties. What was meant for a lethal stab at Liam's back is parried aside, and then a vicious battle begins, three against one, and somehow, it looks like the lapinkin is winning.

"Soft landings, Soulkeeper," Liam says, realizing the danger the both of you are in. He swings you toward the nearby stone stairs leading downward. It's an awkward landing, and you nearly bite your tongue in half upon hitting them and then rolling the final few to the hard ground below. It's a miracle none of your bones are broken, though you'll certainly be sporting plenty of bruises come tomorrow.

Assuming you live to see the morrow...

You stagger back to your feet, fighting off a temporary wave of disorientation. You need to get back to your group. The lapinkin, you don't see him anymore. Is he dead? Your group, they're alive, still fighting, hopefully winning. You need...but wait, no, you have to be seeing things. Running toward you in the middle of the street, it's Ansell. He's bleeding from a shallow wound across his cheek, and there is a smear of gore on his heavy club.

"Soulkeeper," he says, clearly out of breath from his sprint. "I was told to find you."

"And you have," you say, baffled. "Why?"

So far as you knew, Ansell was assigned to protect the civilians in the mines. Why was he here?

"The owls, they've figured out where we are hiding," he says. "I was told to bring reinforcements from the walls."

You want to laugh. There are no reinforcements. There is no help coming from the many riflemen set up to surround the city. The owls were bad enough, but now the lapinkin have joined in, taking already difficult odds against you and turning them dire.

"Surely the owls cannot fit within the mines," you say.

"They cannot," Ansell says. "But not everyone hid in them. Survivors are fleeing to the city entrance. Henli is holding the line at the mine entrance, and told me to tell you that not even the Sisters could convince him to abandon the people when they need him most."

You hold back a curse. You want to help, but you also know that the greater battle is out here.

"Go back to the mines," you say. "Tell Henli to make do with what he has, and then do whatever you can to keep him alive and fighting."

Ansell looks relieved. The battle around him means nothing. He doesn't fear death. He is only content to have a task he understands.

"To the mines, then," he says. "Shall I go now?"

You look back to your group. The riflemen have resumed firing with their diminished numbers, though their aim is now scattered, firing at any and all owls that might be nearby. When you scan the outer wall, it seems the lapinkin are focusing their attacks around the city gate. You feel a sinking feeling in your gut upon realizing why. They're not there to win the fight. They expect the owls to accomplish that task. What they're there for is to prevent anyone from escaping. They are to keep the population penned within so the owls can do their work.

Homes have started burning. Owls dive all across the city, crushing in rooftops in search of prey. Smoke fills the air, from both the homes and the constant barrage of flamestone. There is need for you everywhere, but most severely at the gates. Should worst come to worst, and people must flee Roros for their lives, there needs to be a way out.

"Go, and good luck," you tell Ansell. "I'll be on the wall. Come find me if you survive."

You load your pistol with lead shot and flamestone as you run toward the main gate. There are two lapinkin near the interior stairs that lead up, and they are making quick work of the skeletal crew of guards that remain to watch over it.

One against two. Not the best odds. You look for Lyssa, hoping she is near, but see no sign of her. You pray it means she is fighting elsewhere.

Elsewhere. That's all. Not what the dark corners of your mind fear to believe.

You shift your run as you get closer to the wall, sticking to the dark recesses of the homes. If they don't see you coming…

You pause just shy of the open gap between the final home and the wall. It seems in the chaos of the fight, your approach has gone unseen. You lift your pistol and aim for the nearest lapinkin. He's landed atop the stone, but his attention is not yet in your direction. Slowly you hold your breath, steady your grip against the pounding of your heart, and pull the trigger.

Your aim is true. The lead shot strikes the lapinkin square in the chest. The impact of it rocks him backward, and you see the faintest spray of blood. He sways on his feet, then collapses, his body slumping off the side to vanish from view.

The fight now equalized, you holster your pistol and sprint for the stairs. You need up there before the other lapinkin knows he's in danger. You climb the stairs two at a time, and are halfway up before the lapinkin realizes his companion is dead. He was too distracted by the owls, the fires, and the thunder of flamestone singing a thunderous song in the bloody night.

He does, however, finally see you and spin. He's a good twenty feet away, and he readies his spear. His pink eyes seem to glow in the night, a color much too close to blood for your liking.

"Murderer!" he shouts, lifting his spear.

You pause and lift your sword in return.

"As if there's no blood on your spear!" you shout at him. It baits an attack as you hoped. He flings the spear, its speed shocking even with you being prepared for it. You retreat a single step while shifting your body sideways, all the while sweeping your sword in an arc before you. The hit jars your hands and arms, but you parry aside the spear so it strikes the stone at your feet instead.

You have no time to move, though, for the lapinkin follows up the throw with a burst of wind, leaping with the same velocity as his spear. His ears flap behind him, the three locking rings rattling of iron. You see his fist, see his bared teeth, see his glare.

And in return, you stand firm. Let him see your resolve. Let him meet the reflection of your cold steel in the moonlight. You angle your sword so that he will impale himself upon it if he collides with you, and you trust him to react accordingly. Sure enough, he shifts at the last possible moment, landing at the step before you and then leaping backward. You flex the muscles of your legs to endure the blast of air that follows, pushing against you, threatening to topple you off balance.

It passes, and you give chase, reaching the ramparts just in time to be greeted with a tremendous gust blasting from the lapinkin's palms.

Enduring it will only lead to a vicious tumble, so you drop to your knees and lower your head. You feel the wind blast against you, furious as a tornado, but much of its fury passes overhead.

You uncoil in explosive fury, but the lapinkin is faster. His fist strikes you across the jaw, a second punch to your stomach, and then comes the blast of wind that follows his command. Your momentum shifts, and you start to fall down the stairs...

But unlike him, you still have your sword.

You jam the blade straight down through his collarbone and into his chest, and when the gust hits, you use his own body to hold you steady. Blood flows across you as bones rip and tendons tear, but your footing remains. The lapinkin, however, is a ruined mess. When you rip your sword free, he collapses in a heap at your feet. With a kick of your heel, he goes rolling down the stairs, leaving a trail of blue blood upon the steps.

Murderer, you think, and look to the carnage that has besieged the town. How anyone could look upon these defenders and declare *them* murderers baffles you. At least, it would, if you were not so tired.

But it seems your presence upon the wall has not gone unnoticed. You see the diving owl moments before he arrives, and the pure white of his feathers fills you with dread. You recognize him, and when he pulls up from his dive with a flaring of his wings and beating of feathers, the missing eye only confirms it. Yont, the supposed champion of the Queen of the Winged, has come for the revenge he promised.

31

Yont's claws dig into the stone of the wall as he lands, blocking the entire passage.

"Soulkeeper," he says. Hatred seethes in his lone good eye. "Is it a blessing or a curse that brings you here?"

No riflemen, no guards, not even Ansell to fight alongside you. Alone, you stand before the champion and lift your sword.

"A little bit of both," you say. "Still planning to eat my innards while I watch?"

Yont lowers his head, his spine flattening in preparation for a charge.

"I have eaten well already," he says. "But your suffering will taste extra sweet."

"I'm flattered."

He lunges at you, his wings tucked to his sides and his beak snapping. The stone rattles from the scraping of his clawed feet. The air shakes from his piercing cry. The noise of it nearly roots you in place, but inaction means death. You leap aside, your sword flailing uselessly in front of you. It strikes his beak and bounces off. Pain shoots through your shoulder as you hit the rampart's side wall.

No thinking. You immediately drop to your knees and then roll. Yont's beak closes around the rampart, and if you thought it would harm him, you were wrong. The stone breaks between his beak, showering the ground with dust and gravel. You come up from your roll swinging, hoping to clip his neck, but the owl is too quick. He hops back while flapping his wings, the wind buffeting you and robbing your slash of power.

The owl beats his wings once more while swinging his feet around, claws hooked and reaching for you. The space is so small between you, the ancient bird, so frighteningly fast. Instinct drives your actions, and you pivot again to the side of Yont's missing eye. Whatever advantage you can find, you must take. The feet clasp air, and you punish the miss with a desperate hack across the tough skin just above his claws.

There is no satisfaction to be found in the blood that spills across your sword. Yont shrieks, louder, sharper, and before you can follow up with a thrust for the soft, exposed feathers of his underbelly, he flaps his opposite wing, shoving his body directly into yours. You struggle for balance, fail, and fall backward toward the rampart wall.

The broken portion of the wall, gapped and crumbling from Yont's bite.

You drop your sword to grab for anything, thankful for the thick leather of your gloves as your fingers momentarily scrape along the stone before finding their grip, halting you with only your feet dangling off the side. That you are on Yont's blind side is your only salvation, for he cannot see you, and to find you, he hops back while flapping his wings to momentarily hover in the air just off the opposite side of the rampart.

"Yes, struggle," Yont bellows as he dives again with his feet leading. You roll out of the way just in time to watch more stone get blasted from the rampart, leaving a huge portion of the interior wall open to a long fall to the ground.

"Squirm, and flail!"

He circles around, taunting you. His attempts to grab you are half-hearted, as if he wants to prolong your desperation. Another chunk of the rampart wall goes tumbling over. There's nothing to protect you, nothing to hide behind.

You grab your sword and pull it from the rubble. If you're going to die, you're going to die fighting.

"Do everything to live, human," Yont says, the wind of his wings beating against you as he fills your entire vision with his incredible wingspan. He slowly lifts off into the air. "And find it all…futile."

You clutch your sword in both hands, needing the strength. You glare into Yont's good eye. No fear. No surrender. If the damn owl plans to eat you, he's going to learn how poor a meal you'll make.

"Come on," you say, though he likely cannot hear you over the beating of his wings and the chaos of the battle around you. His arrogance is your best chance. "One mistake. Come at me. Come get me."

You stand there, legs tense and sword raised. Yont beats his wings to gain a bit more height and then dives. You have but a heartbeat's time to see him swoop upward, curling his body so his legs can rise up, claws reaching.

You've dashed aside to avoid every single attack. Never stood your ground. Never challenged him. He's anticipating the same again, expecting you to use the lack of his eye against him. Before his claws wrap around you they are already curling, seeking to grab you in the middle of a dodge that never comes.

You don't flee. Instead, you take two steps and vault right off the rampart, to meet the owl in midair. You twist your sword, reverse-gripped with both hands clutching the hilt with all your strength. The reaching claws slide to either side of you as you pass between them. You collide, and though the force of it is enough to rob the breath from your lungs, it only adds to the power of your sword as it plunges deep into Yont's chest. The owl screeches, but that first pain is only a prelude, for your fall continues, and now all your weight is held aloft by your grip upon the embedded hilt.

The sword tears through feather and bone as it rips a gash open across the belly of the furious champion of the Queen of the Winged.

Yont spirals downward, slamming the both of you back down atop the wall. You release your sword, figuring it much too deep to retrieve amid the tumble. Pain flares across your body as you bounce twice, elbows, knees, and hips hitting stone awkwardly and certainly leaving bruises. You remain limp, at least at first, but then realize where you are headed.

A frantic grab is all that keeps you from falling to your death. You hang off the edge of the rampart, your legs dangling in the air. You grit your teeth and pull, trying to raise up and over to the relative safety of the rampart.

The rumble and crack of stone is your only warning to Yont's arrival.

"Miserable worm," he says, his voice noticeably weaker. Blood stains the entire lower half of his body, and you see a patch of feather and skin hanging loose from his belly where you rent him open with your sword. How he still stands, you have no idea. It is as if hate alone keeps him alive.

His foot settles beside your hands. His claws carve a groove into the stone. Another step as he settles nearer. His yellow eye fills your vision as he lowers gingerly. He's in pain, terrible pain, but enduring it as he must, if only so his beak can slowly approach your fingers and their white-knuckle grip on the rampart's edge. You feel the warmth of his breath. You hear his pained wheezing.

His beak snaps for your left hand. You release, and hang from only your right arm. Pain swells in your shoulder as the tension heightens on the socket. The fall will kill you.

So will the owl.

He snaps for you, seeking to cleave your fingers from

your other hand. You release, the beak hits stone, and for the briefest moment it feels like all time stands still. You hover in place, starting to fall, your right hand moving to avoid the bite. Your left hand, reaching up, reaching, reaching…

Grabbing Yont's nostril hole upon his beak.

The weight is excruciating on your left arm, but you hold on as if your life depends upon it, because it does. Yont shrieks, and with your combined weight and his momentum, he threatens to teeter off the side of the wall. His wings flap, and though he could easily carry the both of you to your deaths, his survival instincts take over. The push of his wings pulls him away from the edge, carrying you with him.

The two of you tumble back atop the rampart, and you roll across a great smear of blood. You flinch, expecting the hooked claws of his feet and the sharp point of his beak to assault you, but there is nothing.

Gingerly, you rise to your feet, while the owl remains still atop the wall. He's breathing, but shallowly. His lone eye glares at you. A bit of blood leaks from his mouth and nostrils, a far cry from the amount coming from his torn belly.

"Stubborn humans," he says, and then coughs. The motion ripples through his feathers. "Will you give us no homes? Must every field and every forest be yours to claim?"

The slaughter of the night adds a fire to your words.

"This is our town," you say. "Our home, that you assaulted at night."

He tries to rise up but cannot. His body will not obey despite his obvious struggle. Even now, he wishes to bring his claws to bear against you.

"These were *our* lands," he says. "You chased us off them. Drove us west. And when that was not enough, when nothing would sate you…"

He collapses back onto his side.

"Your Sisters banished us. Outside the Cradle.

Outside time itself. A prison. Their prison. All for you…for their beloved…children."

What he speaks is heresy, but you've long realized the Keeping Church's understanding of the world cannot endure the return of these children of the dragons.

Another cough, even weaker.

"Your…sword," he says, each syllable labored.

You slowly limp to where you dropped your sword. With aching fingers holding the hilt, you lift it high.

Yont's eye closes.

"Give me…a warrior's death."

You position the tip of your sword against his chest, higher than your last cut, to aim for his heart. The steel sinks underneath the blood-stained white feathers.

"Farewell, champion," you say, and push the blade up to the hilt.

Yont's entire body stiffens, and then relaxes. His breathing halts. His feathers fall still.

You pull your sword free. The noise of battle is distant. All you hear is the pounding of your heart in your ears. Shadows fill the skies. The flash of flamestone fires in return.

Miserable. Pointless.

"Why?" you mutter. "Why *any* of this?"

"Robin!"

You turn, still feeling trapped within a nightmare. Ansell is back on the wall, running toward you, lithely stepping over both broken stone and the bodies of the dead.

"Are you in need of assistance?" he asks upon arriving. He sounds a little out of breath, but that is all. No other sign you are the midst of a battle, or that he has blood splashed across his neck and chest, blue blood, that of an owl or lapinkin, you suspect.

"I'm pretty sure we all are," you say, and gaze upon the town sprawling before you. Multiple homes are in flames.

Others have their rooftops smashed inwards. Owls dive among the streets, seeking prey, and there is no one to fight them off. They are free to hunt, to kill. At least the lapinkin still seem relegated to the walls, but that won't last long. Most of the riflemen squads are half their original number. The wind and the spears will make quick work of them.

"What shall we do now?" Ansell asks.

You don't want to sink into despair, but it is hopeless, utterly hopeless.

"We fight until we fall," you say. Your grip tightens around the hilt of your sword. "It's all that we can—"

The sound of a bell washes over you, so loud you fear your eardrums will burst. You drop to your knees and clutch your hands over your ears as, above you, the owls twist and dive.

Seconds later, the ringing ends, and you can hear yourself think.

"Where in Anwyn's name did that come from?" you ask.

"From the gate," Ansell says, still maddeningly calm. "We have a visitor."

You climb back to your feet and peer over the wall. Sure enough, a stranger stands just beyond the gates of the city.

He is tall, shockingly tall, at least seven foot at a minimum, and that does not count the height of his great rack of antlers stretching from the sides of his head. He looks like a muscular deer, yet he walks on two legs, not four. Strips of colorful cloth hang from his horns, matching the color of his flowing robes. His arms are lifted above him, his fingers curled inwards.

"Human and dragon-sired, take heed!" he shouts. His voice carries across the battlefield, an impossible task given the chaos, yet somehow, it does.

And then he slams his hands together. A bell materializes out of thin air high above him, carved of brass and majestic in its detail. Hundreds of figurines line the sides, creatures of all sort, some you recognize, many you don't. The bell hangs from a translucent yoke, ghostly and blue. It turns, the clapper hits, and then the sound washes over you a second time.

Even prepared, it is agony to your ears and mind. The bell disappears as the strange newcomer lowers his arms. There is no doubt both those in Roros and the skies above are aware of his presence.

"I am a messenger of King Cannac," he shouts. "And I come with a single demand to all who listen. This bloodshed must end. This violence must halt. Put aside claw and sword. Tonight, we will have peace." He points to the sky. "Have I your promise, Arondel?"

A brilliant white owl swirls down to land before the deer-person. Blood has splashed across her feathers from the many humans she has killed.

"Cannac is a fool to call for peace," she says. "But out of respect for him, I will honor it, if the humans do."

The messenger bows to her, his hands lifting ever so slightly so his fingers and thumbs touch in the empty space between his antlers. When he rises, he addresses Roros next.

"What of humanity? Who will speak for you, and the surrounding villages?"

An awkward silence follows. Battle-worn soldiers look about. The mayor is in hiding, and the overseer, imprisoned. In the distance, you see Lyssa holstering her pistols, and she gestures toward you. Her message is clear enough.

"Pretty sure this is overstepping my authority," you mumble as you climb down to the gate. The soldiers positioned at it both bow their heads in respect before pushing it open. You're glad they seem in agreement, and not angry at the halting of battle. Sure, you were losing, but once the bloodshed starts, there's always those who would rather fight to the death and take as many with them than accept a potential peace.

You walk the short space between the gates and the waiting messenger.

"I am Robin, Soulkeeper of the Three Sisters," you say, deciding to make this as legitimate as possible. "And with what authority has been granted to me by the Keeping Church, I vow that, so long as our lives are not endangered and our people go unharmed, we shall seek peace between us."

Arondel glares at you, at least, you suspect the owl is glaring. The messenger, however, looks relieved.

"There will ever be trials and disagreements," says the messenger. "But know that Cannac would have us walk a road of peace, not one of war. I only pray we do not walk it alone."

You look back to Roros, to its broken rooftops, its smashed homes, and its blood-soaked streets.

"So do I," you say, and bow to the messenger. "So do I."

32

"You sure it's safe to go?" you ask Lyssa two days later. The pair of you stand just outside the gates of Roros, the morning sun pleasantly warm upon your faces. The previous day had been for mourning, and the night, filled with funeral pyres the two of you built to burn the bodies of the dead after their souls were taken during the reaping hour.

"Is *anywhere* safe?" she asks in response. Her tone is a mixture of exasperation and playful mockery. "I'll be safe on the road, if that's what you're worried about, Robin. Even if the owls decide to be petty little assholes and hunt outside Roros's walls, I know how to hide from them at night. I owe our Vikar information on what's transpiring here in the far north, as well as knowledge the mining of flamestone will resume soon."

And resume it had, much to your surprise. You'd thought after the fierce battle, people would want to take time to grieve and mourn. Instead, with the rise of the sun, the miners had taken to their work with an air of celebration.

It's a return to normalcy, Lyssa had said when you questioned their good cheer. *That's all anyone wants right now. To live as we always did before the world changed and became something frightening and new.*

"Any chance you can take Ansell with you?" you joke.

"Such cruelty to the poor soulless, even after he saved your life against the lyndwyrm." She smirks. "Sorry. He's your problem, not mine, just like William is."

Given the upheaval of having an overseer arrested, William has chosen to remain behind and assist the town mayor with negotiating with the diplomat that had arrived to halt the battle, the supposed 'messenger of King Cannac', whatever that meant. King of who, you assume only the deer-like people since the various races appear to have their own rulers, such as Queen Arondel for the Winged.

"So be it, but let Vikar Forrest know I'm working extra hard here to clean up all the messes, all right?" you say. "I don't want him thinking I'm relaxing away the hours instead of returning with you to Londheim."

"I'll make sure he gets the message," Lyssa says with a wink. "Take care, Robin."

With that, she begins her journey south. You watch her go for a minute or two, sad to lose both her wit and her pistols. Eventually other duties call, and you return to the mansion where William is busy holding a thousand meetings. Much to your surprise, he seems jovial about it all.

"What can I say," he says once when you bring it up amid your boredom while listening to the many requests for aid, repairs, and potential trade with towns to the east that have yet to send wagons. "I like my work when my work is meaningful."

Come a break for dinner, when it is just the two of you, he leans back in his chair and eyes you warily.

"Will the peace hold?" he asks. "Those owls certainly seem unhappy, and I don't like that the lapinkin were among their number."

You shrug. "When that diplomat arrived and gave his order, the others listened. Until we can speak with him further, we have only guesswork."

The man nods.

"It's heartening though, isn't it?" he says. "To know that among all these various races that there are those who seek peace? Maybe that means our future doesn't have to be bloody. We don't need a war."

You smile softly at him. "I pray you are right, and that we have need far more of diplomats like you than killers like me."

*

You dream.

The world is dark, and your bed, hovering over brightly lit emptiness. You are awake but not. You are still, but you cannot shake a sensation of flying over a vast distance.

Words rumble through your ears, thousands upon thousands without meaning or purpose, at least not at first. Slowly they begin to take shape, accompanied by phantom images in the darkness. You see rolling hills, their valleys filled with densely packed oaks. Amid their branches you see little winged creatures buzzing about.

Faerie-kind.

You see snow-capped mountains with roads carved along their sides. Half-human, half-deer people trudge through the snow, crates and logs on their shoulders as they build homes for themselves.

Dyrandar.

You see the grand canyon carved into the ground by the passage of the crawling mountain that has halted at the gates of Londheim. Little foxes walking on two legs and dressing in colorful garments hurry about, digging holes, adding doors, and putting up coverings made of sticks and mortar.

Foxkin.

A grand plains, flat and sprawling for hundreds of miles. The grass sways like a verdant ocean. Amid them walk men and women, their eyes pure black, their bodies covered with reptilian scales, only they are not scales, but firm layers of grass. They move and shift as if without bones.

Viridi.

Next are hills you recognize, those in the space between the mountains and the city of Londheim. Unfamiliar is the grand castle sprawling out of the earth. Grass grows from its rooftops while vines sprawl across its rock walls. Flowers bloom between the many windows, their colors carefully arranged to create images of forests, rivers, and familiar rabbit warriors wielding spears from their perches atop the clouds.

Lapinkin.

You feel paralyzed in your bed, awash in wonder, buried in names, some you recognize, most you do not. They come faster, overwhelming you.

A fungal creature deep underground, half-submerged in water, walking through rows upon rows of grand columns bearing a thousand carvings.

Trytis.

Stone men with four legs and two faces, emerging from the ground to surround a distant human city. Their hands lift to the heavens as words glow across their stone flesh.

Aeryal.

The grand fleet of owls soaring from the forests to encircle Londheim, not attacking, not yet.

The winged.

A bird-like woman clothed in gray trousers and black coat walks the streets of Londheim. She wields two sickles in hand, their silver gleaming in the moonlight. Black wings stretch from her back, the feathers transitioning into shadows and smoke halfway across.

Avenria.

Little orbs of water, leaping in and out of the river that runs alongside Londheim.

Waterkin.

A spidery woman wrapped in webs in the heart of a cave. Colorful scales cover every inch of her body, but they are soft and flutter with her movements like soft petals of a flower.

Araloro.

The darkness returns, so it is only your bed hovering over the cavernous emptiness. You lay there, wishing you could move. You should be afraid, but you are not. A strange calm settles over you. Peaceful. Curious.

The fireflies arrive without sound or fanfare. First a few, then dozens, then hundreds, swirling together into a tremendous funnel at the foot of your bed. Golden lightning arcs between them, creating a dazzling display.

And among them, humans.

You can move. The sense of freedom comes sudden and unwelcome. You sit up, your hands at your sides, and stare at the fireflies.

"Who are you?" you ask.

The answer is a lone word that shakes the darkness.

Gloam.

It feels like a dam breaks within your mind. Memories once blocked now return. Your first night spent at Roros turns crystalline clear. You remember the strange stone creatures speaking their words and molding your language. You remember the name they spoke, and the titles they gave. Two titles, they gave the dragon, but you would hear it from the mysterious entity's own mouth.

"And who is Gloam?"

I am the Dragon of Thought, whom you humans named the Dragon of Heresy.

A dragon, yet before you is a swarm of lightning-kissed fireflies. It makes no sense.

You look upon my truest self, Robin, not the creation of flesh I built for myself in an age long past.

Your blood chills, and you feel the first inkling of fear. The dragon can hear your thoughts, but what else would you expect from one who bears such twin titles? Here in this strange realm, you are at its mercy.

"What is a dragon?" you ask.

We are the mothers and fathers of our children, they whom you named dragon-sired. They are the beloved I have shown you, the reawakened, the returned.

"Why?" you ask. "Why now? And returned? From where?"

You seek answers, Soulkeeper. That is good, but with answers comes knowledge, and with knowledge, a demand for action. Stripped of ignorance, you lose your innocence. Are you willing to bear that burden? Would you still ask your questions so carelessly?

You've never been one to fear the truth, nor cower before a challenge.

"I am not afraid," you tell Gloam.

The fireflies shift up and down, their revolutions growing momentarily twisted. It feels unsettling. It feels like laughter.

You leap ahead, Soulkeeper. You ask why we return, yet give no thought to what first banished us. But I shall answer. The imprisoning sleep has been lifted. We Dragons of Creation return, and with us, our children.

You fear you know the answer, but you must ask it nonetheless.

"And who imprisoned you?"

The revolutions slow. The lightning arcing through the fireflies turns a crimson color.

Your beloved Sisters.

You believe Gloam. His anger is too pure, too true. Part of you is convinced the being could not lie even if it wished to do so. What unsettles you now is…why? What crime had the dragons and dragon-sired committed that would have your Sisters…

WE COMMITTED NO CRIME.

The cry knocks the breath from your lungs. Your bones turn to ice. Your flesh stills. You are a statue upon your bed, unable to move, as rage washes over you.

As quickly as it came, it passes. The crimson fades back to a pleasant gold.

Your trust in your Goddesses is childlike. Immature. Learn of them, and of us, and perhaps you will grow.

You hold little doubt as to why the dragon bears its second title of Heresy. You want nothing more than for it to leave and grant you peace. You feel like a fly buzzing around a horse, pitiful and insignificant.

"Why are you here?" you ask. "Why do you visit me?"

The swarm hovers closer, and the fireflies slow. You see they are not insects, not as you would understand them. Their bodies are a metallic silver, their wings, so thin as to be semi-transparent and crafted of emeralds, sapphires, and rubies.

Because my aeryal deemed you worthy of my words. I come to see why.

You sit tall in your bed, attempting to be as proud as possible under such strange conditions.

"And how would you judge me?" you ask.

The swarm circles, faster and faster. They are but blurs in your mind, flashes of silver intermixed with hints of color. The lightning bursts. The world trembles. Within it all, you suddenly see eyes, and a face.

You brought peace once. Will you choose peace again?

33

You wake.

You are in your bed, drenched in sweat. Your heart races, and you gasp for air as if you'd been drowning. Your windows are dark, morning still far away.

A dream, you realize, rubbing at your eyes and wishing your heart would calm down. It seems that is not in your destiny, not yet. A knock on your door.

"Miss?"

"I'm awake," you say. The door opens, and Whistler steps inside and quickly bows in apology.

"I know the hour is early," he says, "but there is an urgent visitor awaiting you beyond the city walls."

*

The sun has barely risen as you walk past the guards at the open gate and walk the roads. Your visitor is not far, sitting patiently with a crown upon his head. You are tired, battered, and bruised, but nothing in all the Cradle could prevent the smile that spreads upon your face.

"How'd you find me?" you ask.

Wotri tilts his head to one side.

"You insult me," he says. "Why would doubt this nose?"

You laugh and fall to your knees as the wolf king bounds over to you, pausing just shy so he might lower his head and press his forehead to yours. He's so huge now, a towering, regal beast.

"Well met, Soulkeeper," he says. "I pray your days have been kind?"

A night of wings and smoke flashes through your mind.

"I have known better," you say. "And I pray 'better' is what awaits me in my future. But what of you, Wotri? How have you been?"

In answer, he glances over his shoulder. Amid the waving grass, you see he is not alone. At first what seems like only a few wolves lurk behind him, but that number grows as more and more stand tall. They were bowing, you realize. There are dozens now, including some pups that remain crouched on the road, flanked by older wolves. You look up to Wotri, your smile growing.

"Your kingdom," you say. "You found it."

"Indeed, I did," he says. "Scattered and broken, but even we few are enough to birth a new kingdom. Over it, I will rule. Even if it may take an age, I shall watch the lands blossom with our pack, and the grand hunt resume its majesty."

"Your hunt..." You slowly stand. "And where will we humans stand in regards to that hunt?"

Wotri's eyes narrow, and he sniffs at the smoke still rising above the damaged city. Even now, the burning of debris and pyres for corpses continues.

"There are those among us dragon-sired that seek war. I am not among them, little Soulkeeper." He nudges you with his nose. "I would have us be friends, if you accept us."

There are political implications to consider, proper channels and authorities to manage such agreements, as well as the risks of acknowledging yet another king among these non-human factions. You don't care about any of that.

"Of course I accept," you say, and throw your arms around the wolf's neck. After a momentary tenseness, Wotri relaxes, and he brushes his head against you as you hold onto his fur, smelling the scent of fallen leaves and rushing springs upon him.

You remember the demand of the dragon come to you in your dreams, and you give him the answer you were unable to give before the dream collapsed.

"Peace," you say. "When given the choice, I will choose peace, and may all the world accept it."

Wotri's lips peel back, his nose scrunching in what you understand to be his equivalent of a smile.

"Then consider us your allies, friend Soulkeeper, now and forever."

Despite his crown, despite his regal nature, you sink deeper into his fur, holding him as you would a companion. A friend.

"Thank you," you whisper.

The future is still troubled, and you fear the repercussions to come of the arrival of the dragon-sired...but Wotri has given you exactly what you needed this cold morning.

He has given you hope.

"Thank you."

A Note from the Author:

So this was a strange little experiment, wasn't it?

Some of you may have played it, many not, but years ago I worked with Delight Games to create a sort of choose your own adventure of my already existing Paladins books to release on mobile platforms. And it did really well! But the thing about that game was how it was taking existing books, never written with choices in mind, and trying to add choices and outcomes to it. People liked it, but it did a lot of things weird for the specific genre. It was in third person, not second, it was in past tense, not present, and it contained multiple POVs instead of one main narrative.

Now given you just read a book in second person present tense, you can probably figure out what this started as. When deciding what to write, there was never much question. When I wrote my Keepers Trilogy, there were aspects I had plans to touch on at some point that I just never found a way to fit into the narrative (the origin of the flamestone being one such example). And so in my spare time, I cranked out an occasional chapter, returning to this world I first visited with Soulkeeper.

Coming home felt fantastic, honestly. The Keepers Trilogy has some of the weirdest, most enjoyable world building I've ever done. Getting used to second-person present tense? Way harder, but it was fun to embrace that challenge.

Now the second most obvious thing should be is that you just read a book and didn't play a game. Well…yeah. To keep things very short, plans fell through on creating my own standalone app, and the program I created my working demo of was not capable of handling some basic aspects it needed to handle if the app was to release for free (which was always the plan). So here I was, after about a year, with this entertaining novel revisiting one of my favorite worlds, sitting there on my hard drive. And it was killing me. There are parts of this story I absolutely adore, and Wotri in particular is one of my favorite characters I've ever written. The idea that no one would ever meet the King of Fur and Fanged? No, that can't be.

And so here we are. I went through the choices creating was is effectively a 'canon' storyline, named the main character, and created this novel. Was the experiment a success? Well. Only you can be the judge of that, but I pray you had fun.

Though I will never say never, I do not expect there to be more of Robin, at least for the immediate future given the six(!) novels I currently have contracted out with Orbit Books. If you enjoyed this world, and a lot of the elements and mystery within, I highly recommend you check out the Keepers Trilogy, starting with Soulkeeper. A lot of characters within Night of Wings And Smoke were brought directly from there, either as cameos like with Devin, Tommy, and Puffy, or for more direct involvement such as with Soulkeeper Lyssa. So if you want to know more about the Dragons of Creation, King Cannac, or what's going on with the Three Sisters, that is where your answers await you.

As always, thank you, dear reader, for coming with me on another journey. You have given me your trust to tell you a tale, and hopefully I rewarded your time well with one you will remember.

David Dalglish
May 24th, 2024

Printed in Great Britain
by Amazon